# THE TURQUOISE SHOP

FRANCES CRANE (1890-1981) was an American author and a former writer for *The New Yorker*. Crane was invited to leave Nazi Germany in the late 1930s after writing a number of unfavorable articles about Adolf Hitler. After settling in Taos, Crane introduced private investigator Pat Abbott and his future wife Jean in her first novel, *The Turquoise Shop* (1941). The Abbotts investigated crimes in a total of 26 volumes, each with a color in the title, with settings around the country and globe.

ANNE HILLERMAN grew up in Santa Fe and Albuquerque, the eldest of the family's six children. Before becoming a best-selling mystery writer, she worked as a newspaper reporter, editor, columnist and restaurant critic. She was also a magazine and book editor, travel writer, and the author of several non-fiction books. She helped organize the acclaimed Tony Hillerman Writers Conference. In 2013, she published her first mystery, *Spider Woman's Daughter*, which continued the adventures of Navajo law enforcement characters created by her father. Her seventh mystery, the 26th in the series, *The Sacred Bridge*, was published in 2022.

# THE TURQUOISE SHOP

## FRANCES CRANE

*Introduction by*
## ANNE HILLERMAN

## AMERICAN MYSTERY CLASSICS

*Penzler Publishers*
*New York*

Published in 2022 by Penzler Publishers
58 Warren Street, New York, NY 10007
penzlerpublishers.com

Distributed by W. W. Norton

Cover image: Andy Ross
Cover design: Mauricio Diaz

Paperback ISBN 978-1-61316-365-8
Hardcover ISBN 978-1-61316-354-2

Library of Congress Control Number: 2022906577

Printed in the United States of America

9 8 7 6 5 4 3 2 1

# INTRODUCTION

ONE OF the great joys of discovering a skillfully constructed novel is the story's ability to put the readers inside the skin of the characters. We get to live in the place and time in which the fictional world unfolds. In the case of Frances Crane's *The Turquoise Shop*, readers travel back to the 1940s and a small town in northern New Mexico filled with pleasantly quirky folks and a pair of murders to be solved.

Novels give us the gift of seeing the world through new eyes, the eyes of strangers or, in the case of a series, the eyes of characters we've come to know. Well-crafted books entertain and, if we are in the hand of a writer of Crane's caliber, teach us something as a bonus. Good books even transform us for the better in subtle ways. Surrendering to a good book allows us to leave the stresses of the day behind. As a reader, by the time I reach the final chapter or have to give in to sleep, often to my surprise, the day's troubles seem less troubling.

It gives me special delight to dive into entertaining books by authors I haven't encountered before. I am grateful to Otto Penzler for introducing me to this charming vintage mystery, the first in Crane's popular, long-running detective series. Because Frances Crane lived in Taos, New Mexico, for a stretch of her adult life, it isn't difficult to imagine that she based her fictional Santa Maria on Taos. Her depictions of the town's plaza as the center of commerce and socializing, the soul-stirring beauty of the mountains and mesas beyond community boundaries, and the happy isolation from chaos of big city life—all these are spot on. The setting certainly reflects the way things were in the high altitude of Taos and many other small towns in Northern New Mexico decades ago.

In fact, Crane's careful depictions elevate two of the setting in the book into something close to characters. The Turquoise Shop, the cozy gallery trading post that Jean Holly runs as a business and gathering place for people with news to share, could be modeled after any number of galleries in Taos or other New Mexico art towns. (Jean Holly, by the way, is the future Mrs. Patrick Abbot.) Crane also give us a mysteriously deadly cabin on the rural outskirts of town. But even more intriguing is the site of the second murder, a much grander place and the home of another central character, Mona Brandon. Anyone who knows much about New Mexico's rich history as an arts colony will recognize the similarities between Mona's fiction hacienda and Taos's Mabel Dodge Luhan house.

Rich in history and much-praised for its beautiful, authentic adobe architecture, the house has been a center of Taos arts and education for nearly a century. The rustic and relaxing ambience of the place situated at the end of a quiet road not far from the center of town reflects the taste of the woman herself. Sometimes referred to as New Mexico's Gertrude Stein for her skill at bringing together talented, creative people, Mabel's guests included author D.H. Lawrence, who said his time in Taos changed his life. She hosted a Who's Who of creative talent over the years including Georgia O'Keeffe, Ansel Adams, Willa Cather, Marsden Hartley, Aldous Huxley, Robinson Jeffers, Mary Hunter Austin, Frank Waters, and many more who shared drinks and conversation at legendary parties. Biographers have characterized salon hostess, art patroness, and writer Mabel Dodge Luhan as a self-appointed savior of humanity and a woman of profound contradictions: generous and petty; domineering and endearing. She died at this spacious home more than sixty years ago.

Today, despite the passage of time, the house appears much as it did in the days when Mabel admired her views of the sacred Taos Mountain from the third-story solarium.

Frances Crane lived in Taos during the Mabel days and she uses both the home and Mabel herself as inspiration. The hacienda as portrayed in the book is even grander than it was in real life. Among other modifications, the author adds a swimming pool fed by local hot springs. But reimagined as the character Mona Brandon, the legendary Mabel doesn't come off quite as sweetly.

Mona also lives in a grand hacienda and shares many of Mabel's less complimentary traits. Mona's personality is decidedly darker than the legendary Mabel's, as benefits a central character in any good mystery.

For me, in addition to the wonderful setting, another facet of the book's appeal is Crane's ability to bring to life the other unusual people who live in her fictional Santa Maria. As a nearly life-long New Mexican, I can vouch for their authenticity. Crane's characters, like some of us real Northern New Mexicans, are tolerant of and even oblivious to the unusual aspects of both our own behavior and that of the humans around us. Santa Maria, like many small real-life New Mexican towns, is known for its oddballs. Even protagonist Jean Holly is on the eccentric side. For instance, she tells us she doesn't have a car because she believes she'd have no time to use it. And then she complains about how long it takes her to walk anywhere!

In *The Great Taos Bank Robbery*, the title story of his collection of non-fiction essays, one of New Mexico's best-known authors, Tony Hillerman, also captures some of Taos' eccentric charm. Although the story, based on eye-witness accounts from the local newspaper, is set in the 1960s, Hillerman's characters are as out-of-the-ordinary as some of Crane's. And this little piece came before Hillerman switched to mystery fiction!

Hillerman's true story concerns an abandoned attempt at robbery followed by a slow-speed car chase, with characters cut from the same cloth as Crane's crew. The news about the incident appeared in a local newspaper during the time Crane lived in Taos. If she were around today (she died in 1981), I would ask her if the story of a man wearing a dress, high heels, and fishnet stockings over unshaven legs, holding a gun beneath his purse, and politely standing in a teller's line to do the robbery, gave her any reason to reconsider her move to Taos.

In addition to the cigarettes and cocktails, relaxed pacing, and exceptionally modest behavior between the would-be lovers, the novel has some dated descriptions referring to gender and ethnicity that are now rightly deemed inappropriate. For example, the book consistently calls Hispanic residents "Mexicans." The appellation ignores both the reality that the characters are based on people whose families have been in Taos for generations and also the links some of these families have to New Mexico's Spanish settlers and explorers, and to ancient Taos Pueblo. And, I bristled to read Detective Patrick Abbott call the competent, educated twenty-four-year-old Jean Holly a "child." Perhaps Crane's first readers didn't find this jarring; like the friendly, fictional Turquoise Shop itself, the novel reflects its time.

As a writer who also works with a fictional married couple as crime solvers, I found the clever way in which Crane leads us to the possibility of romance and collaboration between Jean and Patrick Abbot very endearing. I liked Jean from the first, and Patrick, too, although he is mostly revealed through Jean's love-struck eyes. Crane wisely leaves much of their background for subsequent books in the series. Like the best authors, she teases her readers, making us wait to see if the two will collaborate on another crime-solving mission, and to discover if and how their relationship could unfold.

In *The Turquoise Shop* the two share nothing more than drinks, ideas and pleasant conversation about murder. They don't marry until book three in the series.

I understand from my own experience as an author that there are advantages and pitfalls to a couple solving crime together. My detectives, Jim Chee and Bernadette Manuelito, married each other in Tony Hillerman's final novel but began their romance long before I took over the series. That spared me the job of writing about Bernie as an awkward, love-struck rookie cop or about Chee's earlier failed romances. Using a married detective couple eliminates the need to at least hint at romance as part of each novel. Instead, the challenge is to deepen or stress the relationship as an on-going subplot, while the paired detectives unravel the central mystery and decode the other challenges that round out the novel. It's a matter of going deep instead of going wide, and Frances Crane proves herself to be an expert at this.

Finally, we all know that enough new mysteries arrive each year to keep us going 24/7, barely squeezing out the time to read them. What's the point, one might ask, of bringing back this old classic? The reason is a return to reading for pleasure, relaxed enjoyment and pure, stress-free entertainment. *The Turquoise Shop* provides a time travel experience back to a simpler and fascinating world. As both a reader and a writer, I am grateful to the American Mystery Classics series for giving *The Turquoise Shop* another chance to shine.

ANNE HILLERMAN
Tucson, Arizona
April, 2022

# THE TURQUOISE SHOP

# CHAPTER 1

THAT MORNING as I walked from my house on the mesa to my shop on the plaza the mountains were piled-up purple velvet on a dark sky. October had been warmer and drier than any of the eight I'd spent out here, but this morning looked like the end of that. The wind stirred ominously, and on the plaza it was casually twisting the last of the cottonwood leaves from their branches. November as a rule was pretty cold in Santa Maria. In November everyone started turning out in sheepskin coats and high boots, except Mona Brandon, who always dressed up, and all day long there were likely to be little pools of melted snow around the fireplace in The Turquoise Shop. My shop, where people gathered and talked.

Talk was right, I thought, as I headed toward the Castillo Restaurant for my usual orange juice, toast and coffee. Talk certainly was my chief commodity in winter. I never did any business to speak of from October till May. My outlook this year was bleak, and thinking about it made me feel more desolate. Just the kind of thinking that I'd be doing on a morning like this. Maybe it was the weather. I wished it would snow and get it over with.

The Castillo had two entrances, but inside, the bar and

restaurant were so intimately connected by a wide archway that they might as well have been one room. I sat down at my usual table. Rose Dominguez flashed me one of her queenly smiles and sailed out to fetch my usual breakfast.

Then I saw the O'Haras at a table toward the back. I waved. Michael grinned. Sonya sort of twisted her slant-eyed face.

"Looks like snow!" Michael called genially.

"Sure does."

"Hope it lays off till we're back from Santa Fe."

"You going to Santa Fe?"

"God willing. Do anything for you there?"

"No. But thank you."

Sonya had said nothing. She was like a plump, jealous shadow of her popular redheaded husband, and not especially liked in Santa Maria. They'd come out from New York three years ago and lived in Mona's studio cottage just outside her east gate. I never have understood Russians very well, which might be why I didn't care for Sonya. Oh, I didn't say so. When you have a shop in a small artists' colony like Santa Maria you don't run around speaking your mind, or pretty soon you wouldn't have a shop.

I finished, signed the bill, told Rose I'd see her at lunch, said *adios* to the O'Haras, and in a moment was cutting diagonally across the plaza to my shop. I kept eyeing the gloomy sky through the bare lace-work of the cottonwoods. Then, in the center, where the paths met in a circle around that birdbath which Julia Price once said Mona Brandon swapped the town for her warm swimming pool, I met Gilbert Mason.

I braced myself.

"Hi, Jeanie!" Gilbert said. Affably, which meant trouble.

"Hello."

"You're late!"

"Monday's privilege, Gilbert."

"You seem in a hurry."

"You just said I was late."

He turned and walked beside me, shifting the briefcase he always carried to his other arm, and thus disclosing the worn place it had made inside his left sleeve. I also knew why he looked so pleased with himself. He was all set for some of his malicious gossip. Nothing doing. For I knew exactly what he wanted to talk about. So I'd sit tight.

Gilbert sensed it, so he shut up like a clam, too, and we walked in step, the leaves skittering away from our feet, not saying a word till we were opposite the shop. Then, as usual, I got to feeling sorry for him. I thought of his good qualities. For one thing he was so clean. His thin hands, which were always fretting with that briefcase, had a scrubbed look, the nails a little blue as from soaking, the tips scraped with a file till very white. I remembered that he washed his poetic hair every day. The old worn coat buttoned so snugly about his slight body was immaculate. It was a funny thing, really, that anybody whose mind worked like Gilbert's should always smell like soap and water.

So I gave in first. As usual.

"Looks like snow, Gilbert."

"Does it?" he sneered, and I was sorry pronto that I'd weakened.

We crossed the pavement and stepped onto the sidewalk in front of The Turquoise Shop. I shot a checking-up glance at the show window, which extended save for the door entirely across the front of the shop. It was satisfactory, that is as I'd left it Saturday night. I didn't open on Sundays at this time of year. The building was an old adobe. Characteristically, neither the window nor door was quite in alignment with each other or the sidewalk. The walls were ivory-white, the door and the window facings painted turquoise. Above the door a little black iron-work sign swayed in the slight wind and showed in silhouette the name of the shop, and beneath in tiny letters was my name, Jean Holly. Versatile Michael O'Hara had made the sign for me a couple of Christmases ago.

I fumbled in my big saddle-leather bag for my key, taking my time, making it plain, I hoped, that I wasn't feeling hospitable.

"Funny if she couldn't buy herself out this time," said Gilbert.

It was not what I expected. So I fell.

"Who?"

"Mona. Who else does any buying in Santa Maria?"

I peered grimly into my bag for the key.

"Stop putting on an act!" Gilbert snapped. "You know what I mean. You always know everything ahead of everyone else. Except me. I know first because I use my brain. You're second because everybody gossips in your shop." He was resting a shoulder against the door-facing, waiting for me to open the door. "You interest me, darling," he said, insultingly. Gilbert always called you darling when particularly nasty. "Even though you run a shop you interest me. Because we're just alike, you and I!" He paused to let the compliment sink in. "We want no part of the messes of Santa Maria. We want merely to sit back, look on and have fun."

I took out the key and put it in the lock.

"Santa Maria isn't a bad show any time, what with people always scratching and screaming behind other people's backs," Gilbert said. He lowered his rather high voice. "But I've gotten fed up with small stuff like that. Now it's taking a turn more to my taste." He waited for me to ask what. I merely turned the key. "I mean murder," he said.

He was eyeing me intently. I could tell even without glancing at him because I knew his tricks.

"I said murder," he reiterated softly.

I said, "I'd rather you didn't come in this morning, Gilbert. I'm going to be awfully busy."

Without another word Gilbert turned and walked away. As he crossed the street I felt as though I had struck a child. I know this doesn't sound logical, but I often felt furious with him and sorry for him at the same time.

# CHAPTER 2

I WENT into the shop, a large rectangular low-beamed room with the usual tables and cases, now covered with the gray dust sheets I'd spread over them on closing Saturday night. The air was thick with stale smells. My cleaning woman, Lotta Dominguez, had been here and had swept the floor and laid the fire in the adobe fireplace at the back left-hand corner of the room, but it would take a rousing fire to air the place. I left the front door ajar, crossed to the fireplace, and knelt to put a match to the shavings. I kept thinking of Gilbert. He was so poor. I thought about his threadbare clothes and the stark little house where he lived alone. I felt sorry again that I'd been harsh. I had no real cause, except my hating to get mixed up in any way in the local messes, which certainly wasn't reason enough to offend him. He could have sat by the fire while I did the regular straightening up.

The fire was already burning, filling the room with the spicy scent of the piñon wood, when a soft sly step behind made me jump and wheel about.

It was Gilbert. He laughed because I looked scared.

"Something on your conscience, Jean? Or just on your mind?"

"Nothing I know of," I said.

"You couldn't've been thinking about murder?"

I started into the back room to take off my coat.

"You know just as well as I do," Gilbert said, coming to the fireside, "that the murdered man was Tom Brandon."

"Nonsense!" I said.

I stopped, but I didn't look at Gilbert.

"All right, Jean. Where *is* Tom Brandon?'

"I've no idea."

"You're his agent," Gilbert said.

"I'm nothing of the kind," I said, facing him again. "I once sold some of his pictures. I've still got a few in the shop."

"It's enough for him to keep in touch," Gilbert said.

"Should be. Hasn't been."

"And of course it never entered your pure girlish mind that the mysterious companion of our Carmencita, out there in the desert, was Tom Brandon. Oh, no!" Gilbert was smiling his sweetest. "Well, what difference does it make?" he said then. "He's dead and buried. There's been an inquest and a verdict. 'Killed by some sharp instrument, probably a knife, by person or persons unknown.' Exit the admirable Brandon!"

He seemed to think this was funny. I took my coat and bag into the back room, or store room, behind the main shop, hung the coat on a hanger, put the bag on top of the safe, and then got into a clean denim smock. I buttoned the smock and came back to find Gilbert still standing by the fireplace, laughing.

"Who cares?" he asked then. "But it's interesting just the same. How does Mona fit into this new picture? Did she want him off the scene because she's in love with O'Hara? Or as her final triumph over Carmencita?"

I didn't answer.

"I've got some interesting evidence in this briefcase," Gilbert said. I still said nothing. "I see I am boring you," he said then, and again pranced from the shop. This time he didn't return.

# CHAPTER 3

I stood with my back to the fire, hearing it crackle, feeling the gay warmth and smelling the piney smell. Through the wide window I noticed how the stormy sky made a backdrop for the haphazard-looking row of buildings across the plaza. Each side had its assortment of stores, shops and offices. Some were adobe, some brick, some wood, some had portals, some none, some lined up with each other, some didn't. All Santa Maria was like that. The streets ran any old way and the houses were all shapes and sizes and made no effort to align with their neighbors or the streets.

Julia Price said that Santa Maria looked like a community style asylum built by the inmates. In which case, Daisy Payne said, Gilbert Mason would be inmate number one, though not because he did any building, and Gilbert retorted that the honor was *ipso facto* Daisy's. Their feud never had a lull.

I started folding up the dust sheets.

Instantly, the whole world began to change as the gorgeous colors of my Indian and Mexican things—emerald, yellow, crimson and bright blues—sprang to life. The fire was leaping now. I could feel the dead currents of air moving toward the chimney. My depression went with them. It had certainly been the weather. Already what Gilbert had said seemed just one of the crazy things he said.

Of course the idea *had* occurred to me, but mildly.

I wondered how many others would think of it?

I hoped not too many. Not seriously, anyhow.

I'd told myself I had worried a little because of Carmencita. I was glad when the inquest cleared her of suspicion. She was not exactly a girl whose character was enough.

I had no real affection for Carmencita, as I had for her sister Rose. But her looks justified her existence. Well, she was going settle down. Good thing. She was going to marry that Ortega boy who had started a little grocery near the plaza. He would do well, too. Carmencita's beauty would fade, she would get fat, have lots of children, and her mystery would take wing forever. About time. Funny about that man in the desert. She lived out there with him about a year now and no one had ever once set eyes on him. That was why, now and then, somebody would get the notion he was Brandon. It was ridiculous, no one in his right mind could ever believe it, but if a man vanished for three years, and all letters came back marked address unknown, you couldn't help but kind of wonder.

There wasn't anything, I thought, putting my arms around the stack of folded covers, that you could do about the imagination, but in any case I wasn't going to sit around worrying about anything devised by Gilbert Mason's. My own gave me bother enough.

I carried the dust sheets into the back room, put them on the box where I always kept them and picked up a pair of cotton gloves and a chamois. Each day I made it a rule to go over some of the silver and turquoise jewelry in the long glass case across the back of the shop. I'd wipe each piece with the chamois, and once in a while clean them all with silver polish.

I came back out and perched on the stool behind the case. I put on the gloves. A car with a California license was parking at the curb. I took a tray of rings from the case and set it on top. A man got out of the car and stood gazing at something in the show window. He was tall, lean, and thirtyish. He wore western clothes, a suede jacket, flannel shirt, bandanna, and corduroy pants that fitted his long legs snugly and were belted low on lean hips. His Stetson was on the back of his head.

I picked up a ring and the chamois. I knew his name was Patrick Abbott, and he'd been out at Warner's Dude Ranch for about four days. Everybody knew that, by the grapevine, and also that he was an artist. That's all anybody knew so far, but as I sat now looking at him I thought what a shame it was that the best-looking guy that had hit Santa Maria in a blue moon had to be another artist. I've got nothing against artists. It's just that there were so many around Santa Maria.

Then I saw he was coming in the shop and wished I had checked on my lipstick when I was in the back room.

# CHAPTER 4

HE DUCKED as he entered the door. Then he took off his hat and tucked it under the arm holding his portfolio. His dark brushed-back hair grew in a peak.

"Good morning," he said.

He had a deep easy kind of voice.

"Good morning."

"May I see the picture in the window, please?"

"Which one?" I asked, laying down the chamois.

He smiled. "There's only one. Don't bother to get up. I'll get it."

He took a long step and reached for the picture. I picked up the chamois and finished wiping off a ring.

"May I sit down?"

"Do."

There were two big skin chairs and a corner seat by the fireplace. My customer put his hat and the portfolio on one chair and took the corner seat, the best place because it looked towards the window. He crossed his long legs and concentrated on the picture. I worked with the rings. It was nothing which taxed the intellect, however, so I was able to concentrate on Mr. Abbott. His eyes were blue-green, deep-set under straight black brows, the flesh of his face was spare, and there were lines in his tanned cheeks and around his eyes from the sun.

"Cigarette?" he asked suddenly.

"No, thank you."

"Mind if I smoke?"

I was astonished that anyone was left alive polite enough to ask. "No," I said. "Go right ahead. I just don't want one,"

He took a cigarette from his pack and lit it and again fixed his eyes on the picture. I went on working with the rings and after a while, and entirely against my own determination, I got to think about that murdered man again. If Gilbert should start talking, and people took it up, I'd soon be hearing it in the shop. Probably I would anyhow. People would probably drop in and after a while say offhandedly, "Tell me, do you ever hear anything from Tom Brandon?" "No," I would say, "Nothing." "How long has it been?" they would say then, and I would say exactly, knowing full well that they all knew my occasional letters to him had been coming back to me now for three years. "How strange," they would say then. "What could have happened to him, do you think? Where could he be? After all, you would know if anybody knew, Jean. You were one of his agents. You have a few of his pictures. An artist might want to disappear from his wife, perhaps, but he wouldn't be likely to abandon his agent, would he?" And then their eyes would strain out towards the desert, to the southeast, where the mysterious Arkwright had lived with Carmencita. "Well, why not? Stranger things have happened. And no one ever saw this man Arkwright face to face, save Carmencita, and she's not talking. Carmencita never did talk, you know. Would it be possible for a smart girl like that to know as little about a man she lived with for a whole year as she pretended at the inquest? Such a nice man, Tom Brandon. So kind. Singularly without temperament for an artist. I wonder if he was in love with Carmencita. An artist is a fool about a face. But Mona herself is so beautiful."

"Is this for sale?" asked my customer.

I jumped. "Oh, yes. The price is on the back."

He turned it over. "Fifty dollars? Seems very cheap."

"Is."

"Why?"

"The artist needs the money."

"It looks like a fine piece of work."

"Everything he does is tops," I said.

"O'Hara," he said, reading the signature. "I'll take it. Have you anything else of his?"

"Not at the moment. He's not exactly prolific."

I was glad he was buying that picture. It was a delicate yet vivid portrayal of two Indians riding their pintos across the desert. It was done with great economy of line yet catching the poignant excitement of the scene as only Michael could.

"You say he lives here?"

I hadn't said so, but I did. He wondered then if he might go to Michael's house and see if he had anything more on hand. I told him the O'Haras had gone to Santa Fe for the day. He said he'd have to pay with a check. He came over to the counter and wrote the check with his fountain pen, on a bank in San Francisco, and signed it Patrick Abbott in a small precise handwriting.

Then he brought his portfolio and laid two watercolors on the case.

"What do you make of these?" he asked.

I hesitated. Too long.

"I suppose I need teaching?"

"Did you do them?" I asked. It was silly. I knew he had. I felt embarrassed.

But Patrick Abbott remained entirely at his ease. "Are you an authority on art?" he asked.

"Me? Of course not."

"But you sell it?"

"Oh, no, I don't. Not to any extent. But Michael's a good artist and a nice guy, and I like to help him out. That's what I've always done, really. I haven't room to show pictures, but when I like a person and his work I like to have some of his things around."

He was listening as though every word I said had importance. "You are an artist?"

"No, indeed," I said. I laughed. "I wanted to be. That's why I came to Santa Maria. I was eighteen. But I got wise to myself pretty soon and started this shop."

"Like it?"

"Crazy about it. Doesn't make sense. You can't imagine a worse sort of business, Mr. Abbott. But if I didn't have it I'd have to teach school or something and probably couldn't live in Santa Maria, and I'd hate that."

"Nice place, Santa Maria," said Patrick Abbott. "So simple."

"Simple?" I said. Then I said, "I know what you mean. It was, too, when I came here eight years ago. But now it's getting too much talked about. Tourists come from all over, which means that Santa Maria will be spoiled, like Santa Fe and Taos."

"Tourists should be good for your business."

I sighed. "It's a vicious circle," I said. I resented the notoriety Mona Brandon had given Santa Maria, because it was she who had put the little village in the public mind, and kept it there. That brought tourists. But if tourists didn't come I'd have to shut up shop. If I didn't have the shop I couldn't live in Santa Maria. I adored living in Santa Maria. In spite of occasional gloomy Mondays. Life was very complicated, and I was about to say so when Jim Trask came into the shop.

# CHAPTER 5

MR. TRASK was six-feet-four, with blue eyes, sandy hair and a weather-beaten face. He wore jeans, high laced boots, and a plaid jacket. The brim of his old sombrero boasted a time-honored curl.

"Morning, Miss Holly, ma'am," he said, in his soft southwestern voice. I said good morning. "Kind of looks like snow." I said it did.

Mr. Trask glanced at Patrick Abbott, who was standing at the left of the glass case. I introduced them. "Mr. Trask is our sheriff," I said. "Mighty glad to know you, Mr. Abbott," said the sheriff.

"Glad to know you, Mr. Trask," Patrick Abbott said. They shook hands.

"Fact is, I saw your car parked outside and stopped in here just to get acquainted," said Mr. Trask. He paused for an instant, then said, "Sergeant Gilbey was in this morning from state police headquarters. I was telling about a murder case that's come up here and he thought you might be interested, Mr. Abbott."

I stared.

"I'm here for a vacation, Mr. Trask."

"That's what he said."

Patrick Abbott smiled. "I stopped in at your state headquarters on my way up here to say hello. I wasn't looking for a job, Mr. Trask."

The sheriff grinned rather sheepishly. "It's not a job, Mr. Abbott. We don't have the money for a special investigator, I reckon. But the circumstances are kind of peculiar and the sergeant had a notion you might be interested to hear about them."

"Of course."

"We could talk right here. If Miss Holly don't object."

I said to make themselves quite at home. It was the first of several similar conversations which they held in my shop during the next few days. I have always felt proud that the sheriff honored me with his confidence enough to speak quite frankly in my presence to Patrick Abbott about something of which at the time the town itself knew very little.

The sheriff mentioned that he had started out as a Texas Ranger. Patrick Abbott said his father had been a Wyoming sheriff, but that he himself called San Francisco home. I knew Mr. Trask quite well. He had a job he liked and be did it to the best of his ability on the money he had. The county, however, was a very poor one. It was infinitely large, but mostly desert and mountains.

I glanced out and noticed that the plaza was thickening with its mid-morning traffic. A good many cars of all descriptions had angled in at the curbs. Indians, Mexicans, ranchers, artists and townspeople loitered about. The Indian and Mexican women carried shopping bags and went from store to store. The white (or Anglo, as we called them) women didn't carry bags, but went into the stores empty-handed and emerged with their arms crowded with packages.

I saw Julia Price park her Buick in front of the Jefferson Hotel. I was glad she'd come back. She had left for Hollywood only two weeks ago saying she was gone for the winter, but she'd got back yesterday morning.

Mona Brandon skimmed around the square in her Cadillac. The top was down. I caught the metallic gleam of her hair under a tiny fur hat. Her Indian boy, Luis Martinez, was at the wheel.

Carmencita Dominguez crossed the plaza, cater-corner.

I forgot the desultory talk by the fireplace as my eyes followed the Mexican girl's slim proud figure on the diagonal crossing of the square. She wore navy trousers, a black leather jacket, and a black sombrero sat jauntily on her jet-black hair. I noticed the whiteness of her skin and her wide-apart gray eyes and her gun.

"I wanted to talk about a murder we had here last week, Mr. Abbott," I then heard Mr. Track saying, and my ears snapped to attention. "Victim was an old tramp of a fellow who lived out on the desert. Called himself Arkwright. We had the inquest, but I'm not quite settled in my mind that everything's okay. Like you to go out some time and look the place over with me."

"Tell me about it first," Patrick Abbott said.

# CHAPTER 6

THE BODY had been found in the desert about ten miles southeast of Santa Maria. The throat had been cut from ear to ear. There was a little mountain river not far from where it lay, which, two miles further down the valley, passed the house where the dead man had lived.

"How do you get there from Santa Maria?" Patrick Abbott asked.

"To the house? You go four miles south on the main Santa Fe Road and then four miles east along a trail past Mrs. Price's ranch. I didn't reckon a car could use that trail. I just happened to hear, though, that a couple of cars went through there last week. Anyway, this man Arkwright never used the trail. He hid out for some reason. There was a Mexican woman who lived with him and who walked back and forth to town for anything they needed, or else walked as far as Mrs. Price's and rode in with her. However, I'm getting off my story. The body was found by a neighbor named Gomez. He had lost a sheep and he saw buzzards hovering around the spot and went to investigate and came onto the body. He went home and told his wife and then got in his old jalopy and came to town to get me. The D.A.'s down in Phoenix—his wife is bad sick there—so I took the coroner and Doc Johnson and we went right out, but the man had been dead for some time. Four days anyway, the doctor said. It's been pretty warm and what with the varmints in the desert there was hardly anything left but bones."

"When was this?"

"Saturday. Day before yesterday."

"Did Gomez identify the body?"

"No, sir. He had never set eyes on the man. His farm was a couple of miles on down the river, but he seldom had any occasion to go up that way. Carmencita, the Mexican woman, identified the dead man after we brought him to town."

"Know Arkwright's first name?

"Carmencita said it was Albert."

"How did she identify him, Mr. Trask?"

"By his clothes. Also by a small-like scar on the back of his head."

I had a twinge of memory, something I had forgotten trying to make itself remembered, I guess, but nothing happened.

"Carmencita," said Abbott. "What's her other name?"

"Dominguez." The sheriff seemed surprised.

"Any relation to the pretty girl in the Castillo?"

"Yes, sir. Older sister."

"I'm putting you off your story," Patrick Abbott said. "Go ahead. I'll try not to interrupt again."

"Do it any time you like, Mr. Abbott. Well, the body had been lying on its face. The face itself was all gone. We managed to get a picture of that scar on the scalp and some hair and that's just about all. Hair was dark brown. He had first rate teeth. No fillings or anything. We were sure it was murder because the wound was too long and too deep to be self-inflicted and because we couldn't find the knife. We were pretty sure it was a knife. A heavier implement would probably have got at the bone. There was an empty wallet near the body and we assumed that the motive would have been robbery because Carmencita said the man carried lots of money."

Patrick Abbott flicked an ash at the fireplace.

"Is Carmencita as pretty as the one in the Castillo?"

"Some think so and some don't, Mr. Abbott." I got off my stool and took a picture from a drawer and laid it face down on the glass case, and then went on with the silver. "But anyway she always has been too good-looking for her own good, I reckon."

"How's that?"

"Well, she's got a kind of reputation, Mr. Abbott. And she's been in the pen for theft."

"Was she married to this Arkwright?"

"No, sir. She says not. I don't think she had anything to do with the murder. She had an alibi. She had left the man for good the day before the doctor figured he was murdered. She's been staying in town with her aunt, see, and she accounted satisfactorily for all her time."

The aunt was my part-time help, Mrs. Lotta Dominguez.

Patrick Abbott asked if it wasn't pretty hard to prove an alibi covering so much time, especially when no one could tell exactly when the man had been killed. The sheriff agreed, but said that everyone at the inquest had been convinced that she had told the truth. They had all been struck by her sincerity. It was quite different from her usual manner since she had been in prison. She had always claimed, he said, to have been innocent of the crime for which she had been sent up, and had made things worse by pretending to have a grudge against the world ever since. But she had been convincingly simple and sincere at the inquest.

"You say no one knew the man except Carmencita?" Patrick Abbott asked.

"That's right."

"Seems peculiar."

"Very, Mr. Abbott. Her story is that after she was paroled she went to Santa Fe and worked as a waitress in a tavern outside the town. She claims that the fellow walked in one day to eat, that was about a year ago, and they got to talking and made a date. He seemed to have plenty of money so she quit her job pronto and went to live with him in a tourist camp. We checked that. He registered himself as John Simpson, Los Angeles, California, printed it, and he stayed there for one week just a year ago, and the owner of the camp said he was a quiet enough fellow and had an old Ford car. He forgot to take the license number. It seems Carmencita only stayed at the camp a couple of days. Then, according to her story, and it checks, she came up here and rented that house out there. It belongs to a banker here in Santa Maria, by name of McClure. McClure said Carmencita didn't tell him that anyone was going to live with her in the house, but she paid down a year's rent in advance and McClure is tighter'n the bark of a tree so I reckon he didn't ask no questions. Fact is," the sheriff said, pausing after this unusual flow of talk, "nobody thought much of it. It's natural for Carmencita to come back here and if her friend was kind of shady and they kind of hid out, that was natural, too, I reckon."

Patrick Abbott nodded. "How did the man get up here from Santa Fe?"

"Oh. Well, Carmencita said she rented the place and then sent him a letter to General Delivery, Santa Fe. Two nights later he walked in. According to her he said he had sold the car and had come up by bus, which made her sore at the time, because, she said, if she had known they weren't going to have a car she wouldn't've picked such an out-of-the-way house, even though he had specified wanting a place somewhere away from other people. Also he wanted a house up there near the reservation and the woods on beyond, she said. We asked her why. She said he liked the view and liked to fish.

"Well, I took the usual steps. We had the inquest. I sent what exhibits we had to state police headquarters for expert examination, only there ain't much."

"What about clothing?" Patrick Abbott asked.

"He wore jeans. Blue, with brass buttons. Usual stuff. Had a change of the same at the house, also some woolen underwear, corduroys, and a lumber jacket. Every stitch bought here in the chain stores. Carmencita says he burned everything he wore when he came here and why not, because it was dirty." The sheriff chucked his cigarette stub. "Well, I figured the fellow was a bum, carrying too much money maybe for his own good. There's a narrow strip of Indian reservation between that place and the woods. I wondered maybe if the Indians thought he might be spying on them when he went up that river fishing. It makes Indians mighty sore to be spied on, Mr. Abbott. Early this morning I went out there again. Somebody had been in the house."

"Was it locked up?"

"No, sir. Only nobody ain't likely to go to that house just now, after what happened. But somebody had been there, and the funny part is that there was nothing missing but a small picture from the bedroom wall, and—"

"What kind of picture, Mr. Trask?"

"A saint, sir. Mexicans hang one in every room. But it wasn't the missing picture that bothered me as much as something else. There was a spot on the floor of the sitting room, Mr. Abbott, that looked liked ink. Still does. Only now that spot is black and I'd swear on a stack of Bibles that when I was out there the other day that spot was bright green."

Patrick Abbott sat forward in his seat. His eyes went green themselves, a trick of the muscles, as I was to realize later on, a sudden narrowing when he became exceptionally alert.

"What can I do to help you, Mr. Trask?"

"If you could take the time to go out to that house with me, Mr. Abbott, I'd be mighty obliged. I reckon you'd see a lot I probably missed." He hesitated. "I reckon I ought to tell you that some people seem to think the dead man was a man named Brandon who used to live here. I doubt it."

Patrick Abbott said he'd be glad to go. They made a date for nine the following morning.

# CHAPTER 7

PATRICK ABBOTT remarked that he had hoped to keep his profession a secret while on his holiday in Santa Maria.

"Don't worry. I won't mention it. And Miss Holly is one woman that don't talk. There isn't another person in Santa Maria I'd think out loud before the way I've done here, and go away knowing I wouldn't be quoted."

I glowed, thinking it a great compliment. But honestly I didn't let down my back hair with anybody but Julia Price. Julia wasn't careful of her own secrets but she was a rock about other people's.

Patrick Abbott also asked the sheriff a few questions about the Indians. Mr. Trask had told him that a corner of the Indian reservation was not far from the Arkwright house. On the mountains nearby was a forest which belonged to some land syndicate in the East. Our Indians, Mr. Trask said, were quiet, but any Indians might commit murder if they thought their religious doings were spied on.

I expected Patrick Abbott to leave with the sheriff. Instead he lit another cigarette and sat down.

"I thought you were an artist, Mr. Abbott?" I said.

"I hope to be, Miss Holly."

"I think your pictures are pretty good, for a detective."

"Thank you," Patrick Abbott said gravely.

"But just what goes on? I mean, have you come up here to detect something and are only pretending to be an artist? If so I can give you some advice. Just don't show your stuff. Nobody will think a thing." He regarded me earnestly and I hurried to explain. "For instance we have a poet here for whom everyone has the highest regard, that is for his work, yet no one has seen a line he's done in all the years he's been out here. But we're sure he's a genius. You know why? Because no one can say he's not all he pretends to be."

Patrick Abbott smiled appreciatively, but his reply was calm as ever.

"But I'm not here on a case, Miss Holly. It's really a vacation. And I do want to be an artist."

We talked then about Michael as a possible teacher. I said maybe he'd be home this afternoon and told him where they lived. He said if I saw O'Hara first please to mention the lessons. I said I would.

"Well, what do you think of that murder?" I asked then.

"Sounds very interesting," he said.

"Interesting is a funny word for murder," I said. I slanted a glance at the portrait upside down on the counter, the one I had taken from a drawer while Mr. Trask was talking.

"You think so?"

I said, "Do you think Mr. Trask is right in not following the thing up unless the clues merit it?"

"He has no choice."

"Suppose that man were someone people here used to know? Someone who was hiding out, for some reason?"

"Is that probable?"

"Oh, I don't think so," I said quickly. "But murder is murder."

I realized how stupid this sounded then, and quickly picked up the picture on the case and carried it over to Patrick Abbott.

"What's this?" he asked.

"Carmencita."

He held it in both hands and said, after a moment, "She reminds me of someone."

"Perhaps you've seen her on the plaza?"

"No," he said. "That's not it."

I said the artists used to love to paint her but she wouldn't pose any more. He asked who did this portrait, and I said his name was Brandon. He asked if Brandon was related to the woman who owned the big house he passed on his way from town to the ranch and I said very very casually that he was her husband, only nobody seemed to know exactly where he was now. Patrick Abbott looked for a good while at the picture, and after a while he rose and laid it casually on the case and remarked that if I'd tell him where to find the logs he would fix the fire.

# CHAPTER 8

HE HAD just moved into the store room when Mona Brandon came in. I stepped behind the glass case as Mona tripped across the room, conscious of her yellow hair, a tiny fur hat matching a jacket, a blue skirt, over-sweet perfume and little footsteps. Her rather square face was quite expressionless. She had blue eyes, a white complexion, sparkling teeth, regular features, and beautiful clothes.

"Hello, Jean," she began, on entering. She left the door open. When she went out she would also leave it open and I would have to close it. "I want to give you an order." Her eyes kept roving. They came to a stop on Patrick's hat and portfolio, and then returned to me, not quite the same, for they had noted something which was not self-explanatory. "I'm going to give your jewelry-stuff as Christmas presents, Jean. It looks like junk, but that's the style now." I winced, as I loved many of my things. "I want about twenty-five pieces. Some of them antiques. About a third of them for men. They go East. Bring whatever you've got to the house this afternoon at five."

"What price things do you want?" I asked.

"I want to spend in all about five hundred dollars." Gosh, I thought. "Better bring about forty things so I can make a choice. Oh, on approval, remember."

She was already leaving the shop, taking for granted that I'd do as she ordered. Why not? I needed the money and she knew it. She was a good customer.

"Five sharp?" I asked as she left.

"Sharp." Then she faced about and said, as if it were an afterthought, "I'm giving a party for the O'Haras tomorrow night. Nine to one. Like you to come."

"Thank you," I said.

Patrick Abbott came out of the back room with a log in each hand. Properly a green one and a dry one, the way we burn them here. He put them on the fire and kicked them into place.

Mona sailed right back to the middle of the room.

"I don't know just why I had to get a party and Christmas presents on my mind at the same time, except that I've decided suddenly to leave for New York next week." She glanced archly at Patrick Abbott's back. "If there is anyone you want to bring to the party . . ."

"I can't think of anyone," I said.

Patrick Abbott faced about. He took out his handkerchief and wiped the dust from his hands.

"We haven't met," Mona said.

I introduced him. Patrick looked positively delighted. Mona, thrilled. She said if he was going to be in town tomorrow night to come to her party. He said he'd like that very much.

"Why don't you bring Jean?" Mona said. She sounded poisonously sweet. "Jean is a problem for us, Mr. Abbott, having no car. Well, *adios,*" she said, and went out.

"Is she the wife of the man who did the portrait?" Patrick asked, after seeing her out the door.

I nodded. I was angry. That crack about the car evened her up for having to ask for the introduction. She knew why I didn't have a car. I had no time to use a car.

Patrick went to the chair and picked up his Stetson. He creased the crown and set it on his head.

"I'm rather sorry I can't take that Arkwright murder case," he said.

"Mr. Trask can handle it, can't he?" I said edgily.

"Of course."

I looked at him. His eyes were twinkling.

He picked up the portfolio and carefully inserted Michael's picture inside and tied it up.

"May I take you to the party, Miss Holly?" he asked.

"Oh, you don't have to pay any attention—"

"But I want to. How about dinner with me first, too?"

"Well. All right. It's the style to have dinner at the Castillo before Mona's evening affairs. You wear your best clothes, by the way. Why don't you come over a little early and see my house and have a cocktail?" I explained to him where I lived and how to get there.

Just then Mona's car skimmed past the window. Luis Martinez was at the wheel.

"Mrs. Brandon has a handsome Indian chauffeur," Patrick Abbott said.

The sting of her words came back. I said, "He isn't her chauffeur, exactly. She says she adopted him." I didn't mean to sound disagreeable, but I knew I did. I looked at Patrick Abbott. He was laughing at me.

# CHAPTER 9

AT NOON I put the screen in front of the fire, locked up, and crossed the plaza to lunch at the Castillo. I wasn't mad any longer, or sunk, the way I'd been this morning. The clouds were as grim as ever, so my better spirits must be due to the prospect of a five-hundred-dollar sale, or meeting Patrick Abbott.

There were always lots of people on the plaza at noon. Today the dull light made the color and variety of Santa Maria even more striking than usual. Dark chiseled male Indian faces looked out of their pale swathing blankets. Anglos in cowman clothes were everywhere. Some were actually cowmen, but more were male or female artists, polishing off a dizzy western outfit with masses of silver and turquoise bracelets and rings. Mexican girls promenaded, fluttering sooty eyelashes and swinging neat hips.

The Castillo was the rendezvous at lunchtime for the artists. Its cream-colored walls, dark beams, and wild west bar made them a pictorial setting.

I went in and sat down at the table Rose always kept for Julia Price, Daisy Payne and myself. They hadn't yet been in. I nodded at people here and there about the room. Gilbert Mason sat gazing at his coffee cup, at the little table midway back where

he always ate alone. Rose was at the bar waiting for some cocktails Joe Padilla was mixing. Through the front windows I saw
the Santa Fe bus come in. Some women got out and went into a
huddle in front of the Jefferson Hotel.

"Hi, Miss Holly!" It was Rose. She poured me a glass of
water.

"Hello, Rose. How's tricks?"

"Okay," she said. "What you eat, Miss Holly?"

I said I'd have the roast-beef plate, salad and coffee, which
would be quick. She wrote it down and went away, walking as
always like a queen. She was a brunette, and a very different
type from Carmencita.

"Is all, Miss Holly?" Rose asked, when she brought my food.

"Yes, thank you."

She took a quick look around.

"Miss Brandon ask me to help at party tomorrow night," she
murmured in her lilting, softly accented speech. "You think I
ought to?"

"Why not?"

But I knew why not. The Dominguezes might be off Carmencita but they were off Mona Brandon more, and had been
ever since she let Carmencita go to prison.

Rose tossed her raven hair.

"I think I go maybe. I want to see inside that house, Miss
Holly. My mama have a fit if I go, but maybe she not find out."

I said, "I'm sure you must be glad about Carmencita's going
to get married. Such a nice boy."

Rose's pretty lips curled.

"I think Juan Ortega too good for Carmencita. I have no interest in anything she do, and my mother cry if we speak her
name even. I go wait on peoples now."

She meant those women tourists, who were coming in now and filling up the tables between mine and the front windows. Rose was very busy, very pretty, and very efficient as she got them seated, filled their glasses, and imperiously took their orders. I sat eating my lunch, thinking how grimly Carmencita's family had turned against her. Yet they had sided with her when Mona had her prosecuted a few years ago now. It must have been the way she'd carried on after leaving prison, first in Santa Fe, and then living out there with that Arkwright, and so on. Carmencita had pocketed a diamond bracelet belonging to Mona Brandon and had paid for it with two years in prison. Rose was about sixteen, I thought. Carmencita, with a lifetime of experience behind her, couldn't be more than twenty-two.

I was signing for my lunch when a lusty "Hiya, Jean!" sounded through the restaurant. It was Julia Price speaking as she came in with Daisy Payne.

Julia Price was a divorcée and had settled near Santa Maria because she liked the country and the climate. She was thirtyish, with big brown eyes, a little chin, and red hair which she had touched up occasionally. Today she wore corduroy pants and jacket, cowboy boots, and a Mexican sombrero on which was embroidered a cowboy throwing a steer. Daisy Payne was older than Julia, with a small biscuit-shaped face and pale blue eyes and fair hair. She was dressed in a tweed skirt, a plaid jacket and a red velvet tam o'shanter with a long feather on it. She wore high yellow laced boots. There was a sheath in her right boot for a knife. The one Daisy always carried in it had a turquoise matrix handle and a long thin flexible blade. I don't know how I happened to notice as they crossed the restaurant that the knife was missing.

Daisy was English, but had taken out her American papers.

She had come to Santa Maria some years ago with her mind made up for a wild west experience, and she always went armed to the teeth. Besides that knife she carried a revolver in her handbag. Her gun's handle matched that of the knife. I had had them made to order for her.

I had to get back to the shop. They said they'd stop in after lunch. Daisy said she wanted to buy a ring to send to England.

I'd been back in the shop a few minutes and was poking at the fire when some of the clubwomen tourists came in. They started milling around the way people do who are merely killing time. Two of them bought some postcards, wrote them in the shop, then asked for stamps, which I gave them from the cash register.

I stood behind the jewelry case not thinking much about my customers, but looking out the windows. Then the women sort of clustered round and started asking questions about Mona Brandon. This always happened. The questions were always the same. They asked if it were true that she had adopted an Indian, and why. They wondered why anyone so worldly would want to build such a be-you-ti-ful house in a place like Santa Maria, and if it was true that her Indian slept in a gorgeous Louis Quinze bedroom rolled in his blanket on the floor. Since I didn't know any of the answers I said yes or no, according to what I thought they wanted, and I carefully refrained from stating my own opinion of Mona's suburbanish mansion. Still, I could see the tourists' viewpoint. When the bus crossed the saddle to the south and began the gentle twenty-mile descent towards Santa Maria, travelers could see Mona's house long before they could pick out the town. At that distance Santa Maria was like a careless handful of adobe shapes the color of the desert, but Mona's huge house was conspicuous with its red tile roof, seven acres of irrigated greenery, and broken glass glittering on the top of its high walls.

The tourists left. Then Julia and Daisy came in.

They were angry at each other. I could tell because Julia's brown eyes were bigger than usual and her little chin quivered. Daisy said that she wanted an inexpensive ring to send to her niece.

I set a couple of trays of rings on the glass case and while Daisy was looking these over joined Julia, who was smoking by the fireplace.

"Have a good trip to the Coast?" I asked Julia.

"Lovely. But I wanted to come back the minute I got there, and about did. Had my hair done a new shade."

She snatched off her sombrero.

"It's beautiful," I said.

"Inhibitions never bother Julia," Daisy sniffed. "Why tell people?"

"I dye my hair for beauty, not to deceive, Daisy."

Daisy fidgeted. Everything irritated her today. "How much is this one, Jean?" she asked, holding up a nice old Zuni wedding ring set with pure azure turquoise.

"Price is on that little tag, Daisy."

"Six dollars? Here's a ten, Jean. Will you please box the thing ready for posting?"

I put the ring in cotton and a cardboard box and even wrote the many-jointed Yorkshire address for Daisy. Then I put the new ten-dollar bill in the cash register and gave her four dollars in change.

"I hope you haven't lost your knife, Daisy," I asked her then. She frowned and made no reply. Julia winked at me behind her back. They left the shop, but a moment later Julia stuck her head in again.

"You going to be home tonight, Jeanie?"

"Sure. Come for supper?"

"Thanks. I'll bring along some gin or something." She rolled her big eyes and went.

# CHAPTER 10

I HAD Mona's Christmas order on my mind, so I got into my smock again and brought out some velveteen pads, cleaning things, and tissue paper, and put them on the glass jewelry case. Then—and with a thrill of secret pleasure—I fished out of the safe two cardboard boxes full of antique silver jewelry. The stuff was tarnished pretty badly, but the polish would soon fix that.

I'd just dumped them all in a heap on the case when Patrick Abbott came in. "Mind if I park here again?" he asked. His way of asking made you want him to do anything he liked, and of course I liked having people around, unless their kind of talk bothered me, like Gilbert Mason's. I said for him always to make himself at home. He stood beside the case and asked me questions about the silver. I'd selected five rings, three bracelets, a necklace, and two pairs of earrings from the antiques and put the rest back in the box. I showed them to Patrick Abbott and explained why they were exceptional. Many of them dated back to the days when the Spanish dons lived like feudal lords on vast estates in our Southwest.

"This necklace came from the Dominguez family," I said then, handing it to him, "Don Carlos gave it to his first bride, who made the long journey out here from Spain to marry him.

She was pure Castilian. They say Carmencita resembles her. Gray eyes, ivory skin, black hair." Patrick Abbott took the necklace in his large shapely hands and gravely examined it. "Wait till I polish it," I said then. "You can't tell much about it, the condition it's in." It was not the necklace I'd included in the selection for Mona Brandon, but I thought I would polish it up and put it in the case for a while.

Patrick hung his hat on a peg over some beadwork belts and got out his cigarettes. I started babbling like a brook. "I'm sorry you weren't in here a while ago," I said, squinting at a bracelet of heavy coin silver. "Julia Price and Daisy Payne were here. You must meet them. Daisy's rather a character. She gets very strong likes or dislikes and rather rides them, you know. She's nuts about Mona, and also about Julia, who is just the opposite of Mona, you might say. Julia's Mrs. Price, she owns the ranch next that place where that Arkwright lived." I chuckled. "Julia bought a place in the country to cure herself of being so social, but she stays most of the time in town, turns up almost any time of day or night."

"She sounds nice," Patrick Abbott said.

"Julia's marvelous," I said. "Daisy is all right, too. But she's cranky. She has an endless feud on with Gilbert Mason, much to his delight."

"Mason?"

"You haven't met Gilbert? He's our poet."

"Carries a briefcase? Needs a haircut?"

"He's the one," I said. "I hope I haven't put you off Daisy. As a matter of fact I like her very much, but she makes herself a lot of trouble with all her strong notions. Julia's from Chicago. They've both been here almost as long as I have."

"Eight years?"

I smiled at his remembering. "That's my record. They've each been in Santa Maria seven years. Mona Brandon the same. All the artist crowd and its hangers-on came from somewhere else, you know." I looked up and met Patrick Abbott's level glance. "There's something about polishing silver that makes you talk like a sewing circle," I said. But that wasn't it. His personality invited confidence. From the first I forgot my usual caution when speaking to Patrick Abbott. I said what I thought and felt safe doing it, and understood.

"If I'm going out in society I'd better have the dope, hadn't I?" he said.

"You'll have it," I said. "Don't worry, you'll be getting it from all directions pronto."

He drew on his cigarette. "I hope it doesn't get around that I'm a detective."

I laughed. "I'll keep quiet."

"First real break I've had for years. And I walk right into a murder case!" He laughed. "Even before that I promised to do a little looking round while up here for a friend in the Secret Service, but that's nothing, merely a matter of sending him a wire if I stumble onto anything really important. Murder's a different proposition."

"Aren't you even going with Mr. Trask to see the house?"

"Of course. Two pairs of eyes are better than one and I might see something he missed."

I said, "Let's hope it really was murder for whatever cash the poor man had. Almost anybody in this country is poor enough to turn to crime in a moment of stress if it meant a little ready money. It's funny about Santa Maria. Almost everybody is really poor, including the Anglos. Oh, there are a few well-to-do families among the business people, but mostly there are poor people at one extreme and at the other Mona Brandon, who's so terribly rich. They say she doesn't even know how much she owns. She was born rich, she married money the first time, and that husband died leaving her richer . . ."

I broke off, wondering why I'd mention a thing like that. I felt sure that he was not interested.

"Did you have to go to school and learn to be a detective, or what?" I asked then.

"I went to the University of California. Afterwards to a special school."

"What courses did you have to take?"

"Oh, ballistics, photomicrography, forensic medicine."

"Heavens. Then what?"

"Then I got a job with an agency. After five years I went to Europe for a year and studied methods in London and Berlin and Paris, then came back and worked for myself . . ."

He broke off, for Luis Martinez, swiftly and silently, as was always his way, had walked into the shop.

# CHAPTER 11

THE SHOP door was an old thing which habitually sagged and groaned, yet Luis always opened and closed it without its making a murmur.

"I buy Hopi belt in window, Jean," he announced bluntly.

"Which one?" I asked, already starting a defense. He never had any money.

"I fetch." He took two long steps and reached the belt. He held it up. "How much?"

"Fifteen dollars. The price is on that ticket, Luis."

Disdain briefly tinged his handsome face. Then he began examining it meticulously. The Indian wore his shining black hair cut in bangs across his copper-colored forehead and looped in a kind of bun on his neck. His clothes were gray flannel trousers, a white soft shirt, brown shoes, and a blanket of thin Scottish wool, at the moment draped like a crushed scarf across his shoulders.

The Hopi belt was scarlet, hand-woven, and embroidered with tribal symbols in emerald, black and white.

"You keep for me, Jean?" Luis asked suddenly with a surprising note of tenderness in his flattish voice.

"Don't tell me you aren't going to dicker, Luis."

"It too much. But it fine thing."

"I know it is. No, I won't keep it. I've already got a shelf full of things reserved for you in the store room."

"I get money, Jean."

"That's what you always say."

"Mona give me maybe fifty dollar Christmas."

I frowned. "Luis, those things already in the storeroom add up to a hundred and three dollars and thirty-five cents. You haven't even got the thirty-five cents. Either you must pay for them and take them away, or I must put them back into stock."

He ignored my long speech. "I got have this belt, Jean," he repeated, in his monotonous Indian voice. "You keep five minutes? I be back."

He went out, moving with his cat's grace and his uncanny soundlessness.

"Poor Luis," I said, to Patrick Abbott. "He's crazy about Indian things. But he never has a penny."

"How's that?"

"Mona doesn't want her place cluttered up with Indian stuff."

"His clothes cost plenty," said Patrick Abbott. "His pants and shirt looked like London. His blanket's an import, and incidentally that tartan it's made of is supposed to be exclusive with the royal family."

Then Luis came back. He laid down three five dollar bills and went off with the belt. I was dumbfounded and said so.

"Mrs. Brandon gave it to him," Patrick Abbott said. "She's standing near the Castillo."

I leaned to the right a little and saw Mona and the O'Haras talking together. So they'd got back. I saw Luis joining them. I could see him showing off the belt.

"You mean he just made a touch? And got away with it?"

"That's how it looked," Patrick Abbott said.

Maybe Gilbert was right, I thought then. Maybe she was really crazy about Michael, I meant. Maybe she didn't want Michael to see her being mean to Luis.

# CHAPTER 12

NOT LONG after Luis Martinez was in Patrick Abbott left the shop. I'm used to having people hang about like that, but I might as well admit right now that I had seldom had company I liked as much. I finished making the selection for Mona, polished each and wrapped it separately in tissue paper, and then put them in a two-handled Navajo basket for carrying them to her house.

At half-past four I checked over the money in the register, put the change in the safe in the back room, then made out a deposit slip for the bills and sealed it with them in an envelope which I would drop in the bank's night depository. I kept out the check for Michael's picture, meaning to give it to him directly, for as I was finishing up I could see the O'Haras and Mona in her car in front of the Castillo. That meant a ride to Mona's, too. The silver was rather heavy for the long walk.

But by the time I was ready they had gone. I locked up, dropped the envelope into the bank, and headed along the road towards Mona Brandon's.

Usually I would enjoy such a walk after my day in the shop. It was only a mile, and though I had to walk in the road this one was well-kept, not full of holes and ruts like the one which led out past my own house. But this afternoon even the prospect bored me.

The town ended a couple of straggling blocks beyond the plaza, then there was what might be called country, with only Daisy's house, and, further off the road, Gilbert Mason's cottage, between the plaza and Mona's big place. There was a light at Daisy's and Julia's car was parked in front. Her house was a short distance off the road. On my way back, I decided, I would stop and ride back to my own house with Julia. A little further away, in a field, Gilbert's house looked white and lifeless and very little. It was reached by a path which led past Daisy's English-looking place. I walked on. And now the gloom itself was like something crouching against the earth. The desert looked weird and immense, Mona's walled estate like an oasis in its nothingness, and the mountains loomed dark, without color or shadow, just hugeness.

I walked along growing more and more depressed, wishing that someone would come along and give me a lift, but no one came. It required twenty minutes to walk the mile to Mona's gate. And it was locked, as usual. I rang impatiently and had to wait for the gardener, Pedro, to let me in. He was sorry, he said. He had not been told, he apologized, to expect anyone. Mrs. Brandon had just come in a few minutes ago. I walked on along the shrubbery-swathed drive and noted by my watch when I rang the front doorbell that I was five minutes late. One of Mona's Mexican girls opened the door.

"Hello, Rita," I said. "I hope I'm not too late, Rita."

She looked apologetic. "No, ma'am. But Miss Brandon say she sorry. She not see anyone, Miss Holly."

"But I have an appointment."

"She say leave things and she let you know."

I got mad. It was so typically Mona. All the time of her own in the world, and pulling a stunt like this.

"Tell her she'll have to come to the shop," I said.

I spoke quietly, but I gripped the handles of the basket and sailed back along the drive. I could feel my anger pounding at my throat. I kept getting madder as I marched along, setting my heels down hard, clicking off the winding distance to the gate. It was again locked. That made me madder than ever. When Pedro came back and said something friendly about the weather I'm afraid I snapped at him.

I knew why Mona had done this. It was just one of those things, like her crack about my having no car, which Mona was always doing to put you in your place. She would do a nice thing, like giving me the order for this silver, and then make me pay for it by being nasty in little things. I was too independent.

Well, she would see! If she wanted these things she would now come to the shop for them, like anybody else.

Anyhow Julia was at Daisy's, and I'd stop there myself. But halfway to Daisy's an old car rattled behind me and stopped.

"Hi, Jeanie!" somebody called. It was Michael. "How about taking the load off your feet?"

"Oh, Michael!" I said.

So I didn't stop at Daisy's.

"We were out of coffee," he said.

"I sold your picture, Michael. Patrick Abbott bought it. He's the one staying out at Warner's. The check's made out to me. I'll endorse it when we stop. You can cash it at one of the stores, probably."

Michael laughed.

"I was born under a lucky star, Jean. I just see my finish and something like this happens. I didn't have even the price of a pound of coffee."

We were getting near the plaza. In the gathering haze the street lamps seemed to float disembodied from their posts.

"Sonya and I thrashed it all out today, Jean. I'm through out here. We've decided to go back to New York. I've had an offer from an advertising agency, not too good, but it will do as a start. We haven't decided if we'll leave right away or wait till after Christmas."

"After Christmas, please, Michael."

He made a chuckling sound. "Depends on the job. I wouldn't leave at all if I didn't have to. Mona suggests our going next week. She's driving through, which means free transportation."

"It's a shame," I said about their leaving. "I know how you love Santa Maria. Your work is so marvelous."

"Nice of you to say so, Jean. But why pretend? If Mona didn't give us the cottage free we couldn't have hung on this long."

"It's not exactly free, Michael. You painted the frescoes in her bar, and several oil portraits of Mona."

He angled in at one of the chain grocery stores. I endorsed the check. He said to wait and he'd drive me home. He went in the store and came out with a big paper bag of things which he put in the back seat. He put five dollars on my lap. My commission, which I didn't want—I was rich compared with the O'Haras—but I knew it would offend him if I didn't take it. He drove on along the rough adobe road to my house and got out and opened the car door for me. My black Persian cat was waiting for me at the gate and Michael picked him up and Toby purred against his neck.

# CHAPTER 13

I picked up my black Toby and started up to the house. I felt good now because Michael had been pleased with the check. It wasn't much, but it meant a month's living, if they didn't leave at once, with the way they lived. I was over my temper now and thought I'd acted silly about Mona and the silver. I should have left it with Rita.

I opened the door. The house looked gay and friendly. There was a bright fire flashing on the colorful rugs and pictures. I could smell the spicy smells of dinner. Apples were being cooked, and ham.

I put the basket of silver on the desk in one corner, stuck my head into the kitchen to ask Mrs. Dominguez to set a place for Julia Price, and then had a hot bath. I had just gotten into a wool shirt, flannel trousers, and moccasins when Julia arrived.

She looked tired, much less buoyant than usual. She handed me a bottle of gin.

"Can I have a bath, Jean?" she asked, as she took off her sombrero.

"Sure. There's hot water, and you know where to find towels. I'll make some cocktails. Martinis?"

"*Muchas gracias.*"

She emerged refreshed. Her bright hair made a halo around her funny face. Two martinis made her cheerful. But she was quite reticent, for once, and dinner was over and Mrs. Dominguez gone for the evening before she spoke about what was on her mind.

Julia sprawled in the wing chair. I was across the fireplace, on the sofa, with my back to the long window and its geraniums. We were both smoking.

"I'm worried about Daisy," she said then. "Something *mucho* screwy there, Jean."

"Oh, you know how she is, Julia."

She shrugged. "Oh, I know, all right. I've fought with Daisy about more things than all the rest of you put together. If fights make friends Daisy and I will always be pals, but this time it's serious."

Julia stared at the fire. Her big eyes and her little chin were even more comical when she was solemn.

"It started over Luis Martinez," she said.

"You two must have started a thousand fights about Luis, Julia."

"Uh-huh. And this one started out according to the time-worn pattern. Daisy said as usual that Luis was nothing but a savage and that Mona was wasting time and money trying to make him anything else. I said as usual that it was Luis who was being wasted and that the life he led was nothing but a superior sort of slavery. Daisy said that Mona's adopting him meant that he would have a fortune some day so my goodness, and I said did she really adopt him, or did she just say it, and—"

I cut in. "And in the end you apologized, as usual, and said what did you know about it, really, never having adopted an Indian, that being about the only mistake you never made, you said. So what."

Julia giggled. "You know our fights by heart, Jean."

"You hear a lot sitting around your own shop," I said. "Why worry about it, Julia? Daisy will be all right tomorrow." Julia looked gloomy.

"Jean, did you notice how Daisy acted when you asked her about her knife being gone?"

I nodded.

"Well, that's all part of the present mystery. Also, there's a calf in it."

"A calf?"

"Daisy bought a calf."

"What does Daisy want with a calf?"

"Well, that's what I wanted to know. She said the alfalfa was taking over her place. I reminded her that this is late October and the frost would soon settle the alfalfa. She told me to mind my own business. I told her to go to hell. Then she said she already had the calf now but not to tell anyone that she had it. I said a calf was a hard secret to keep, in a place the size of Santa Maria. She said it was really that she didn't want people to know where she got the calf. Well, it was all so cockeyed that I went ahead, pinned her down, and she finally told me that she had bought the calf from Carmencita."

"Carmencita?"

"Complicated, what? I accused her right away of being afraid she'd have Mona in her hair if Mona knew about her buying calves from Carmencita. Daisy hedged. You know how tight Daisy is, Jean. Well, that explained her getting it from Carmencita. It seems she complained about her alfalfa going to waste, and her boy—who is your Mrs. Dominguez's Tony, you know—said why didn't she get a calf. Daisy asked where she could get one. He told her that his mother said that Carmencita had one out at that Arkwright place that she could have for a dollar if she would go and get it. So Daisy got into her station wagon and went for the calf pronto. It was late in the afternoon, getting toward sunset, so she decided to try that trail on past my place. It's seven miles shorter that way. But I said wasn't the trail impassable and she said it practically was only she didn't know it before, and fortunately a station wagon like she uses has extra clearance.

"Well she got there and Carmencita wasn't there. No one seemed to be there, she said. She said she knocked, no one came to the door, and of course Daisy being such a lady she didn't even try the doorknob to see if the house was locked up. But she could hear the calf bawling in a shed not far from the house. She went there, and it was all by itself and half starved, which touched Daisy's English heart, so she found a piece of rope and tied its little hoofs together and slung it over her shoulder and carried it to her car. She's strong as a horse, of course. Well, she was going to bring it back to town and find Carmencita and pay her for it, of course, and was wondering if her procedure was entirely ethical when she got back to her car and there . . . honestly, Jean, I've got no business telling this."

"Suit yourself," I said, knowing she wouldn't stop now.

"Well, who should be there but Mona and Michael O'Hara. In Mona's station wagon. No way they could get by, or even go back, till Daisy backed up and turned around."

"Well, what of it?"

"The trouble is the way Mona took it. She got in a state, made Daisy promise not to tell about seeing them, said Daisy knew how Sonya would act if she found out."

"And how!" I said, grinning. "What were they doing up there?"

"Mona said she was inspecting the lane with the idea of fixing it up so that Santa Maria would have a shortcut to the Picnic Rocks."

"Mona's benevolences take strange shapes, Julia."

"Sure. Remember the birdbath?"

"Oh, now, Julia! She didn't give that to Santa Maria, in exchange for her warm swimming pool, really."

"She didn't give the town anything else for those warm springs."

"Have it your way. But do be fair. She has done some nice things. For the hospital, for instance, and she finances Gilbert, and gives the O'Haras the house."

"You've made me feel mean," Julia said.

"Well, I'll be mean myself to even up for it," I said, "and say that my guess is that she is fixing up the trail past your place so that you'll have traffic past your house, and so that Carmencita will be ousted from her love nest, but she calls the road kindness to Santa Maria. Only, Carmencita had already left that place, hadn't she?"

"Yes, but Mona didn't know that then," Julia said.

"When was this?"

"Last Wednesday. Carmencita left on Tuesday. Well, anyhow, Daisy believes what Mona tells her. She says they went on past the house and forded the river and took the long way back. Daisy came back the way she'd gone. Incidentally there is a deep dry arroyo just in front of the Arkwright house and Daisy's car was parked in it, which was why they didn't see it till right there. Well, back in town Daisy found Carmencita and gave her the dollar and the calf did what it could while still so young by the alfalfa and Daisy loved it for itself any how. And then they found that man murdered on the desert." Julia set her little chin. "And things happened."

"What?" I asked, a funny little anxiety starting inside me.

"Well, Daisy thought she ought to tell the sheriff about being out there. Seems they figured that the man must have been murdered about that time, and Daisy thought they ought to report. They didn't have any evidence of any kind but maybe some one had seen them out there and it would look pretty funny if they didn't tell on themselves first. So she went to Mona about it. Mona flew in a rage. Daisy got mad herself and said things and then she says Mona snatched that knife Daisy carries in her boot and waved it at her. She called Daisy a nymphomaniac and accused her of going out there to see the man. Can you imagine? Nobody but Mona could have thought of that. But it sure settled Daisy. She's afraid to squeak."

"Well, it should have opened her eyes to Mona."

Julia sniffed.

"Well, it didn't. She thinks now that Mona was just wrought up. For it seems that Mona laid down the knife pronto and began to weep, so Daisy was sorry for her. Mona said please for her not to tell about being at Arkwright's. She said it would not only set Sonya against her, but would start people talking again about Brandon and Carmencita. Mona said she had suffered so on account of that that she would kill herself if she had to go through it all again, that people would say she was up there spying on Carmencita. Daisy swallowed it all like a fish. And, of course, at the inquest nothing came out about their having been out there, so apparently it was just as well she didn't report it. But Daisy forgot her knife at Mona's, and when she went back for it Mona declared it had never been there so Daisy figures now that Mona had a lapse of some kind during which she grabbed the knife and that she remembers nothing about it."

"You don't say!"

"The thing that worries Daisy most though," Julia said slowly, "is that she suspects Arkwright was Tom Brandon. Otherwise, Mona wouldn't take it so hard."

I looked at Julia steadily. She was looking at me the same way.

"Has that occurred to you, Jean?"

"I don't mind telling you it has."

"You don't really believe it, Jean?"

"No. Do you?"

"Certainly not," Julia said. "Of course Daisy is not going to mention it, either."

# CHAPTER 14

It was nine o'clock. Julia got up suddenly and said she had to go home, that she'd been in town all day and hadn't yet got really rested from her trip to California. She put on her jacket and her black hat and I got my flashlight to show her along the flags to the gate. I stood in the dark then watching her drive away down the hill.

It was so dark I couldn't see my tree, another cottonwood, and when Toby mewed near by I could see at first only his eyes, then the darker blob in the dark which was himself. I could have used the flash, naturally, but Toby hates it, so I waited till I could see him then picked him up and carried him inside the house. I sat down by the dying fire and thought about what Julia had told me. It didn't mean a thing, any more than Gilbert's storytelling meant anything. It was just one of those things which Mona did, and the funny thing was that old Daisy never seemed to get wise to her.

Then I heard a car coming up my hill.

I thought it was Julia, coming back. I went to the door and opened it and was standing there when Patrick Abbott got out of his car and came along the flagstones.

"Remember me?" he said. "Sorry I couldn't phone first. But you have none."

"That's right," I said. "Come in."

He looked down at me. "I'd like to go that honky-tonk west of town. I wondered if you'd come with me."

"Saturday night's the night," I said. He didn't say anything. "All right," I said. "Come in and find yourself a drink while I change."

"You're all right as you are, aren't you?"

I was, except I don't like to dance in slacks, if we were to dance. So I went into my room and quickly changed to my tweeds, fixed up my face a little, and changed my moccasins for oxfords. I needn't have bothered for as it happened we didn't dance.

When I came out Abbott was playing with Toby. "You like cats, Mr. Abbott?"

"I like this one."

Toby purred loudly. Patrick Abbott stroked his head and put him down. I picked him up and took him outside, then locked up and put the key under the flower pot to the left of the stoop. Patrick Abbott wanted to know why I left it there at this hour and I said force of habit. We drove back to the plaza, headed west two miles, and arrived at Bill's Place. There was almost a fog now and the rosy neons made an infected looking patch of red against the night.

We went in and sat down at a table near the dance floor. The noise from the jukebox was terrific. Loud noises make me sort of dizzy, so I was in the place a minute or two before I noticed that Carmencita and Juan Ortega were one of five or six couples dancing in the open space at the back of the room.

I said, "So that is why we are here, is it?"

Patrick grinned. "You win. Mind?"

"Why should I? But don't tell me you've fallen for the Ark-wright case?"

"No."

"Then why are we here?"

"I saw them walking on the square. I felt interested. I over-heard them say they were coming out here and I thought maybe you'd like to come, too."

"And tell you all about her. Yes?"

"Certainly not. It's enough just to look at her. I told you she reminded me of someone. I can't think whom."

She was dancing with her pale cheek against her boyfriend's brown cheek. Her eyes were closed. Her skin looked very white and her long thick lashes and cleanly arched eyebrows very black. She wore a red-and-blue checked shirt and navy trousers which fitted her sleek flanks and tiny waist as though made to order. Her black leather jacket and the holster with her gun were hanging over the back of a chair at the table next ours, and her sombrero was on the seat.

Bill himself came for our order. Patrick Abbott asked for a whiskey and soda. I had cognac and a glass of water.

"Why was Carmencita sent to prison?" Abbott asked suddenly.

"The sheriff told you. Theft."

"I got the impression that the circumstances must have been exceptional."

I was feeling pretty irked because of what Julia had told me this evening about Mona and Daisy. So I told him all about Carmencita, how she had had a job at the Castillo, like the one Rose had now, and had picked up a little extra for posing for the artists. Then Mona had hired her as a parlormaid in the big house, and Tom Brandon had been keen about her looks and had painted goodness-knows-how-many heads of her. Mona had got jealous. Then a diamond bracelet had been found in an apron pocket which Carmencita had just taken off preliminary to leaving the house for her free afternoon.

"Who found it?" Patrick asked.

"The housekeeper. A Scotswoman of impeccable character. The Mexican servants all liked her, still do. But Carmencita contended that she was framed."

"Did Mrs. Brandon have her prosecuted?"

I nodded. "And Santa Maria didn't like that part of it. You have to make allowances, you know, give people a chance. The thing that made people really mad was that Carmencita couldn't get probation because Mona wouldn't agree to it."

"Was Brandon in love with her?"

"People said so. Mona was insanely jealous, in any case, and it oughtn't to have been Carmencita's looks entirely. Most people would prefer Mona's."

Suddenly the ear-splitting music stopped dead. Voices which had been speaking loudly abruptly ceased. In the lull the various couples shuffled to their tables. Carmencita and Juan walked with their arms about each other. They seemed genuinely unaware of not being alone in the room. I'm sure they didn't see me, or they would have stopped for a moment at our table. They sat down and fell at once into a whispered talk, leaning close to each other, holding hands under the table. The room itself without the distracting noise of the music and the movement of the dancing was suddenly ten times more nakedly drab and ugly. The gray walls showed their dirt and grime. You noticed that the light came from grimy bulbs dangling from flyspecked cords.

Patrick Abbott signaled Bill and gave him a quarter for the jukebox, and the dancing started again. A waltz this time.

*Ramona.* Carmencita and Juan promptly got up and danced. "She's in love with him," Patrick said.

"I think so, too," I said. "Juan's a nice honest hard-working boy, and I expect it will work out all right."

"I still don't fathom her fascination, Jean."

"Maybe it's because she looks so good," I said.

"That's it!" Patrick said then. "She's a type the early Spanish *padres* favored as the madonna. You see faces like hers in the old cathedrals, in Spain."

We sat for a good while in Bill's Place. When Carmencita noticed me she nodded, but they didn't come to our table. She was happy, I thought, and I was glad that she was going to get married now and settle down.

No one would ever call me clairvoyant.

# CHAPTER 15

NEXT MORNING I woke and saw through the open casement windows that it was gray again. I got up and dressed in the tweed suit I'd worn to Bill's Place last night, with a brown sweater. Then I fed the cat and headed to the Castillo for my morning toast and coffee.

As I walked down my hill and along the road to the plaza the sky looked like a piece of slate. I kept hearing things—the goats bleating in the meadow at the foot of the mesa, their little bells, a worn record of the *Varsoviana* playing in one of a cluster of Mexican houses on the mesa some distance north of mine.

"No snow yet," Mr. Kaufmann said, at the Castillo.

"Not yet," I said.

Rose's eyes were defiant.

"I'm going, Miss Holly! My mama find out, but all the same I'm going to Miss Brandon's tonight."

Before she brought my coffee and could relate more details, Dr. Johnson came in. His thin face was twisted with fatigue. He called to Joe Padilla to fetch him a double whiskey and then sat down at my table. He said he needed company. When Rose came back he ordered a man-sized breakfast and then said he'd been out all night. I supposed that he didn't want to bother his spoiled wife to get up and cook for him, or he would probably have gone straight home from whatever he'd been doing, which, after he'd had his whiskey, he said was an accident case.

"The Santa Fe bus skidded off the road into The Canyon," he said. There were all sorts of canyons hereabouts, but The Canyon was the big one on the way to Santa Fe. I instantly pictured a lot of crushed people, but the doctor said that a tough little tree had caught and held the bus until the sheriff and two of his deputies and himself had effected a tedious rescue. "It took us all night," he said. "Jim Trask is a hero. He went down and stayed in the bus till we got everybody out. They all had bruises and shock but that's all, except the driver, who has a concussion."

I asked if there was anything I could do. He said not today, but that no doubt the whole town would have to go out and play bridge with the victims after a day or two. He said they all wanted to sue the bus company right away and they'd have to stay in the hospital till the company ascertained how badly they were hurt. I walked across to the shop, thinking about those women, nothing more serious on their minds yesterday afternoon than whether Luis Martinez slept rolled in a blanket, all unaware that in a few hours their lives were going to depend on whether or not a silly little tree let a bus plunge down into a canyon. Their escape seemed miraculous.

I had just started the fire when Patrick Abbott came in.

"Mr. Trask can't get away to go out to that Arkwright house this morning," he said, "so I think I'll try to find O'Hara and talk about art lessons."

"Oh, he's going away," I said. "I forgot to tell you."

"At once?"

"Mona's talking of going next week. They may go with her."

"I might as well talk to him, just the same."

We were standing, I near the fire, he in the middle of the room. Then Gilbert came in. He slammed the door.

"Hello, Jean," he declaimed, importantly. "You going to be alone soon?"

Patrick Abbott looked down at Gilbert, his glance sort of skimming over him before it came back to me. His calm expression did not change. Gilbert might have been a fly. I introduced them. They didn't shake hands. Patrick Abbott, without another word, went out.

"Fresh guy," said Gilbert. He sat down in the corner seat. I dropped my things in the store room and came back and started folding up the dust sheets. "What's he doing around here, Jean?"

"Taking a vacation."

"That's what he says, is it?"

"Really, Gilbert. That's what he told me. Should I have cross-examined him?"

"If your intellect wasn't equal to finding out the truth in any other way, why not?" Gilbert's sallow fingers started their tattoo on the briefcase. "Listen, Jean, what's behind this party at Mona's tonight?"

"She told me it was for the O'Haras."

"Why should she give a party for the O'Haras?"

"I believe they are going away."

Gilbert's sickle-shaped grin slid into his puffy cheeks.

"Oh, no. He won't go away now, Jean. He's just getting things nice."

I went on folding dust sheets. I worked slowly.

Gilbert said slyly, "Would you like to see what I've got in my briefcase?" I didn't say anything. I took the sheet from the turquoise case, folded it in half, folded that, and folded that. I could hear the faint chitter of the buckles as Gilbert opened his briefcase. I heard the soft rustle of paper, then the cracked sound of coarser paper being handled. "Here you are, darling!" he said then.

He held up a knife. It was the one from Daisy's boot. The long wicked blade was stained with a dark substance. Gilbert sat holding it by the turquoise-mounted handle, waving it back and forth.

I stood like a statue, the gray muslin cover slackening in my two hands.

"Where did you get that, Gilbert?"

"Wouldn't you like to know?" he sneered.

"What's on it?"

"Just what you think."

I felt sick. He saw it. He laughed and wrapped the knife back in the newspaper. "Daisy's had her fun, Jean. She's made me wretched for years. Now it's my turn."

"What are you going to do?"

"That's my business."

"I thought it was Mona you were going after, Gilbert," I said then.

He said, with intense bitterness, "I've got them both where I want them, at last. You didn't know I hated them both, did you?" He paused. "I suppose everything comes your way if you wait long enough." He paused again. "I will tell you one thing, Jean. This knife was found out on the desert. Yes, about ten miles southeast of Santa Maria, near the place where a man was murdered who called himself Arkwright. Daisy was in love with Brandon. Remember?"

"You would remember that, Gilbert," I said.

I felt tense and strangely anxious. I thought about Daisy's going out there for that calf. But I couldn't think of Daisy's committing murder. That wasn't possible. When I thought that, my tenseness lessened. I knew then as definitely as though I'd seen him do it that Gilbert had picked that knife up at Mona's and stained it with something and put it in his briefcase to do exactly what he was doing here. Then I didn't feel sick any more. I got a dustcloth and put on some cotton gloves, thinking how Gilbert strolled around Mona's place as he liked, paying no attention to her annoyance at the way he made himself at home. I pictured him discovering the knife shortly after she made that scene with poor Daisy and nabbing it for this very purpose.

Suddenly he left the shop. I stood quite still, my eyes trailing Gilbert's slight figure as he crossed the plaza, but my mind busy with old half forgotten things. Daisy's infatuation for Tom Brandon. Mona's treating it as a joke. Nobody taking it seriously, Daisy being one of those caricatures who are funny when in love.

# CHAPTER 16

THE REMAINDER of the day was as dull as the weather. Julia didn't come in. I wondered if I ought to tell her about Gilbert's having Daisy's knife. But she couldn't resist telling Daisy and then there'd be a row. Gilbert loved make-believe. He was just having fun with the knife.

Later I asked Patrick Abbott if there were other things which looked like blood on a knife, not mentioning what knife, and he said sure, lots of things. And of course anybody knew that it wasn't hard to get real bloodstains, if wanted. Yes, Gilbert was amusing himself. Too bad that old silliness of Daisy's had to bob up again, but if it didn't get around much no harm was done. All that sort of thing had been hard on Brandon. He had been a kind man, quiet, tall enough and good-looking, more interested in his work than anything else.

He enjoyed the confidence of the Indians to an unusual degree and was accorded the rare privilege of admission to the reservation without a guide. There was no greater compliment to a man's character. I always suspected that incompatibility, plain and simple, was at the bottom of his trouble with Mona. She liked excitement. She loved ordering the town in, as she was doing tonight. Strutting her stuff. Well, she'd rather overreached herself in the case of Carmencita. That was the last straw, I had always thought, and the thing that made the actual break with Tom Brandon. But, of course, that was only my idea of what happened.

At noon I walked over to my house to leave a note asking Mrs. Dominguez to press my black lace. The sky maintained the same steel-grayness as this morning. I wondered if Patrick Abbott would like Mona's house. It was enormous for a place like Santa Maria. The studio itself was larger than the attractive adobe cottage they had lived in while she was building the big house, the one where the O'Haras lived now.

Mona had been an only child with a large inheritance. She had been married, shortly after she came into her own money, to a much older man who had twice as much. He had died several years later, perfectly honorably in bed of pneumonia, and a year after that she had married Tom Brandon, for love. He was an artist. She adored that. They had come to Santa Maria. She had built the house and after he had gone she'd stayed on playing patroness to Santa Maria and its artists. No, there was nothing against Mona except her selfishness and unkindness.

Back in the shop that afternoon I rearranged shelves and started making an inventory. About four o'clock Carmencita came in.

She carried a package wrapped in a newspaper and asked if I would lend her two dollars. She would leave this picture, she said, indicating the newspaper-wrapped parcel, as security. I gave her four half-dollars from the register.

"*Gracias*," she said then, quite humbly.

"I hear you're getting married, Carmencita."

Her gray eyes lit up. "You like to come to my wedding, Miss Holly?"

"Of course. When is it?"

"Soon. I let you know."

"What would you like for a present?"

She thought it over. Finally she said that if it wasn't too much she'd like one of the bedspreads in Penney's window. I'd been seeing them all week, they were made of a shiny rayon brocade and priced at a dollar-ninety-eight, and the one she preferred was watermelon pink. It was the worst of all!

On my way home that evening I bought the spread and asked the store to send it to her at her aunt's house.

# CHAPTER 17

EVERY BIG party has its aftermath of disaster, serious or small, but of course nobody sits around thinking about that before the party. I didn't like Mona's parties, but I couldn't afford not to go, and always I went through a period of minor collapse before dressing for one of them, in which I slumped beside my fire and rebelled.

Her fanatical admirers, like Daisy, the banking McClures, and Dr. Johnson's dressy young wife, accepted Mona in toto because she had so much money. Others of us who had our livings to make or who were easygoing like Julia didn't care to make a situation, which an absence without good reason would indeed make. I must say she did herself well at these parties, spending without stint, getting in a good dance band, filling the house with flowers, giving us champagne and English biscuits and Russian caviar. The harder things were to get the more likely she was to get them.

Mona liked to boast that the Indians would only come from the pueblo to dance at her affairs, and that they danced dances for her entertainments that were parts of secret ritual never before witnessed outside the sacred *kiva*. This wasn't so, of course. They were just their regular dances, the ones anybody could see when they held a fiesta at the pueblo, but we didn't argue, and anyhow it was quite true that they would dance as evening entertainment only for Mona Brandon. Luis arranged it, she paid them well, and they used the money communally to buy machinery, horses, and other things needed on the reservation.

I was still sitting by my fireplace, chaining one dismal anticipation after another, when Mrs. Dominguez came through from the kitchen on her way home. She was a big brown motherly woman, a member of the colorful Dominguez clan by marriage only.

"Anything else, *Señorita?*"

"Nothing I can think of."

"I locked up back. Doors and windows."

"Windows?" I said, surprised.

She shook her head. "It's that murder, Miss. You better be careful. Maybe bad men about."

"Lightning never strikes twice, Mrs. Dominguez."

"When there is one, *Señorita,* there will be three."

I was careful not to smile. Her superstition was genuine. "Carmencita was in the shop today." I said then. "She does look happy."

Mrs. Dominguez bobbed her shawled head.

"*Si, si.* She is happy. But I wish she marry soon, Miss Holly. She waits now till she have money, for wedding dress and veil. Valencia say she have bad luck unless she get married in church with a dress and veil. I say she got good man and she better take him quick. *Buenas tardes, Señorita.*"

"Good night, Mrs. Dominguez."

On thinking back I wondered why I didn't give her the money right then for Carmencita's dress and veil. It might have prevented a tragedy. But at the time my only reaction was to reflect that whatever Valencia, the village fortune-teller, had told Carmencita, she would do.

After Mrs. Dominguez had gone I dressed. I still had plenty of time. I lay long in my bath, brushed my hair a lot, gazed at myself after I put on the black lace. It was old, but black lace does something to me, makes me feel young and exciting, instead of twenty-six and getting set in my ways.

Patrick Abbott turned up at seven o'clock. He wore a dinner jacket and no hat. He made the daiquiris, measuring the bacardi and the lime juice and the shaved ice with grave precision, the way he did everything.

# CHAPTER 18

By the time we got to the Castillo people who had dined were beginning to go on to the party. Gilbert Mason was sitting alone at his little table, glooming over another cup of coffee, dressed in his other suit, a black lounge suit, and wearing a white shirt and a purple artist's tie. I introduced Patrick Abbott to three or four groups of people as they stopped to speak to us on their way out. We ordered steaks. The service was slowed down by the absence of Rose Dominguez and Joe Padilla, both gone to help at the party. We were the last to leave the restaurant. Then, at Mona's gate, Pedro cocked an eye at Patrick's California license and refused to let us in.

"Pedro!" I reproached him.

"Oh, it's you, *señorita.*" He opened the gate. *"La señora* was very firm tonight, *señorita,"* he apologized.

We drove along the winding drive.

"If she's so afraid, why the dense planting?" Patrick asked.

"I don't think she was, at first."

"How's that?"

"Well, she put the iron grilles on the ground floor windows and the broken glass on the wall after Tom Brandon was gone. Maybe she was scared, living alone."

"Hasn't she got a big staff?"

"Yes. But their quarters are in the back wing. Mona's suite is in front, above and to the left as you go in the front door. Luis has a room in the middle of the house."

We were moving slowly along the drive. The murk was almost fog here on the grounds.

"By the way," I remembered to say, "Mona has the place specially guarded during functions like this. Don't wander in the shrubbery. You might get shot."

"Does the shrubbery look like being wandered in?"

I laughed, noting the wet gleam of laurel leaves in the headlights. The planting seemed to catch and hold the dampness. And at times the haze thickened like drifting smoke, masking the leafy growth.

We approached the house. We could not see it clearly in the murk, but I was so familiar with it that it loomed solidly before my eyes as usual. It was made of pink stucco with a red tile roof, shaped like the letter H, with two wings and a connecting portion. It was only two stories high but covered a lot of ground. The kitchens and the staff occupied the back wing. The dining rooms, small sitting rooms and upstairs bedrooms filled the bar of the H. The front wing contained the drawing room, library, two reception rooms, and a bar, all on the ground floor, and on the second was Mona's personal suite and the big studio, which was directly above the library and the bar, which were to the right of the hall as you entered the front door. The house faced north. There were two wide halls on each floor, the main one extending from the front door through the central portion of the house, and a cross hall the length of the inner side of the front wing. In the center, between the two wings, were flagged terraces.

There were three entrances to the grounds. The main one, by which we had arrived, a kitchen entrance, and the little gate in the east wall through which a flagged path led from the big house to the O'Haras' cottage. The swimming pool, which was enclosed by a tight hedge of spruce and holly, was in that corner of the grounds and reached by a branch off the flagged path.

Pedro's boy Pepe was at the front door to take the car to the parking space back of the house. We stood for a moment before ringing. The windows were closely curtained inside. In the haze, the lights burning on either side of the door were like globes of phosphorous.

Patrick Abbott said, "This house is wonderfully built. You'd never know that anything was going on inside." He rang. Rita opened the door.

I greeted Rita too warmly, did the same to the Padilla girl in the reception room, then stood at the glass fussing with lipstick, eyeing my old black lace, hanging my bag on my arm then taking it in my hand, in other words suffering a spasm of the party-feeling I always got here. Patrick was waiting as I came back into the hall.

We walked along the hall in the direction of the entrance of the drawing room.

There was no one at all in the hall just then save Gilbert Mason, who was teetering on his heels at the far end opposite the dining room, studying a row of pictures. I knew those pictures. They were steel engravings done years ago by Tom Brandon.

The drawing room was full of people, many of whom were strangers. Mona was standing in the middle of the room under the crystal chandelier. I was aware of the four life-size portraits of herself which hung in this room, and then of Mona herself, under the crystals, in an emerald green frock. Behind her stood Luis Martinez in a white satin shirt with full sleeves, black broadcloth trousers, the red Hopi belt, and masses of silver and turquoise jewelry.

Sonya O'Hara wore cheap pink net, her only evening dress, and redheaded Michael was in his navy serge.

"Mona looks wonderful," I murmured.

"The Indian's the one," Patrick Abbott said. "He makes a stunning background for Mrs. Brandon."

We were near them now. Mona put out her white red-tipped hands. "Jeanie, darling! I'd about given you up." She kissed me. "So nice of you to come!" she said to Patrick Abbott, giving him the hands. "Have you met the O'Haras, Mr. Abbott?"

"This morning," Patrick said. He bowed to Sonya. The men shook hands. There followed one of those meaningless tangles of talk. Patrick said he had been fortunate enough to secure one of Michael's pictures. It had to be explained to Mona who seemed not entirely pleased.

Presently she remembered to introduce Luis Martinez to Patrick, and Luis's beautiful manners at once put some sort of ceremony into everything. Mona said then it was time for a drink and to start the dancing. She sent Luis to tell the dance band in the studio to start the music, and she slipped her hand into Patrick Abbott's arm. I saw some friends from Santa Fe and went to speak to them. The blur of seeing so many people all at once was wearing off now, and I started around saying hello, feeling too bright, too glad, too this and that, the way everybody was. We began moving along in a crowd out of the room, into the halls, toward the bar and the stairs opposite the entrance of the bar which led to the second floor and the studio. I ran into the Johnsons about the time I got into the crosswise hall. The doctor looked rested and replied to my inquiry that all the bus patients, except the driver, were coming along fine.

I felt a cold hand touch my bare arm.

It was Gilbert. He fell in beside me.

"I've got to talk to you, Jean," he whispered.

"Some other time," I mumbled.

"Hello, Mason," said Dr. Johnson.

"Good evening, Gilbert," Mrs. Johnson said, coldly.

"Come have a drink with us," suggested Dr. Johnson.

Gilbert ignored them both, didn't even speak. "It's urgent!" he insisted, in my ear.

"How do you like my new dress?" Mrs. Johnson asked.

"It's beautiful, Lily," I said, and simultaneously Gilbert was saying, "It's about what I showed you in the shop. For God's sake keep mum."

"I shall, Gilbert."

"Naturally, I know what I'm talking about, Jean," he went on. "She did it. But our glamour girl—you-know-who—goaded her into it. I know all about it. Every little thing. But we'll keep it to ourselves, shall we?"

When we got to the place where you turn right into the bar or left up the stairs, and we turned right, I noticed that he was not there. I was not sorry. Gilbert is not the best company at a party.

"Oh, here you are, Jean." It was Patrick Abbott. "Shall I get you a glass of champagne?"

"Thanks."

I introduced the Johnsons. The crowd pushed us toward the semicircular bar. Again I felt the blur which comes over me in crowds. I was conscious of black glass, chromium, people, too many people because the wall-sized mirror behind the bar made everybody two. I noticed that the doors onto the west terrace were closed, and the grilled windows curtained. I saw Julia and Daisy on stools at the far side of the bar. We made our way there. Rose Dominguez, in a *china poblana* costume, was serving drinks. Joe Padilla, mixing cocktails, was dressed as a *charro*.

After we had joined Daisy and Julia, Gilbert appeared again, just as Daisy, turning to speak to me, knocked her bag off the counter. It hit the floor with a thud.

She saw Gilbert. "Pick that up, will you?" she said. It sounded like an order.

His puffy face paled. "Pick it up yourself!" he said.

"Rude!" she snapped.

"I wouldn't touch that thing with a pole!" Gilbert screeched. "Some day it's going to shoot somebody."

"Hysterical fool!" Daisy screeched back.

I saw with amazement her thin hand shape itself into a claw. I thought she was going to strike him.

Patrick Abbott picked up the bag.

# CHAPTER 19

ON LOOKING back over what I've written I feel a little ashamed at the way I've lammed Mona's parties, because we all had a grand time at that one after all. Mona had gotten in a well-known radio dance band which happened to be spending a week in Santa Fe. The music was swell. And Patrick Abbott certainly could dance. The studio was big enough to accommodate a lot of people comfortably. I suppose that was why Mona built so large.

The orchestra sat on an improvised dais under the curtained north window, opposite the main entrance to the studio. There was an exit near the dais, a door from which a small staircase led down into the library below. But the guests used only the main door from the hall. The orchestra played all the new ballads, all the cowboy tunes, groups of the Strauss waltzes. When they made a square dance of southwestern tunes like "Rancho Grande," "Silver on The Sage," and "Heart of The West," Michael O'Hara called it, and when they danced the first *varsoviana* he danced it with Mona. The quaint old dance, with its triple time and accent on every second measure, has an old world dignity, and redheaded Michael in his old navy suit and artist's tie, dancing the *varsoviana* with Mona, so expensive and so elegant, looked like something in a play. The Artist and The Lady.

I was one of a few people honored by being asked to dance by Gilbert Mason. He walked me stiffly around the outer edges of the crowd, not deigning to adjust his step to the rhythms of the band.

The dancing went on and on. Waltzes— "The Merry Widow," "Beautiful Lady," "Vienna Woods," "Artist's Life." A Spanish group— "Ramona," "A Little Spanish Town," "Monterrey." Past hits— "Two Sleepy People," "You Wore a Tulip."

Mexican boys ran around with trays of drinks and tiny sandwiches. You drifted down to the bar and back again. It was nice. It was gay. It was really a grand party.

Then the orchestra leader lifted his baton.

"Please take seats along the wall after this dance," he said. "There will be a program of Indian dances. Mrs. Brandon would prefer you all to remain in the room. After the program the dancing will resume and meanwhile supper will be served continuously in the dining room."

When the band went out I joined Julia, who was near the main entrance into the studio.

"Have you seen Pat, Julia?"

"He's in the bar. Talking with Dr. Johnson."

"Where's Daisy?"

"Down in the dressing room. Said she was going home."

"Anything wrong?"

"No. I guess she's still upset about that row with Mona. I don't think she'll really go home though."

We found chairs and sat down. The McClures, and then the Warners, from the ranch where Pat was staying, were on our left. Mrs. Johnson was with them.

I noticed Sonya and Michael and Mona sitting down across the room from us. The band was then filing out the little door near the dais, going down through the library and on to be fed, no doubt. I couldn't see Gilbert, not that it mattered. But knowing that Mona liked people to stick around for her shows, I did have a good look around for Gilbert. But, of course, it would be just the time he wouldn't be caught dead here. Then the Indians came in through the main entrance and lined up facing each other down the middle of the room. Three old Indian men sat down crosslegged with their drums near the dais. The drums were kettledrums. I counted the dancers. There were thirty-six.

They were naked save for tunics wound snugly around their thighs and hanging only to their knees. They wore ceremonial belts, beads, bells, and silver necklaces, and their copper cheeks were splashed with red or white paint. The drummers started beating out the rhythm. The dancers started treading the simple pattern of the dance. Up and down, up and down, clapping hands, jogging round and round in foursomes, suddenly letting out ear-splitting whoops and hollers.

"Good Lord!" breathed Julia, in my ear.

"The noise makes me dizzy," I muttered back.

"It's terrific!"

"Have you seen Luis?"

"Not since we first got here. Why?"

"Just wondered. He usually hovers round at a time like this."

"Maybe he's opposite," Julia said. "I saw Mona and the O'Haras near the far end of the dais just before the Indians came in."

I had seen them too, of course. The tall Indians, dancing close together, made a screen. It was not important. I was just a little curious about Luis's not being here.

There was a lull. Then the Indians began all over again, did the same steps in the same order, stomped, whooped, hollered.

Daisy came in. Somebody had taken the seat Julia was saving for her, and glad of the excuse I gave her mine and slipped out of the room and downstairs. I saw Patrick Abbott and Dr. Johnson sitting at the bar. Not wanting to horn in, I crossed the spot where the two wide halls intersected and walked on past the staircase opposite one door into the drawing room, which led up to Mona's part of the house. There was a door beyond these stairs which opened onto the east terrace. On an impulse I opened the door and stepped out, and was glad at once that I had, for the air had cleared, quickly, the way it can when a wind comes from the desert.

I walked across the terrace. The noise the Indians made could even be heard here. I felt the cold then on my bare shoulders and started back into the house. But I had just put my hand on the knob when I heard a scream.

I went on into the house. I supposed it was the Indians. Just part of their jolly little entertainment.

I strolled back toward the bar. I happened to notice the time by the clock near the intersection of the halls. It was twenty past eleven.

I thought again about the scream, thinking that it would be repeated ten or twelve times maybe in the dance, which was at present shaking the house. It wasn't.

I turned into the bar, happening to notice Daisy's evening bag lying under one of the tables, and then Patrick Abbott saw me and said, "Was hoping you'd show up."

"You're missing the show, Pat."

Dr. Johnson said, "We'd better go up, Abbott. Mrs. Brandon doesn't like people to play hookey." He got up and went.

"Don't you want a drink?" Pat asked me.

"I could do with some coffee."

He was drinking coffee himself. Rose poured a cup for me and put some ice in it to cool it quickly.

"Anything wrong?" Patrick Abbott asked me.

"Wrong?"

"Something in your face," he said.

I sipped the coffee.

I said, "The fact is, I *was* thinking of something. I thought I heard somebody scream."

"Thought?" Patrick said, cocking a brow in the direction of the Indians.

"I suppose it was one of them," I said. I explained where I'd heard it. "Sounded like a woman," I said.

"The skylight in the studio is open," Patrick said.

"I wondered if it wasn't," I said.

Then Gilbert Mason came in from the west terrace. He went to the bar and asked Rose for brandy.

# CHAPTER 20

THE PARTY ended at one o'clock. As we were waiting on the front terrace for Patrick's car to be brought Michael and Sonya came out.

"Give you a lift?" Patrick Abbott said.

"Thanks," said Michael. "But we've only got a step, you know. We take the shortcut through the side gate."

"But yes! I should like to ride, please," said Sonya.

Pepe whirled the convertible around the circle. Patrick tipped him while the rest of us piled in. We drove away. "Why not come to my house for a nightcap?" I said.

"Thanks. Too late," Michael replied.

"But yes. I would like to," said Sonya.

"But, Sonya—"

"We shall not stay long, dear," said Sonya. "Mr. Abbott can drop us on his way home to the ranch."

So they came. We had a lot of fun at my house, too. We built up a fire and we cooked bacon and eggs in the kitchen. We made coffee and toast. The men talked art. Michael had already agreed to give a few lessons in the time he had left. Patrick said he could get a room at the hotel as a studio. North light, Michael mentioned. We talked about the party. It had been a great success, we said. Sonya was definitely nice. She started singing funny little Russian songs.

Only one disagreeable thing happened, and that was when Toby, my cat, getting in from a prowl just when they were leaving, sunk his teeth into Michael's hand as he stooped to pick him up.

"I thought Toby liked me!" Michael said, astonished.

"He's just being Persian," I apologized for Toby, who had beat it. I brought the iodine, but I was careful to let Sonya apply it to her man.

# CHAPTER 21

AFTER THEY had gone I stood on my step watching the twin ruby taillights glide down the short steep lane, turn left and grow smaller until they disappeared into the village. I could still hear the purr of the motor when it was well beyond the plaza. Then the nearby sounds asserted themselves, the mooing of a cow, the little silvery bells on the goats, the soft sniffing and whinnying of horses, all in the pasture at the foot of the hill. I heard Toby padding across the leaves under the cottonwood tree. I could smell my chrysanthemums.

The weather had lightened, and the air felt quite dry, but the moon was still only a brighter ragged spot through a cloud bank, and the atmosphere which enveloped the sleeping village of Santa Maria was peculiar, neither one thing or another.

# CHAPTER 22

I DARESAY there are people who can go cleanly from one moment to the next. Not I. The past encroaches on my present which is already crowding the future. Thus as I got ready for bed I was still back in the evening just finished, yet irked by the knowledge that I'd soon have to get up again and go to work. The evening had been really swell. I'd have to eat what I'd said about Mona's parties. Everyone had had a grand time. The music had been tops. Snatches of it blew through my mind as I brushed my hair. I went to bed, but I couldn't sleep.

Half an hour later a car plunged along the rutted road below and turned up my hill. I sat up in bed remembering all at once that my house was alone on this lane. It was Julia Price.

She called from the gate and then came shuffling along the flags. She had mules on her bare feet and was wearing only her nightie and a red quilted housecoat. "Come on in," I called through the open window. "The door isn't locked."

Julia came in and sat on my bed. She lit a cigarette. I sat up against pillows. It was, she said, just past three o'clock, and she was here because she had had a row with Daisy.

"It began even before we got home from the party," Julia said. "I made some crack about Mona knowing how to behave if she wanted to and hadn't it been fun. Daisy said I was revolting. Then, just after I'd dozed off, Daisy came into my room and announced that she had lost her evening bag."

"I saw it lying under one of the tables in the bar," I said. "While the Indians were giving that program. How come she didn't think about it before?"

"I don't know. She's all mixed up. But her gun was in the bag. So she now insisted on locking everything up, saying we weren't safe, that now she had neither gun nor knife, etc. I said I'd have to have my window open and so I'd lock my door on the inside, but she said I had to lock the window and open the door. Finally I said either I'd have my window open or else. Well, I elsed."

"Did you leave your clothes there?"

"Yes. Except my bag, which had my car keys and cigarettes in it."

"Well, the spare bed is all fixed for sleeping in," I said. I got up then and we went into the other bedroom, through the bath from mine, and I opened windows and turned back the covers. I debated again about telling Julia that Gilbert had Daisy's knife but decided against it. I didn't want to start anything. They already had such a feud on—Daisy and Gilbert—that it wasn't safe to add any fuel. But I certainly would tell Gilbert, first time I saw him, that I was going to tell Daisy he had her knife, unless he gave it back to her immediately.

I tucked Julia in, turned out her light, and went back to my own bed, but I couldn't sleep. Now I wasn't thinking of the pleasant things at the party, but the others. Specifically I was thinking of the brief explosion Gilbert gave way to when Daisy ordered him to pick up her bag. I remembered the rage in his eyes, and her hand looking like a claw to strike him.

Suddenly I was diverted, swiftly and completely, by a shadow. The head of my bed was against the south wall. To my left was an open window. At this point the house was flush against the lane. There was a pallid square of moonshine on the floor, and the shadow was in the moonshine.

A pale shadow, because of the pallor of the moonlight, but a shadow, which fitted the square like a picture in a frame. Someone was standing in the lane, looking into the window.

I wasn't frightened at first. I lay watching the shadow with a sort of intensifying interest. I calculated my chances for escape if the shadow should materialize on this side of the sill. Then, slowly, I began to be afraid.

Fear became horror as I realized that the shadow was that of an Indian, or at least someone swathed in a blanket like an Indian, and half a dozen stories flashed across my memory like silhouettes on a wall, stories of atrocities supposed to have taken place within the secrecy of the reservation, of quicksands which never gave up the dead, of a strange bottomless lake requiring an annual human sacrifice.

Then, as suddenly as it had come, the shadow vanished. I discovered that my body was chilling from a cold sweat, and my nails were digging through the skin of my palms. I got out of bed very carefully and slammed down the window. I got back into bed weak as a cat.

Gradually I began to realize that my fright had been foolish. No doubt the Indian had been passing, his shadow would look the same if his back was to the window, he had stopped perhaps to look over the landscape, and the shadow had fallen by accident on my floor. I began to hear friendly sounds, Toby in the cottonwood tree, the little bells below the mesa.

The next thing I knew someone really had come into the

room. I sat up. It was daylight and Mrs. Dominguez was standing there with a tray of food in her plump brown hands.

"I sorry to wake you, Miss Holly. But it almost nine o'clock."

"Good heavens!" I said, jumping up.

"Please eat first, *señorita*."

"Mrs. Price is here," I said, putting a finger on my lips.

I settled back against the pillows and took the tray. Mrs.
Dominguez closed the door into Julia's room and ran me a hot
bath. Then she came back to the foot of the bed.

"Carmencita no come home last night, Miss Holly."

I said for her not to worry. Then I reminded her that Mrs.
Price would want to sleep late, and to give her a fine breakfast
when she woke.

It was another gray day. I had my bath and dressed and hurried to the shop. I got there half an hour late. Mr. McClure was
literally foaming on the doorstep.

# CHAPTER 23

INSIDE THE shop the banker's little hooded eyes ran quickly about the room before he plopped two green banknotes on the dust sheet covering the jewelry case.

"Miss Holly," he demanded, with a sort of schoolteacherish arrogance, "where did these come from?"

I stared. One was a new five, the other a new ten.

"Why, Mr. McClure, how should I know?"

"You deposited these in an envelope on Monday afternoon after the bank was closed. In the night depository."

"Why didn't you bring them in yesterday, then?"

"I was out of town yesterday. They were called to my attention just this morning."

He enumerated the other money I'd deposited in the envelope. The amount was right.

"Well, Mr. McClure, what's wrong with the money?"

"Wrong? It's counterfeit!"

"Heavens!" I said. I picked up the two notes and smoothed them out and stared at them. I turned them over. They looked all right to me. I held them up to the light, fingering them thoroughly and covering them with prints which would confuse the experts later on, but not thinking about that. "What do I do?" I asked them.

"You're out fifteen dollars, for one thing." Mr. McClure's voice cracked a little saying that, for there was no greater tragedy to him than losing money. Even other people's losing it hurt a little, for it made him think it might have been himself. "Where did you get these?"

I thought fast. Daisy Payne had given me the new ten, if it was the money I had put in the bank. Luis Martinez had given me three new fives when he paid for the Hopi belt.

I wondered if Mona had really given Luis that fifteen dollars. It had seemed improbable, anyhow, that she would give him so much. I hated to set the banker on Luis. McClure would go to Mona first. Then if there was anything fishy about the money or its source Mona would be on Luis's bones, too. No harm in putting McClure off, in any case, until I could talk it over with . . . Patrick Abbott! Of course!

"I'm afraid I can't tell you," I said.

"Why not?"

"But how can I be sure where I got that money? All sorts of people come into the shop."

"It looks very odd that there should be only two counterfeit bills turn up at the same time, and both from your shop."

"I suppose so."

The banker flopped his heavy eyelids and reached for the money.

"Mayn't I keep it?" I asked, meaning to show it to Patrick Abbott.

"Certainly not!" he snapped, and looking at me as though I

were a menace to the U. S. government he gathered up the bills and stomped out.

I lit the fire, folded the covers and put on my smock. Then Patrick Abbott came in.

"Hello," he said, stalking across the room and sort of filling it with sense and reason. "Something wrong?"

"Sit down," I said. He leaned against the mantel. I got out a tray of rings. I decided to tell him about Mr. McClure and the money.

He spoke first.

"Nice party, Jean."

"Wasn't it!"

"I was sorry I couldn't get a better look at Brandon's pictures. I wonder if Mrs. Brandon would mind my stopping in to look at them sometime?"

"She'd be delighted, I think."

"Did Brandon ever do any engraving?"

"There's a row of steel engravings hanging in the back end of the main hall."

"I wish I'd known that."

I looked up at him suddenly. "Why?"

He hesitated a moment. "I just wondered," he said.

"You sure you're not here on a case?" I asked.

"Quite sure."

"How would you act, Pat, if you were? I mean would you sail in here being very grand, like Philo Vance?"

"Certainly not," Patrick Abbott said, with his slow grin. "I'd pretend to be anything but a detective, lie low, and watch what everybody did. I'd bide my time."

"In other words, if you were here to solve a crime, you'd pretend to be an artist."

"Of course. But I'm not here to solve any crime."

I said, "You wouldn't be interested in counterfeit money, would you?"

His eyes narrowed, lit up.

"Have you heard of any?" he asked.

"Oh, oh!" I said.

Patrick Abbott laughed then, and lit a cigarette.

"I told you I'd promised a friend to do a small job for him. Confidentially, it does concern money. There's been some counterfeit knocking about up this way and I said I'd try to find out if the Santa Maria art colony had any master-engravers who were misusing their talents."

I said several of our artists did etchings. I laughed because etchings sound like a joke these days. And then I told Patrick about Mr. McClure and the two bills.

He promptly streaked out of the shop.

I went on fiddling with the jewelry. I kept having a feeling that there were other things I'd better be doing, such as pairing a basket of huaraches.

Then Luis Martinez walked in. He came over to the case and extended a brown fist from under his blanket and laid a roll of money on the glass.

"You count money, Jean," he said.

I picked it up. Three silver dollars, a quarter, and a dime jangled onto the case. I spread out the paper money and counted it. It amounted to a hundred and three dollars and thirty-five cents, the exact sum he owed for the things I had laid aside for him in the storeroom.

"You keep things till I take," he said, and started out.

I put the money in the cash register. At least twenty minutes passed before it occurred to me that it might be counterfeit. I suppose I'm just naturally dumb. I took it out and looked at it all, bill by bill. They were all fives and tens, except one twenty. Two were new. I rolled the money up, put a rubber band around it, and went into the back room and put it in my bag. I brought wood back and fixed the fire, and sat down in the corner seat, turning over in my mind what I should do. One thing sure, I was not going to tell Mr. McClure. I wouldn't tell Patrick Abbott, either. At least, not yet, because he was duty bound to report it to his friend in the Secret Service, and the government certainly wouldn't make allowances for poor Luis just because he had the misfortune to live day in and day out in the midst of luxury and temptation yet never had a penny he could call his own.

I lit a cigarette and sat on.

One of Mr. Trask's deputies put his head in, asked if I had seen the sheriff, and went away again.

Mrs. Johnson stopped in for a minute. She was on her way to the hospital to spend the day helping entertain bus patients. I said I wanted to do something, and she said how about coming out for bridge tomorrow afternoon. I said fine if five o'clock on wasn't too late.

Then Gilbert Mason arrived. He seated himself in one of the Mexican chairs.

"Nice party," I said for conversation.

"How stupid you are!" he sneered. "You go to a party and have a wonderful time because you'd hooked a good-looking man and all the girls were green with envy. Did Daisy enjoy herself? Did Sonya?"

"Well, almost everybody did, anyhow," I said.

"Mona didn't like her party."

"Then I am dumb," I said. "I was sure she did."

"She was putting it on. So was O'Hara."

I noticed then how dark the circles were under his eyes, and the way his flesh sagged from the bone.

"You feeling all right, Gilbert?" I asked.

"Mind your own business!" said Gilbert.

It did seem a good idea. But, since he was snapping anyhow, I decided to speak to him about the knife.

"Gilbert, if you don't mind my saying so, I think you ought to return that knife to Daisy. She's in a state of mind about it, and—"

"And how do you know?"

"I'm not free to say."

Gilbert eyed me contemptuously, his pale lips curled.

"You think you're God, don't you, Jean? You sit in this place and everybody comes in and unloads and after a while you get to thinking that you are divinely ordained to tell us what to do. Give her the knife, Gilbert." He mimicked my voice. "Be a sap, Gilbert. Go on, Gilbert, make yourself dirt under her feet." His face flushed and his voice grew bitter. "And you yourself heard the way she spoke to me last night, too!"

"She didn't mean it—"

"Well, I do. I'm keeping the knife. I've taken all from her I ever mean to."

After a while he began talking in a decent tone about writing. There was something very authentic about Gilbert talking about poetry. No one had ever seen a line that he had written, as I've said, but we all agreed that he knew whereof he spoke and in due time would prove it. "I've got an idea," he said now. "A really big idea. It's odd. I mean, you torture yourself trying to get an idea that is worth a year or two of real work and then, like that, it comes effortlessly."

"I'm so glad!" I said.

It was a mistake.

"Please don't interrupt!"

He frowned and for a while wouldn't say anything. I could hear his fingers tapping on the briefcase.

"I'm going to do a narrative poem about Carmencita," he said, then.

"Good subject," I said.

"Rather. First, the great Spanish family. Conquistadors. Its disintegration. Then Carmencita herself, my real subject, her strange beauty, tragic life, and so on. Eventually her murder."

I smiled. "I guess a happy ending wouldn't do for Carmencita."

"It's murder," he said. "Nothing else clicks."

He sat talking for perhaps fifteen minutes, outlining Carmencita's life, her family with ten children in an adobe house of two rooms, girlhood, womanhood, betrayal. The illustrious heritage contrasted with current squalor, and so on. Tom Brandon. Mona, whom he called a jealous ruthless beauty. Mona's power. The trial. Prison. The subsequent life with outcasts like Arkwright, who was Brandon gone to pieces. Then, just when she had a chance for happiness at last, death.

Gilbert had forgotten me. He sat straight in the chair, tapping the case, talking. Snatches come back to me still. Words. The intricate web of circumstances. Magnificent.

Then, abruptly, he left the shop.

Not five minutes later Patrick Abbott came back.

"Carmencita has been found dead," he said.

# CHAPTER 24

"Sorry I blurted it out like that, Jean. Can I get you anything?"

"Gilbert was here," I explained. "Just a few minutes ago. He kept babbling along as usual, only this time he was talking about Carmencita. I thought it was his usual make-believe. How would he know she was dead?"

Patrick Abbott stood over me, by the mantel.

"It's all over town."

"Oh," I said. I felt relieved. After all, Gilbert was only tolerable because there was never any real mystery in his knowledge.

"How did it happen?"

"Apparently she was drowned."

"Drowned?"

Where would anybody drown around here when the weather was so dry? The arroyos were all dry as a bone.

"She was found in Mrs. Brandon's swimming pool."

I gasped, "When?"

"This morning. It happened last night."

I said, "What a way to get her revenge!"

"Revenge?"

"Mona loves her warm swimming pool. She wouldn't like having people drown in it. Specially Carmencita."

I told Pat about the pool, how there had been a crude con-
crete affair up in the hills where the kids of Santa Maria had
bathed, and the young people had gone in on moonlit nights,
and how Mona had bought the land where the two warm
springs were that kept the pool warm in winter and on cool
summer evenings and had diverted the water into the beautiful
swimming pool. The town hadn't liked it.

"Carmencita couldn't have picked a way to kill herself that
could be more disagreeable to Mona," I said.

"You do think it was suicide, Jean?"

"Of course."

"Could she swim?"

"I doubt it. The pool has no shallow portion."

"Was she a suicidal type?"

"Carmencita? I should think she might be."

"But she was happy. She was about to be married. Why
should a happy woman kill herself?"

"That's what Gilbert said," I mused. "Only, of course, I didn't
know he meant what he was saying."

Patrick Abbott said, "Apparently it did happen during the
party last night. I haven't heard many details. In fact, that is
why I came back here, Jean. Mr. Trask asked me if there was
anywhere we could talk. His office is full of people, and if you
won't mind . . ."

"Of course not."

He sat down and got out his cigarettes. I had one too.

"How would you think she got into the grounds last night?
The gates were all locked and guarded."

That made me actually smile.

"Carmencita is a blood relation to two or three people on
Mona's staff," I said. "Pedro the gardener, for one. All that

guarding is a joke, really. Mona doesn't understand these people. She would be far safer without her locks and walls, in other
words, she'd be safer keeping her key under a flowerpot."

"As you do."

"It puts them on their honor. My Mexican neighbors look
out for me."

"I see. Would Pedro admit her to the grounds?"

"Not exactly. But he might be looking the other way when
she walked in, not knowing, of course, that she planned to
drown herself."

Patrick Abbott knocked an ash on the hearth and said quietly, "Carmencita was also shot."

"Shot?"

"By her own gun, apparently. It was in the pool."

I said, "You remember I heard a scream?"

"Yes, but you didn't say you heard a shot."

"Maybe that came after I closed the door. I was just coming
back in the house. It was twenty minutes past eleven as I came
along the hall. The Indians . . ."

"Would a woman scream when about to shoot herself?" Patrick Abbott asked.

Then Mr. Trask came in.

The sheriff was perfectly calm, as always. Patrick Abbott
brought wood and fixed up the fire. It sizzled and the piney fra-
grance from the green log spread through the room. The sheriff got settled with his back to the window and rolled himself a
cigarette.

I sat facing the window. I could see the midday crowds,
gay-looking now under the overcast sky. There seemed to be no
more about than usual, but of course there would be a crowd
gathered around the sheriff's office, a block north of the plaza.

His deputies would be talking to anyone who asked questions. Mona's servants would be telling everything they knew, over and over, and those who heard it would pass it on, and the story by this time would have filtered through almost every home in Santa Maria. We'd never hear the end of this, I thought. It would hang over the town forever.

Mr. Trask began summarizing the known facts. Carmencita's body had been found about nine o'clock this morning by Pedro, the head gardener. He'd started yelling. Two of his assistants came running. They'd fished the body from the pool and had attempted artificial respiration. They didn't find the bullet wound till Dr. Johnson got there, since there was no blood.

"You say they found her about nine o'clock?" Patrick asked.

"We figured that, Mr. Abbott. None of them had a watch, and I doubt if they would of noticed the time if they had."

"Who called the doctor?"

"Luis Martinez."

"*Luis Martinez?*" Patrick said. "Was he one of the men who came when Pedro called for help?"

"No, sir. The Indian was in the house. He heard the disturbance at the pool and went out to see what it was. He saw right away she was stone dead, and went back to the house and called the doctor and myself."

"He said *dead*? Immediately?"

"Yes, sir."

"He didn't help the others try to revive her?"

"No, sir. But that don't mean anything. Indians are smarter about things like that than other people."

"Luis seems to be a smart fellow, all right." Patrick Abbott's voice was almost too easy.

Mr. Trask said that he and Dr. Johnson had arrived on the

scene at the same time. It was then about twenty-five minutes to ten. The coroner rode out with Mr. Trask. All Mona's staff and a good many of their relatives had gathered around the spot. The ground everywhere was trampled and wet from the water from the pool. They'd cleared them all back while the doctor bent over the body and loosened up the clothes, and for the first time revealed the gunshot wounds. There were two, from the same shot, which had perforated the body, entering under the left breast and coming out in the small of the back. There was no blood on her clothes, only a faint pinkish stain on her undervest, so they'd judged she had fallen immediately after the shot into the pool.

There was also a bruise on her left front shoulder.

"You said you found the gun. What about the bullet?"

"The bullet was in the pool, Mr. Abbott. We drained it, using a sieve, and then had no trouble locating the bullet. It might not be the right one, though. I've sent it along with the gun to state police headquarters for examination."

"I suppose you questioned the servants?"

"Yes, sir. We questioned everybody on the place. The coroner grilled them pretty hard. He's a Mexican, though, and I reckon he understands them. We couldn't figure out how she'd got into and around the grounds last night without somebody at least seeing her, but nobody broke down under questioning. Unfortunately by the time we got out there everywheres around had been so tramped we couldn't get footprints. It would seem a plain case of suicide, on first appearances. The queer part is that nobody at all saw her there last night. Half the town was in that house at the time she must of done it, but nobody saw her getting in or walking around, and nobody heard the shot."

"When does the doctor think it happened?"

"Between eleven and twelve last night. As near as he could judge. Also we traced her up to five minutes to eleven last night. She was alive then."

"Having a complete post mortem?"

"Yes, sir. Just as a matter of form. She died, apparently, from the shot, but we want to know if she was drinking or anything like that."

Patrick Abbott asked, "What about motive?"

"Spite might be a reason for suicide," the sheriff said promptly. "But it was a funny time for her to do it. She thought a lot of that Ortega boy."

"Have you questioned Ortega?"

"Yes, sir. His alibi's sound."

Then Mr. Trask went back to the scene of the crime and described what must have happened. The whole staff had been on duty last night. The gardener, Pedro, had been assigned to the main gate. The other two gates were locked. There was no need for anyone to come in through either of them, save the O'Haras, who had come to the party through the small gate, as was their usual custom when going from their house to the big house.

Both O'Haras said they had tried the gate after they entered it, checking it specially to see if the lock caught because they knew Mrs. Brandon was specially afraid of prowlers when she had a big party. They'd used the key which Michael carried on his key-ring. Questioning had revealed that it was the only key to that gate. Mrs. Brandon had lost hers, she said, some time ago. A year ago, at least. There was a possibility it had been found, of course, and used last night. Or it might have been stolen by one of the staff and used without her knowing it.

No one could climb over the wall anywhere without being cut to ribbons by glass. The gate locks were all Yale locks.

"Did you check the gates for fingerprints, Mr. Trask?"

"No use, sir. Twenty people anyhow had handled them, trying to decide how she'd come in."

Once inside, he said then, it would have been easy for Carmencita to conceal herself in the dense shrubbery. There was only one entrance to the swimming pool, a narrow archway in the tight tall hedge, at the end nearest the flagstone path, and entered by a branch of that path.

Then he told us that at ten-thirty last night the outside help, except Pedro, had gone inside to help with the supper. No one had been noticed leaving the house during the evening except Gilbert Mason.

"Mason's a nut, Mr. Abbott. He'd go poking around the grounds just to bother Mrs. Brandon, if he thought it would. But I reckon all he did was go out one door and in another. Rose Dominguez said she seen him come into that bar place from outside twice during the evening."

I remembered our seeing Gilbert enter the bar from the terrace about half-past eleven. He'd asked for brandy. He didn't usually drink.

"You say Pedro was on the main gate all evening?"

"Yes, sir."

"Do you think Pedro might have admitted Carmencita?"

"I think it's quite possible."

"For what purpose?"

"Maybe just to be friendly."

"Would he lie, Mr. Trask?"

Mr. Trask said, "They all of 'em do that kind of lying, Mr. Abbott. Pedro's a good fellow. I've never knowed him to get into trouble. And they don't any of them like all that locking-up Mrs. Brandon does."

"You mean, you believe he let her in?"

"I don't see any other way for her to have got in."

"Where was Carmencita earlier in the evening?"

"Juan Ortega says she was in his store until five to eleven last night. It's a little store where the Mexicans buy and it stays open late. It belongs to Juan and his partner. Seems Carmencita's been in the habit of hanging around there, coming and going, so Juan didn't think anything of it when she left last night, saying she'd be back later. She did say, however, that she'd be back in forty minutes—that's how he knew the exact time—and she'd be rich. He thought it was a joke. He says he said sure, he would be rich too, and they laughed. There was another Mexican fellow in there at that time. Boy we all know. He corroborated Juan's story."

"Does he seem much affected by her death?"

"Yes, sir, he does."

Patrick Abbott took out another cigarette. "If it's a simple case of suicide, spite, or revenge, as shown by the choice of the swimming pool for the act, would be motive enough, wouldn't it, Mr. Trask? Mrs. Brandon, probably, will not care to use the pool again . . ."

"Well, I wouldn't go so far as to say what Mrs. Brandon would or wouldn't do, Mr. Abbott."

Patrick Abbott asked, "Could you determine the exact place where she fell into the pool, Mr. Trask?"

"No, sir. But I judged it must of happened at the end nearest the entrance through the hedge."

"You found the gun in the pool, you said?"

"Yes, sir."

"In the hand of the corpse?"

"No, sir. It had fallen free."

"Did you find the gun when you drained the pool?"

"No, sir. Pedro seen it laying on the bottom of the pool. The water is very clear. He had one of the boys dive for it. Then wiped it dry. That fixed it for fingerprints, if the water hadn't of already."

"She couldn't've been shot elsewhere? And dumped in the pool?"

"Not likely. There was no blood on her clothes."

"What was she wearing?"

"Wool pants, a man's shirt and riding boots."

They talked about the gun. It was a new Smith and Wesson .38. The sheriff said that Arkwright had given her money for the gun, according to her previous story at the Arkwright inquest, to protect her on her long walks from town. "She was a crack shot, and she wasn't afraid of the devil himself," he said. "Nobody saw her on the road last night, so I figure she took the shortcut through the graveyard. I reckon there ain't five people in Santa Maria with that much nerve."

"What was the shape of the wound where the bullet entered her body?"

"Almost perfectly round, Mr. Abbott."

"Fired at right angles, then? Unusual for a suicide?"

"It wasn't quite at right angles. It slanted down a little toward her back."

"You say she drank?"

"Oh, no, sir. Not as a rule. The boyfriend says she hadn't had a drink last night, but I thought we'd have the stomach examined, just to check."

"Are you going to question all the people who were at that party?"

"What would be the point? Apparently no one left the house except Mason."

Patrick said, "There was an awful lot of noise in that house when the Indians were putting on their show. You couldn't've heard a bomb, let alone a gun shot." Then he said, "You say she told Juan Ortega she'd come back rich. Could she have gone there for money from someone and then have been held up for it?"

The sheriff said, "Don't ask me. She had only three pennies on her, in the pocket of her shirt."

"She was desperate for money," I put in.

"How do you know?" Patrick Abbott asked.

"I know because my help is Carmencita's aunt, who told me that Carmencita was putting off getting married because she hadn't enough for a wedding dress and a veil, and that doesn't take very much these days. Also, she came in here yesterday and borrowed two dollars and left me a picture as security."

"A picture?" the sheriff said.

"She said that was what it was. I didn't unwrap it."

But Mr. Trask said crisply, "May I see that picture?"

I got up and crossed the shop to reach it down from the shelf. It was lying on a stack of folded Navajo rugs, at arm's height. I took off the newspaper. I guess the surprise it gave me showed in my face, but I didn't say anything, just walked back and gave it to the sheriff.

He examined it thoughtfully.

"This is the Santo missing from the Arkwright house, Mr. Abbott," he said then. I remembered his mentioning it before, and decided I really was dumb not to have connected it up when Carmencita came in with it.

"When I went back the second time, you know, I figured

that somebody had been to the house. This is mighty interesting. Carmencita must have gone out there for this Santo. I reckon I ought to have guessed it. I don't understand it. I mean, why didn't she come and ask me for the picture?" He handed it to Patrick Abbott. He said, "And, if she went back to the house, why did she change that green spot to black by pouring a bottle of ink on it? And, in shooting herself, why did she fall backwards into the pool? It has been my experience that people shot as she was fall forwards." The sheriff smiled a funny little smile. "Unless I'm a pretty bad guesser, Mr. Abbott, she fell in the wrong direction, and that bruise on her shoulder was from the butt of the gun, to make sure she went into the pool."

"What gun?" Patrick Abbott said quietly. His eyes never left the sheriff's.

"Her gun, Mr. Abbott."

The sheriff stood up. "Well, we mustn't be hasty," he said. "Thanks, Miss Holly, for letting me sit around and gab. Sorry we didn't get out to look at that house, Mr. Abbott. I figured it would keep."

"I'm anxious to go with you to that house, Mr. Trask," Patrick Abbott said.

"Thanks. The first time I can spare a minute we'll go, sir. Tomorrow afternoon suit you? After the inquest?"

Patrick said yes.

The inquest would be held tomorrow morning, but Mr. Trask said this morning's evidence was the more reliable for by tomorrow the Mexican imaginations would have swelled considerably. He let me keep the Santo, but suggested my putting it temporarily in the safe.

He wasn't through the door when Patrick Abbott nailed me, with eyes like green ice.

"All right, young lady. Come clean! What do you know about that Santo that you didn't tell the sheriff?"

"What makes you say that?" I said.

"I saw your face when you unwrapped it. He didn't."

"It did give me a shock, Pat," I admitted. Then I said, "You see, I gave that Santo to Tom Brandon myself."

I watched his face closely. There wasn't a ripple.

"For that matter," I said, "what makes you flutter every time the sheriff talks about that green spot?"

He laughed, his grave face suddenly alive and gay.

"This would be a tough town for any detective," he said.

"Why?"

"Well, for one thing people all seem to know what everybody else will do before they do it."

"How's that?"

"I was only thinking of Carmencita killing herself for spite," said Patrick Abbott.

# CHAPTER 25

Soon after Mr. Trask left the shop Patrick Abbott also went. On leaving he asked if I'd be home this evening. I said I would. "Why don't you come to dinner?" I said then. "If you don't mind a pot roast?"

"Thank you. What time?"

"About six-thirty. I'll also ask Julia Price and Daisy Payne."

We'd be having pot roast, I thought, as I locked up and started toward the Castillo, because I would have to get dinner, and a pot roast could be put in the pot and would more or less manage itself. Mrs. Dominguez wouldn't be much help now till after Carmencita's funeral.

Suddenly I thought of Luis's money. It was in my bag. I had a sudden feeling that I should get it away from the shop. So I didn't go to the restaurant, but went home instead.

I walked along quickly. My footsteps sounded dry against the dry rutted road. It was only a quarter-mile from the plaza to my house but it seemed further. Everything looked ugly today away from the plaza. The world was earth-color. That meant beige.

My house stood by itself, separated by a wide field, or corral, from the little flock of Mexican dobies further north, none of which had windows even toward my house and were reached by another road from the plaza. There was an adobe wall around the corral, which was a raddled sloping piece of beige-colored earth where the Mexicans dumped their tin cans and, I supposed, used to keep their horses, when they had horses.

It was the siesta hour. There was no one about. I saw Julia's car still parked at my gate, and smoke from my chimneys, which meant that Mrs. Dominguez had not gone home as usual today.

That would mean that she had not heard yet about Carmencita. They would be expecting her home, and therefore had not sent the news. Oh, dear.

Julia was eating breakfast from a tray on the coffee table by the living-room fire. She was in her nightie and the red robe. Her orange hair made a sunburst around her funny face. "I haven't had my bath. Waiting for hot water," she said, after we said hello. Mrs. Dominguez stood at a respectful distance, enjoying seeing Julia eat. She rushed to the kitchen to get me some lunch. I went to the closet in my room, stuck Luis's money in the deep pocket of a black tweed coat I seldom wore, washed up, and came back.

Julia was drinking coffee.

"Wasn't I a fool to come barging in here like that last night, Jean?" she said, self-reproachfully. "Why should I let Daisy's ranting bother me anyhow?" I sat down and lit a cigarette. "But she is worse than usual. Why should she take that murder so hard?"

I said, almost in a whisper, because of Mrs. Dominguez in the adjacent kitchen, "Carmencita was found dead this morning. In Mona's pool."

"Dead?" Julia shrieked.

"Should I tell Mrs. Dominguez?"

"Why? Let her *not* know it as long as possible, Jean."

"Maybe you're right."

Julia said, "Of course she did it that way to spite Mona. But how awful!"

"You think it's suicide?"

"Of course, darling. How diabolically clever!"

"How's that, Julia?"

"Her revenge!"

"Funny I should think the same thing!" I said. We were silent a moment. Then I asked, "I wonder where Luis was all last evening?"

"I never saw him once after the dancing started," Julia said. She sipped her coffee. "Funny about Carmencita, I always had a peculiar feeling about her, Jean. I mean, I felt that she was such a conspicuous example of senseless human waste. That is, with her looks and brains and any kind of breaks, she could have been a wonderful woman. She was absolutely fearless, too. I saw her Sunday night, it was terribly late, after midnight, walking by herself out there on the desert."

"Sunday night?" I said.

"I was on my way home. I'd stayed in town all hours telling Daisy about my trip to Hollywood. On my way back my headlights picked up Carmencita about a mile after I turned off the highway. I saw her only for a moment, but it was Carmencita all right. A straight slim figure in man's clothes and a black sombrero. I couldn't be wrong. I supposed she had gone out there for something. I wondered about it at the time. Most Mexicans wouldn't venture within miles of that place after that murder. I suppose she hid in the sage after that glimpse I got of her, for I didn't see her again."

So that was when Carmencita had gone back for the Santo. How strange!

"Have you talked much with Gilbert lately, Julia?" I said then.

"Me, talk to Gilbert?" Julia laughed. "You know how he scorns my intellect!"

Julia wriggled her toes under the crisscross satin straps of her mules. I told her to take any clothes of mine she wanted till she got home. Mrs. Dominguez brought me a salad, a ham sandwich, and coffee. I asked Julia if she and Daisy could come to dinner tonight. She said they had promised to be at the hospital from four until nine o'clock. Mrs. Dominguez announced that the water was hot enough now for Mrs. Price's bath. Julia slithered off in her mules and I went away without telling Mrs. Dominguez about Carmencita.

# CHAPTER 26

I DECIDED to ask the O'Haras to dinner. They had no phone, and I kept an eye open for them all afternoon but never saw either of them. I closed the shop at the usual time and did a little marketing, choosing the makings of my pot roast at the butcher's and grocer's, feeling lucky to find some mushrooms, some lovely lettuce, and a fair assortment of cheese.

I ran into Gilbert just as I was leaving the plaza for home.

"She's bolted!" he said. His eyes gleamed.

"Who?"

"Old Daisy. Well, what do you make of that?"

I felt exasperated. I didn't know what he was talking about, but I was annoyed. I brusquely walked away from him. It takes time to cook a roast in an iron pot on a trivet in a coal fire, which was the way we did them. I'd no time then to waste on Gilbert.

As I expected, there was a note under the flowerpot with the key saying that Mrs. Dominguez wouldn't be back until after Carmencita's funeral. I put away my coat and bag and washed my hands, and tied on an apron to start the dinner.

First I started a fire in the kitchen corner fireplace, which was built two feet above the floor specially to be cooked in. Then

I browned the roast in butter with a little sliced onion in a Dutch oven on the electric stove. By the time the fire in the fireplace was a nest of red coals the roast would be ready to transfer into an iron pot in which it would finish cooking on the trivet over the coals. I fixed the carrots, mushrooms, and onions, and left them to be added to the roast later on. I set the table, an old Spanish oak refectory table which stood in the corner of the big kitchen near the living-room door. I had good silver and my dishes were in a lovely blue pattern which suited the kitchen. The room had a dark split-cedar ceiling over aspen poles, deep window ledges, and red-checked gingham curtains. My menu was right for the room, I thought. Pot roast, hearts of lettuce salad, sweet pickles, home-made strawberry preserves, hot rolls, a cheese plate and coffee. Martinis to start with. Brandy with the coffee.

When everything was going I went to have my bath, then put on a velvet and brocade cocktail suit Julia Price had brought me last year from New York. After that I had to see how dinner was going.

The kitchen was at the back of the house, so I didn't hear a car drive up. I was coming back through the living room when the knocker sounded.

I went to the door.

It was Mona Brandon! Her shoulder-length hair was swept in a golden cloud over a cape of dark small furs.

"Hello," she said, her eyes raking me up and down, "have you seen Luis?"

"Luis?" I thought of that money.

"I was told on the plaza he'd come this way." Her eyes stabbed suspiciously at my velvet and brocade. "I don't know where he'd come then if not here, Jean."

Her tone was horrid. I said nothing.

"I don't know what's happened to Luis lately," she said, still in that nasty tone.

"Do you think I do?"

"I wouldn't know," she said.

I went furious. "Well, he's your Indian," I said. "If you're not able to look after him why not let him go?"

Mona let her eyes give my finery another once-over and then said insultingly, as she turned to go, "I do hope I haven't intruded, Jean." She laughed.

I went back to my room and whisked off the lovelies and got into my blue tweed suit. I could still smell her perfume and hear the mockery of her voice, and I was still touchy when Patrick Abbott arrived.

He smelled like tobacco and fresh air, and was feeling good. He carried a tiny little canvas on which was painted the head of a Mexican child. After taking off his hat and jacket he stood it on a bookshelf.

"Did you do that?" I said, impressed. His eyes twinkled.

"It's an O'Hara."

"Michael is competent, isn't he!"

"Decent, too," Pat said. "I've been with him all afternoon. He labored over me. Says he thinks I can swing it if I work hard enough."

"He wouldn't say so if you couldn't," I said.

"Well, thanks."

"How are you on martinis?"

"None better," he said. We went along to the kitchen and I finished cooking the dinner. Pat made the drinks and we had them in the kitchen. I said I wished I had known Michael was with him because I would have asked them to come to dinner. He said he thought he would have liked to come.

"Was Sonya with you?"

"No."

I think the dinner was a great success, if the proof was in the eating. We finished and afterwards sat by the living-room fire. I'm fussy about good brandy. I like it in snifters, warmed by the hands. It completes a dinner, makes it a small work of art.

It was all good fun. We got reminiscent. I told Pat that I came from a little town in Illinois but that my closest relations now were aunts and cousins, none of whom I'd seen for eight years. He said he was on his own, too, aside from a married sister in Honolulu.

It was just a chatty, poky time, until the bullet came through the window.

# CHAPTER 27

I SHOULD have closed the slats of the Venetian blinds, but I seldom did. The windows on this side of the house looked over the garden and down the hill. Beyond the garden was the wall and then that empty field or corral. Beyond the field were the Mexican cottages, which were all joined together around a patio, without a single window this way. So even with the slats wide open I always felt private enough.

It was about an hour and a half after dinner when we got shot at. Patrick had been sitting in the wing chair by the fireplace, facing the window. I was in a corner of the sofa with my back to the window, facing Pat. Toby had come in and had been lying against Patrick's feet. Suddenly Pat rose and took a small white envelope from the pocket of his shirt. He took a ring from the envelope and bent down to hand it to me.

"Ever seen this before, Jean?"

It was of heavy hand-hammered silver set with a shield-shaped piece of azure turquoise. The Indian symbols traced on the silver meant *Forever Until Death.*

I said I'd never seen it before. I was sure I would have remembered it, as it was old and very beautifully made.

"Where did you get it?" I asked.

"It was found yesterday on the desert, not far from where that body lay. By some Boy Scouts."

"You think it might have been Arkwright's?"

"Might. Or the murderer's. Anything can be a clue. Knowing you've got a good memory, I thought you might know the ring."

Patrick went to the fireplace and rested an elbow on the mantel.

"What makes you think I've got a good memory?" I asked.

His voice matched the quiet of the room as he said, "How about that Santo of Carmencita's?"

"Elementary, my dear Abbott!" I said. "That saint hung in my shop for more than a year."

"You said you gave it to Tom Brandon. Why?"

"He wanted it. Every time he came into the shop he asked to buy it, but I didn't want to sell it. Then one day he came in looking sort of miserable and on the impulse I gave it to him."

"I wonder how Carmencita came by it?"

"I also wonder."

"She went back to the cottage for it. Secretly, after the murder. That was pretty risky. If she'd been caught, it might have made her a lot of trouble."

"Perhaps she was superstitious about that Santo."

"Why wouldn't she ask the sheriff for it, Jean?"

"Mexicans are afraid of sheriffs. Even of Mr. Trask."

"Was Brandon a hermit type?"

"I don't think so. But he wasn't social. I mean, in the sense Mona is, wanting stir and fuss."

"He wouldn't have a hideaway in the desert, then?"

"It doesn't click with my idea of him, Pat."

He was silent.

I said, "I wish I could see that place. I've got a hunch that I'd know if he had lived there. I didn't know him terribly well but I've got a pretty good idea of his personal taste."

"Want to come home with the sheriff and me tomorrow?"

"Love to."

"Okay. I'll ask if you may."

He took out his cigarette pack. I was conscious of his long fingers taking the cigarette from the pack, the casual motions of his hand when lighting it and I saw the used match curving off into the fire. I started then to hand him the ring. He took a step toward me and bent down to take it.

The movement probably saved his life, for that was when the bullet came through the window!

It happened so fast I have to put it together backwards to get it straight. Then reverse it.

There was a pop, a stinging sound, breaking glass, and a final thud as the shot buried itself in the adobe wall.

The pop was when the bullet came cleanly through the window. The glass it broke was on a picture on the opposite wall.

Patrick yelled "Duck!" I saw him take a couple of long steps and switch off the lights. He got something from his jacket, a revolver as I knew later, then quietly left the house by way of the kitchen, after telling me to lie low. Seconds later I heard two shots. Then silence. I thought maybe he was killed. I was paralyzed.

Toby huddled against my feet. There was a tiny red glow on the hearth away from the fire. Patrick's cigarette.

Then he came in. I relaxed as I heard him bolt the kitchen door. Back in the living room he closed the slats of the blinds before turning on the lights. I saw that the inside of his left sleeve was ripped. There was blood!

"You're hurt!" I screeched.

"It's nothing."

Then Toby leaped on him and bit his ankle.

"For God's sake, cat!" Patrick said, kicking him away. Toby beat it for my bedroom.

"I'll get bandages," I said. I felt hectic.

"Later." He was already at the door. "Lock this door. I'll be back."

He went out. I heard long steps, a motor whirring. I went to the bathroom for first-aid supplies. I saw Toby's yellow eyes under my bed. I came back and put the bandages and such on the coffee table by the fire, then went into the kitchen to put the kettle on the slow electric heat. As I returned to the living room the knocker sounded, and I felt frightened because I hadn't locked the door. I stood looking at it, doing nothing.

The latch lifted. The door opened.

*It was Mona Brandon!*

"Well?" she said, eyeing me. She was in the same blue dinner dress, silver slippers, and the fur cape. "Didn't you hear me knock?" she asked, suspiciously, her eyes running over the room, taking in Patrick's things on the chair by the door, and the smashed picture. She came to the fireplace. Her eyes fastened on the bandages.

"What goes on, Jean?"

"Nothing."

The eyes moved to Patrick's cigarette. It was still burning. That's how fast things had happened.

"Won't you sit down?" I asked.

She sat down. "I can't stay a moment. I left the O'Haras at my house, saying I'd be right back. I met Mr. Abbott at the foot of the hill. He seemed in a hurry."

"Did he?"

"We almost crashed. We passed like that." She brushed her hands together. I was then standing by the mantel, trying to figure things out. She hadn't been in my house for years, and now twice in one evening.

"Cigarette?" I asked her.

"I'll have one of my own."

Mona took a long amber holder and a gold cigarette case from her evening bag and slowly fitted a cigarette into the holder. She lit it with her lighter.

I heard the kettle boiling in the kitchen and went to turn it off. When I came back Mona seemed somehow changed.

"I suppose you are wondering why I came here again," she said. "I had to come. I'm so terribly upset."

"Haven't you found Luis yet?"

"Oh, that's not it! It was the way I spoke to you, darling. I came to apologize! I haven't a nerve left. You've heard, of course, about Carmencita?"

Our eyes met.

"It's terrible!" I said.

Mona became herself again. "It's sickening! She did it to spite me, of course. With the whole earth to do it in she chose my swimming pool, knowing that I could never go there again without thinking of her."

She went on, and I listened without a word thinking how like her it was to regard the tragedy as a personal inconvenience. Then she smiled over-sweetly.

"I understand you brought the O'Haras home with you last night after my party. That was nice of you, Jean. Sonya's such a dreary creature."

"She was charming."

Mona eyed me serenely.

"You don't have to pretend with me, Jean. I know Sonya. She's a bitch. Michael and I are perfectly happy every minute we spend together, but that nasty little Russian is impossible. There she is, snooping every minute, watching me with her horrid little eyes."

I said, "I'm not pretending. Sonya was charming last night. For the first time I understood why Michael cares for her." Mona bared her teeth.

"Michael loathes her! He's tied hand and foot."

I looked down my nose. I wondered if she had come to talk about the O'Haras. And I wondered how her being here was connected with the shot.

Mona went wistful again.

"Jean, darling, why can't we be friends? You were my first friend in Santa Maria, Jeanie. What happened? Why do we go on and on sparring at each other?"

"You've got funny ideas about friendship, Mona."

"What do you mean?"

I practically jumped at the chance to express myself.

"Well, here's a minor case of what doesn't make you a very good friend. Suppose you spent a day polishing up a lot of jewelry and then hoofing it a mile on an unpleasant evening to show the stuff to a woman who has nothing on earth to do anyhow but come and choose it in your shop. You close the shop early to be on time. And you're literally kicked off the doorstep!"

Mona raised her white hands.

"But, darling, that was a mistake. I scolded Lupe roundly for letting you go."

"It was Rita," I said dryly.

"What difference does it make?" Mona snapped. "They're all

alike. Liars and cheats. I had scolded her for something else, so to annoy me she sent you away, and then told me you wouldn't come in. I'll dismiss her."

I was shocked.

"You wouldn't, Mona?"

"Why not? She's only a servant."

"Oh, forget it," I said. Now I would worry about what she'd do to poor Rita.

"I meant to come to the shop and explain," Mona said, waving her cigarette holder. "But I've been so busy. First the party. Then this horrible suicide, with uncouth creatures like Trask nosing all over the place. Will you bring the things again tomorrow, Jean?"

"No," I said. "I won't."

"Then I'll come to the shop," Mona declared.

But I knew that wasn't why she had come, either, that business about friendship. She didn't want my friendship that much.

Toby came in from the bedroom. He didn't like Mona's perfume and started to growl. I picked him up and sat stroking him.

Mona said then, in a voice so natural it seemed strange coming from her, "My real reason for coming here is to ask you to tell me where I can find my husband. Jean, where is Tom Brandon?"

"I don't know where he is," I said. Mona seemed relieved.

"I just wondered. I thought you might."

And that apparently was all there was going to be to it. Astonishingly, she let it rest. Temporarily. I remember looking at her and being struck again by the stillness of her face, and then seeing her eyes again begin their eternal roving. She was not looking at me at all, she was looking at the room, her glance taking in the parchment-colored adobe walls, the gay books on their shelves.

Mona smiled at me. Nicely, too.

"This is the way to live, Jean." I said that I was afraid she'd find it pretty simple. She continued pleasantly then, but spoiled it by raving, "So simple and good. I die inside when I think of that great barn I live in. I did it for Tom. I adored him so that I would have done anything to make him happy. But it was all wasted. That woman came. There she was, day after day, in my house, a servant taking my money and running after my husband. I know you all blamed me for making her serve her sentence. But I wonder how many of you would have done otherwise? I loved my husband. He was my whole life." Mona sighed. It seemed as artificial as her talk. "Well, it was all wasted. He went away. I have come here tonight to beg you to take pity on me and tell me where he is."

"I just told you I didn't know where he was," I said.

"You're lying!" she screamed. "You're lying to my face. You know where he is and you always have." Her lips twisted, but her manner smoothed out again, almost at once, and she declared, nonchalantly, "I wanted to test you, that's all. I know where he is. He's dead."

"Dead?" I asked, startled in spite of myself.

Mona smiled. "So you didn't know that?"

"I know absolutely nothing about Tom Brandon."

She appeared to consider, then went back to raving, soulfully this time. "Of course he could not die without my knowing it. We were too close for that. I loved him so. After he went away I was an unresolved chord, a vagrant being, and then suddenly, not long ago, I felt at peace and knew he was dead."

The whole thing was too silly. I looked down my nose.

But intimations of any kind always fascinate me, possibly because I never have any. I wondered how long ago she had felt suddenly at peace, and if it had anything to do with Arkwright.

I felt relieved when a car sounded on the hill. It was Patrick Abbott returning. He came along the flags, knocked lightly, and entered.

Mona was instantly smooth as silk.

"Why, good evening, Mr. Abbott," she said. She held out her hand. Patrick Abbott crossed the room and shook it. Obviously he thought it was a pleasure! "Why, what happened to your arm?"

"I caught it on a nail," Patrick said.

"How fortunate that Jean seems to have known it in advance," Mona said, waving her cigarette holder at the first-aid things.

"Oh, it happened before I left," Patrick said.

Mona stood up. "I must be going," she said. She caught the fasteners of her cape at her throat and stood there swathed in her elegance. "Why don't you two come to dinner soon? Say tomorrow evening?" she asked.

"I can't," I said. I had promised to help out at the hospital tomorrow, thank goodness.

"The day after, then?" Mona insisted.

I looked at Patrick Abbott. He wanted to go. He nodded slightly to impress it on me.

"Thank you," I said.

"Thanks very much," Patrick Abbott said.

"It's a date then," Mona said. She said something about having enjoyed her little visit and about seeing me in the shop tomorrow morning about ten to choose her Christmas presents.

Patrick went with her to the gate. I went to fetch a basin of hot water from the kitchen.

He came back.

"I wonder if she ever found Luis," I said.

"He was driving her," Patrick said.

"Luis?" I said. "Was he out there in the car?"

Patrick nodded, and then hurriedly started searching the floor. "What became of that ring, Jean?"

I hadn't thought of the ring since the shot came through the window. We searched everywhere. It was gone. Later on, after I'd fixed up his arm, he searched again for the ring, but it was certainly gone. I had left the room only for a moment, to turn off the heat under the kettle, but apparently it had been long enough.

I laughed. "So that's why she came," I said.

# CHAPTER 28

PATRICK SAID he'd have to sift the ashes. I suggested his waiting till the fire died down a little more. The fact is, I wanted to know more about the ring. I had some bourbon and ginger ale and we sat down with long drinks at the fireside, and I was just ready to start quizzing when Patrick Abbott said, "What a hell of a nuisance!"

"What?"

"Losing that ring. What chance have I got now of a real vacation?"

"How's that?"

Patrick said, "Mr. Trask thought that ring a real clue to the murderer. Therefore whoever was outside the window saw me with the ring and evidently suspected me of some connection with the investigation and chanced a shot at me."

"Maybe somebody was just playing with a gun."

"You think so?"

"No, I just said it."

Patrick Abbott grinned. "Thanks. It cheers me up. But it might have hit *you*, you know."

"Well, it didn't," I said, wondering if he'd care. "Why would Mona take the ring?"

"How do we know yet that she did?"

I said, "Maybe she fired the shot. Maybe she wanted the ring and shot at you and saw you drop it and then came in to get it."

"But how did she get across the corral to the road and into her car so quickly?"

I said, "Just where did you meet her?"

"At the foot of the hill."

"That's what she said, too. Was Luis with her then?"

"Yes. He was driving. We almost met head on."

"Do you think she fired the shot, Pat?" I said, repeating myself, more or less.

"What would be her motive?"

"Well, what would be her motive in taking the ring? Isn't it all the same thing somehow?"

Patrick said, "Mona didn't fire the shot. She wouldn't've had time to climb your wall, run across the corral, reach the road, and get into her car by the time we met at the foot of the hill. She had on evening slippers and a long fluffy dress. There was no evidence about her clothes to indicate that she'd been sprinting over walls."

"Do you always carry a gun, Pat?"

"Not always," he said.

"Luis could have done it," I said, feeling awful for saying it, too. "Maybe Mona waited for him in the car. Then they came on here to get the ring."

"How about motive?" Patrick asked blithely. "The ring alone isn't enough."

"Well, Luis has been wanting money. Mona's up to her neck in something. She's worried. Maybe she wanted the ring and so—"

"I hardly think she'd take that means of getting it."

"I'll show you something," I said. I went to the closet in my room and took the roll of money from my coat. "Look at this. Luis came into the shop today and paid me every cent he owed on the stuff he has reserved for himself. All this money, a hundred dollars, plus three dollars and thirty-five cents in silver. Where would he get it? Why? Also, Luis, of all people in Santa Maria, would be the one most likely to own that fine Indian ring. Maybe he killed the man and while doing it lost the ring. Did you show this ring to anyone and say you were going to show it to me?"

"As a matter of fact I did. I mentioned it to Michael O'Hara when I had the painting lesson."

"And Michael was at Mona's tonight. She said so! He's told her!"

Patrick looked appreciative. I said then, "What shall I do with this money?"

"Why not put it in the bank?"

"It wouldn't be counterfeit, would it?" Patrick Abbott looked at it, bill by bill.

"It looks all right to me. The bank will soon let you know."

"I hate to put that shark McClure on Luis's trail, Pat."

"Even if Luis were guilty of murder?"

"Yes, even then."

"Well, if anything comes up, leave it to me."

That made me feel better. I put the money back in the coat pocket, meaning to put it in the bank in the morning. Patrick Abbott sifted the ashes for the ring before going. I sat watching him and thinking about Mona Brandon.

Intimations of Tom Brandon's death, my foot! If Arkwright were Brandon and she hired poor Luis to murder him her intimations would be sure ones indeed.

But, honestly, I couldn't believe he was Brandon.

Just before going Patrick dug the bullet out of the soft adobe wall with his knife. It had ruined a nice Japanese print. He put the bullet in an envelope and buttoned it in his jacket pocket. He took Michael's charming Mexican child and hung it over the hole he'd dug in the adobe. A present for the trouble he'd made me, he said.

After he went everything seemed cockeyed.

It was worse later on. It was a dark night, no visibility worth the name. I lay awake, thinking about Luis, how Julia said that Mona had adopted him—if she really had—to show off, how Daisy contended that she had done it out of a genuine humanity, but Gilbert claimed she was pathological. Mr. Trask once said she kept the powerful Indian as a bodyguard because she was afraid. That made sense. But how far would he go for Mona? Would he commit murder? Would it seem like murder to an Indian? Suppose Arkwright really had been Brandon and Mona was in love with Michael. Mona hadn't divorced Brandon, so far as anyone knew. She refused to at first, it was said, because she was afraid he would marry Carmencita. Now it would be his turn. Would he refuse? If he were Arkwright, already holding her up to scorn by living out there with the Mexican girl, would she resort to having him murdered?

If so, Carmencita would be next, because she knew the truth. It had happened in Mona's grounds. Mona knew when the party would get noisy, and when the grounds would be without their guards.

Where had Luis been while the Indians were dancing?

That ring! Luis was a connoisseur, I reiterated.

How did he know the sheriff had it, and had given it to Patrick? That was easy. The famous grapevine of Santa Maria.

Mona would have come to my house seeking him that first time as a blind. The second time she had come for the ring. Luis's being with her was his alibi. He would have had time to shoot and run down the hill to her car.

Mona certainly seemed damned sure that Brandon was dead. She'd been feeling me out, obviously.

Yes, I was sure. I saw it all. I wondered what to do.

"But what about Sonya?" an inner voice put in.

My beautiful structure collapsed. It was worthless. Sonya was still in the way, and she wouldn't be gotten rid of easily. Not Sonya.

Thinking that the imagination is a wonderful time-waster I fell asleep.

# CHAPTER 29

I FELT a gust of sweet dry air across my face. I raised myself on my elbow and through the garden window saw an old butter-colored moon rising over the mountains. It was a decrepit object, but it was clear.

The clouds had moved on. The close oppressive weather we'd had all week was ended.

I slept then, and the morning dawned clear and rosy. I got my own breakfast, fed the cat, and since Mrs. Dominguez would be away left a note tacked on the front gate asking the milkman to get the key from under the flowerpot and take in the milk and put it in the icebox.

I wore my summery blue tweeds and a polka-dot blouse. As I walked down the hill white featherbed clouds rolled serenely across a canopy of pure turquoise.

I had brought the basket of silver back to the shop, expecting Mona to come in at ten o'clock. I forgot Luis's money until I was halfway to the place. I didn't want to go back. I could bank it tomorrow.

I had to take out the ashes and lay the fire myself. I swept up, then dusted. I thought about what all I'd do today. At noon I would pay a sympathy call on the Dominguezes. I must ask Rose where Carmencita was, at their house or her aunt's. In the afternoon I would close up and go with Patrick Abbott and Mr. Trask to see the Arkwright place. I would then return to the shop and some time after four o'clock go to the hospital.

I set the basket of silver on the glass case, then, and sat on the stool taking the pieces out of their tissue paper and laying them on a velvet pad ready for Mona to look at. They were lovely. I was giving the antique pieces away at that price, though.

Michael O'Hara parked out in front and came in. He had an armful of yellow tea-roses.

"With Mona's compliments," he said giving me the roses. I took them. Then he took a letter from his pocket. "And here's a note. Mona says she's terribly sorry she can't come in this morning."

The fine morning went flat as a punctured balloon. I tucked the roses under one arm and with the other scooped the silver up as it was, velvet and all, and dumped it back into the basket.

"How is everything?" Michael asked, as he turned to go.

"Fine. Not much business, of course."

"Wish I could help."

"You can. Bring me another picture to sell."

"Some day," he promised. "By the way, Abbott's okay. He can learn to paint all right, if he wants to."

"Good. I'd hate to have sent you a dud, Michael."

Michael smiled. "He's no dud. Well, be seeing you."

"So long. Thanks a lot for bringing the flowers."

Michael flipped a hand and left the shop. I shot Mona's letter a mean glance and went into the back room to get a container for the roses. I arranged them in a terra cotta bowl and set them in the window. The basket of silver was on the glass case.

I picked it up and carried it back and locked it in the safe just as it was.

I came back into the shop. The letter was lying there on the case where Michael had laid it. I resisted an impulse to toss it unopened into the fire.

Then I ran a finger under the unsealed flap and the contents slid into my hand. There was a check for five hundred dollars, and the note, in Mona's girlish script, said for me to select the pieces myself.

"Your taste is far better than mine anyhow," she wrote. "Don't forget that you and that nice Mr. Abbott are dining with me tomorrow night. At seven."

I went into the back room, unlocked the safe, and got out the basket of silver.

# CHAPTER 30

THIS TIME I made a list. Gilbert Mason came in and seated himself by the fireplace.

"Nice day, Gilbert," I said.

"Is it?"

Then Patrick Abbott entered.

"Morning," he said. "Hello, Mason."

"Morning," I said.

Gilbert said nothing.

Patrick said if it wasn't intruding he'd like to stay to read his Denver paper. He took the corner seat. I asked him about his arm. He said it was nothing at all and waggled it to show me. Then he vanished behind his spread-out paper. Gilbert sat on, very stiff, very annoyed.

Suddenly I saw again how terrible he looked. His puffy flesh had a waxy tinge, and there were black circles under his colorless eyes. I felt anxious.

"You feeling all right, Gilbert?"

"Why can't you mind your own business?" he flamed back. "I never come in here that you don't say that."

"Sorry."

He said, "Hoped you'd be alone, Jean." I ignored that. So did

Patrick Abbott if he heard it. "I suppose you haven't seen Sonya this morning, by any chance?"

"No, I haven't."

"O'Hara's frisking all over the place. Without her."

"Maybe she's got a cold or something."

Gilbert snorted. "If she had a cold Michael would stay at home and nurse her, or know the reason why. There's something fishy there, take it from me."

"Oh, Gilbert!" I protested.

"I happen to have a brain," Gilbert announced, sitting very straight. "What is more extraordinary, I use it. It doesn't take genius, my pet, to know that something is up when a man who hasn't taken two steps in three years without the little wife suddenly starts bouncing about like free people." He dropped his voice. "Something has happened to our Sonya."

"Why not ask Michael?" I suggested.

"That swine?"

I felt shocked. I said that he shouldn't say such things, that it only made people feel badly and got him nowhere.

"For instance, what you said last night about Daisy Payne," I began.

"What was that?"

"That she'd bolted—"

"She has."

I laughed. "I've got to have proof."

"All right," Gilbert said. "Call the bus station. They'll tell you that she left on the bus yesterday afternoon. She took an airliner from Albuquerque last night. She is now in New York trying to get passage to England."

"She would have told Julia," I said.

"Oh, no. Daisy isn't so foolish as to say goodbye." Gilbert began to laugh. "It's all very interesting. After the way she's treated me! But now I've got her where I want her." He rolled his pale eyes at his briefcase.

He went into a tirade about the inquest on Carmencita which had taken place this morning in the court house. They hadn't even called in the people who knew what really happened, he said. I said, "For instance?" and Gilbert replied, "Myself!"

"What do you make of all that?" I said to Patrick Abbott, after Gilbert had suddenly jumped up and left.

"Mason so obviously wants to shock, Jean. It's a pity to let him get away with it."

Less than five minutes later Mr. Trask came in to ask me if I knew where Daisy had gone. She wasn't at home, he said, and her house was all closed up.

"You know anything for certain about that lady, Miss Holly?" the sheriff asked.

"No. Except she's English. She once had a title."

"Are you sure of that?"

"Why, no. But if she's taken out her American papers—"

"Have you ever seen those papers?"

"Why, no."

"Mind you," said the sheriff, "I'm not accusing Miss Payne of anything, but she sure has picked a funny time to leave town."

"Have you talked with Julia?" I asked. "Mrs. Price? She'll know all about Miss Payne."

"No, ma'am. We'll stop by there this afternoon if I don't run into her around town. Well, nothing specially developed at the inquest, Mr. Abbott. The coroner's jury returned an open verdict. Death owing to causes unknown, with investigation continuing."

The sheriff turned to me.

"I understand you're coming with us this afternoon, Miss Holly."

"If it's all right?"

"Glad to have you. We'll go about half-past one."

Patrick and the sheriff left the shop together. Shortly afterward some customers came in, some tourists driving a car with a Texas license. They stayed till one o'clock and bought a number of things. When they'd gone I saw I'd have only the time for a bite of lunch before leaving with Patrick and Mr. Trask. I put the jewelry for Mona again in the safe.

# CHAPTER 31

THE SHERIFF drove an old-fashioned car, which had lots of clearance and used six-ply tires made for rocky desert roads. I sat in the narrow front seat with Mr. Trask, Patrick Abbott in the back. It was a gorgeous afternoon. I noticed Mona's car parked in front of the hospital as we passed. The hospital was a short way off the road but Mona's yellow car was conspicuous. I asked Mr. Trask if he'd had any special news from the bus patients, and he said that most of them would be leaving to-morrow, but that the driver continued in a state of coma. "We won't know exactly what all happened until he comes out of it, ma'am," he said.

Four miles south, we turned left to Julia's. She was at home, dressed in blue jeans and reading a novel in a hammock in the flowery patio. She was delighted to see us and wanted to make it a party.

"We won't have time to stay, thank you, ma'am," Mr. Trask said. "Can you tell me, please, where Miss Payne could have gone to?"

"Gone? Daisy?" Julia's big eyes opened. "Oh, I expect she's in Santa Fe."

"Do you know where she might stay there, Mrs. Price?"

"Yes, at La Fonda. Shall I phone for you?"

"If you will, please, ma'am."

We sat down on the veranda which surrounded the patio while Julia made her call. But Daisy wasn't at the hotel. She wasn't at any of three or four other places in Santa Fe where Julia then inquired.

"She was awfully upset about the Arkwright murder," Julia said, rejoining us.

I saw the sheriff's eyes narrow. "But why, ma'am?"

Julia grinned. "You know yourself how she is about justice, Mr. Trask."

The sheriff reddened. "Well, don't let it worry you none, ma'am. I wanted to ask Miss Payne some questions about that calf she bought."

I said, "Perhaps she's gone to England."

"Oh, no," said Julia. "She's not on good terms with her family."

"Why not?" Patrick Abbott asked.

Julia said, "They resented her becoming an American."

"It does seem rather unusual," Patrick said. "For one of her class."

"Not if you hate parting with money as bad as Miss Payne does," the sheriff said dryly, referring to the English income tax. "The reason I think she has really gone away for some time is that her car is on jacks, ma'am. I put my eye to a crack and saw that the car looked as if jacked up for the winter. I wonder who would have done that for her."

Julia's eyes sparkled. "She'd do it herself. Daisy is very proud of her strength, you know. Well, I'll go to her house this afternoon and see what she has done about that calf. Somebody will have to feed and water the poor little thing."

We stood up to go. I asked Julia if she'd like to come along with me this afternoon to the hospital. She said she would and would pick me up about four o'clock.

The sheriff drove on to the Arkwright house over the trail, instead of going back along the road. We bounced and crawled along a track that was hardly good enough for a horse. In the arroyo near the Arkwright house two sets of car tracks were plain, side by side on the hard dry earth. The sheriff got out and examined them. One set went on past the house and disappeared into the creek. They appeared again on the opposite bank and, as we were to observe later, went on across the desert and joined the main road two miles on.

The men prowled around the house and picked up things and put them in envelopes and held long conversations I wasn't included in. Patrick Abbott dug out a lot of wood around the ink spot. He put this in one of his envelopes. He looked around for fingerprints and on leaving the house took with him an old tin shaving mirror and a razor the dead man had evidently used, both of which showed some clear fingerprints. He wrapped these things in the handkerchiefs he seemed to produce in endless numbers whenever he wanted them, and put them in a shoebox he found on a kitchen shelf. He told Mr. Trask he'd take these things to the state police headquarters so that the fingerprints might be photographed and sent for possible identification by the FBI in Washington.

There was only one idea I could positively contribute and that was that there was nothing about the place which suggested Tom Brandon.

It was three o'clock when I got back to the shop. Julia arrived shortly after four and had a cigarette while I got the shop ready for closing. She was worried about Daisy Payne's having gone away.

"She's gone all right," she said. "Her house is closed up the way she leaves it when she's going away for a good while. And her car is on jacks. I made inquiry at the bus station. They said she went to Albuquerque."

That was what Gilbert had said, I thought. "How was the calf?" I asked.

"Hungry. She must have forgotten the little thing."

"That's not like Daisy."

"None of it is," Julia said. "She should have told me she was leaving. I slept till noon yesterday, as you know, and when I left your house I decided to go straight home and pick up my things at Daisy's later on. When she didn't turn up at the hospital yesterday afternoon I thought she must be just tired out."

I was spreading the dust sheets. "Obviously she went of her own accord since she jacked up the car," Julia said. I got my coat and bag.

"I didn't tell you, Julia," I said, as I locked up and we got into her car, "that Mona gave me a real order this morning. Money and all."

"*Madre de Dios!*" commented Julia.

"I guess she's not so this-and-that, after all."

"No?"

We laughed, understanding each other, and Julia drove in her gallivanting way around the plaza. We came into the highway and headed south.

"I saw the sheriff take you on to Arkwright's by that trail," Julia said. "It's getting to be a thoroughfare."

"I don't think you need worry," I laughed.

"See anything out that way that made you think of Tom Brandon?"

"Not a thing."

We chuckled again. Then Julia said, "I've got a confession to make, Jean. I did a little snooping this afternoon. I thought maybe Gilbert might know something about Daisy, since he lives near by, and also makes it his business to mind everybody else's, so I went on to his house. I knocked. He didn't come to the door. I felt sort of curious about his house. Anyhow I walked around and knocked on the kitchen door. No answer. So I walked in. Everything was neat as a pin."

"It always is," I said.

"It was too neat," Julia said, slowing down as we approached the hospital lane. "It was bare. There's nothing there, Jean. No food, no wood or coal, nothing. I looked."

"He always goes to the Castillo, you know."

"People keep things for an emergency, Jeanie."

"Gilbert thinks he's God lately," I couldn't help saying, "in which case *no* emergency could arise unless he willed it."

I almost told her then about that knife. But I didn't. She would worry more about Daisy if she knew about the knife in Gilbert's briefcase.

We turned into the hospital lane. The building looked attractive in the afternoon light. It was cream-colored stucco with a cedar veranda entirely around the second floor. It was originally a ranch house, and many of the rooms had doors both on hallways and the veranda. Two big wings had been added to the original building, one of them the gift of Mona Brandon. The nurses' home was new, too, and stood a short distance from the main building. There weren't any nurses to spare, which was why they had suggested our coming in to sit around with the convalescent bus patients.

The whole place was surrounded with cottonwoods, bare now, their leaves in russet billows on the ground.

"There's Mona's car," I said, as we drove up. "She's been here all afternoon, apparently."

We parked and went in by the main entrance. There was no one in the office, not unusual when the staff was overworked. We walked upstairs. The sitting rooms, where the bus patients would be assembled at this time of day, were to the right of the stairs, but just as we were about to turn right Julia suggested first having a look at the sunset from the west side of the veranda. We turned left and walked along, conscious of the teeming activity of the place but meeting no one. But as we turned onto the west end of the veranda, the furthest from the busy center of the hospital, a door opened and Mona Brandon stepped out.

She had on a white overall and a starched lined square sheathed her hair. On seeing us she slammed the door behind her and leaned against it, both hands clasping the knob behind her back. She looked frightened.

"What do you want?" she demanded.

"We're looking for a sunset," Julia said.

Mona pulled her lips tight against her teeth. "The nurses have orders to keep people off this end of the balcony."

"Really?" Julia said.

"You've got no business here anyhow," screeched Mona. "Neither of you. Get out!"

"Dr. Johnson asked us to come," I said.

"You're lying! I told him myself to tell you two in particular to keep away from the hospital."

We turned to go back the way we had come.

Then Mona's manner changed entirely.

"I'm sorry," she said. But she still hung on to the doorknob. "I'm fidgety. I've been parked in this room all afternoon relieving the nurses. The bus driver's in here, you know. Someone has to be with him when he finally comes to, to note down anything he says."

We told Mona we quite understood and then walked back in the direction we had come. In the main hall Miss Edwards, the superintendent of nurses, stepped from an open door and on seeing us smiled brightly and asked if one of us would call Dr. Johnson.

"Tell him our bus driver is regaining consciousness," she said. "He's in this room," she added. "And tell the doctor I'll stay with him myself till he and the sheriff can get here to take any statement. Thank you."

"My goodness," Julia said.

Later I asked Miss Edwards directly who was in the room Mona Brandon was guarding. She evaded making an answer.

# CHAPTER 32

I DROVE back into town with Mrs. McClure, the only other volunteer there that afternoon. Julia went home at six o'clock. The banker's wife was a plump friendly sort of woman. She chatted about her kids, a church social in prospect, and the sudden change in the weather. After she dropped me at the plaza I reflected that at least the mysteries weren't getting the local socialites down. Mona queened it over us all, but she didn't go in for the network of small doings of which Mrs. McClure and Mrs. Johnson were leaders.

I stopped at the Castillo for a late dinner. I asked Joe Padilla where they had Carmencita's body and he said it was at home. There would be a wake, of course. I went to the shop after dinner to get the roses Mona had sent me this morning. Fresh flowers were scarce at this time of year. The Dominguez cottage, at the north side of town, was all lighted up and of course seething with people.

As I entered a flock of old women in black shawls were wailing around the coffin. Carmencita's mother sat in the best chair beside the unlit fireplace. She was a stringy, dark-eyed woman, nothing like as old as she looked, and dignified even in grief. Carmencita lay in a real bought coffin, dressed—a gift of the bridegroom—in the wedding gown and orange blossoms she had longed for.

I needn't have bothered to bring my roses. Mona Brandon had filled the place with fresh flowers. They made a fragrant bower of the tawdry room in which Carmencita lay. Mona had also paid for the coffin, so that Carmencita would lie in a real one instead of the usual homemade pine box. What was even more impressive, there was to be a hearse for the funeral instead of the coffin's being carried from the church to the graveyard on the shoulders of young men.

People couldn't get over it. In the kitchen, where my Mrs. Dominguez escorted me for a glass of wine, dozens of Mexicans were eating and drinking and talking of nothing else but the generosity of Mrs. Brandon. The room was dully lit by an oil lamp on the kitchen table. The light fell on the iron cookstove, the gaudy oilcloth on the table, the strings of red peppers and gourds hanging from the beams.

Everyone got quiet and crossed himself as in the front room some old man started singing a *rosario* over the coffin. They would chant a few words and the women would respond with a sort of sigh, then the men would chant again, and the sigh would sound once more through the house like a gust of weird wind. A strange unearthly sound, that sigh. Tomorrow mass would be held for Carmencita in church, with candles at either end of the coffin.

Mexican manners are very beautiful. Even when drinking these people were decorous. I went away feeling uplifted, but afterwards, thinking back on it all, I was unusually depressed. I had a bath, after feeding the cat, and then saw that it was almost eleven o'clock. When I put Toby out for the night I stepped out into the starlight. It was brilliant. I could see the solid bulk of the mountains and the slim beauty of my cottonwood. Then Toby began to spit and snarl and prance around something in the leaves, and thinking it might be a snake I went inside for my flashlight and a broom, but a search turned up nothing save an empty cartridge shell. I picked it up to give to Patrick.

# CHAPTER 33

WHEN PATRICK Abbott turned up at the shop next morning I gave him the cartridge. He put it in an envelope and said it probably wasn't anything but thanks very much.

Patrick sat down, took a sketchpad from his portfolio, and started sketching me as I sat at the turquoise-and-silver case. I felt talkative. I opened up and told him about Daisy's having disappeared, about Mona's queer behavior at the hospital, and about the nocturnal meanderings of some probable Indian or other.

He didn't seem much impressed.

"You say Miss Payne is unusually strong, Jean?"

"Yes."

"And eccentric?"

"Very."

"Then why concern yourself about her going away like that?"

"There are other reasons. Deeper, puzzling reasons."

"What?"

"Oh, I don't want to repeat them. Just talk." I didn't like to quote that stuff about Daisy's being crazy about Tom Brandon once upon a time, and so on. "But she has been so queer lately. It worries us, that's all."

"What would be her motive in disappearing?"

"That's what I want to know."

He was silent. I said, "A lot of people have had the idea that Arkwright might have been Tom Brandon."

"Do you? After seeing that house yesterday?"

"No. But there wasn't anything there that told me anything one way or another, you know."

He didn't say anything for a minute. Then he said, "I suppose such talk arose because of Carmencita. That's just foolish. She was beautiful, but there is no evidence that she was faithful to anyone or anything. Her beauty created an illusion of a kind of woman she definitely was not. She looked like a madonna, but she was apparently quite a wench. That confused people."

"A wench wouldn't suicide, would she?" I asked.

"Why not? Maybe she was tired of life."

"Remember that scream I heard at the party, Pat?"

"It still might have been an Indian."

"Then it doesn't mean anything."

"Nothing in particular. Still, it's a neat bit of evidence."

"You are one of the most exasperating people I ever met!" I snapped.

He looked at me gravely. "You forget that this isn't my case, Jean. So I couldn't talk even if I knew anything."

"You don't want to know anything, you mean."

"Have it any way you like," he said.

And then I said didn't it even stir him into some kind of action to have been shot at through my window and he said, looking at me out of those grave blue-green eyes, that the only thing that worried him on that score was that I might have got shot. I blushed and felt tongue-tied.

After a while I said, "But, frankly and honestly, what do you make of Luis? Don't you suspect him of—well, at least *knowing* too much?"

Patrick Abbott made a long stroke on the sketchpad. "Nothing most Indians do is suspicious, if you look at it from an Indian's viewpoint. I think you should begin at the beginning, Jean, and consider this thing scientifically. Take Arkwright. Who would benefit by his murder?"

"Mona, if he was Brandon."

"But we don't think he was, you know."

"Then whoever stole his money."

"Good. That takes care of that. Now who would benefit by Carmencita's death?"

"Mona, if Carmencita knew Arkwright was Brandon."

"But there you are. We've no proof that he was Brandon. That kills the whole thing."

Patrick smiled and went on sketching.

"Whom do you think Mona's hiding in that hospital room?" I asked then.

"Your guess is as good as mine."

I said, and I made my voice low, "If Mona is in love with Michael O'Hara and that person in the hospital room is Sonya she is the last of three people who stood in the way . . . if Arkwright was Brandon."

Patrick Abbott said, "I like the way your nose tilts up."

It was two or three minutes before I could ask, then, "If this were your own case, how would you proceed?"

"Just as Mr. Trask has. Hold the inquest. Listen to the evidence. And keep right on quietly investigating. You don't find out things by hauling in people and asking them a lot of questions about where you were at such a time and so on. Everybody always has an alibi. You're just putting the guilty ones on their guard."

"What do you do, then?"

"You wait. You observe the actions of anyone who might have cause to commit the crime in question. The conduct of the criminal after the crime often nets him. If necessary you do or say things which will make him betray himself, or so you hope."

"You think in this case—"

Patrick Abbott said, "I was speaking in generalities."

I sighed at the futility of it all, got off the stool and went to the fireplace. I lit a cigarette and sat down. "Now I'll have to begin all over," Patrick said. He tore off the sketch and tossed it at the fire, and began again.

"Have you found any more counterfeit money?" I asked.

"Not yet."

I waited a few minutes and then said, "I suspect Luis is the person hanging around my house at night lately. Maybe the money he gave me has something to do with that?" Patrick sketched on. "Listen, if he did something for that money, something not decent, shall we say, the facts would never come out, Patrick Abbott. An Indian would leave no clues."

Patrick looked up and said, "I think we must assume that Luis's money was come by honorably, until we prove otherwise, Jean. And just to show you that I am not entirely indifferent to what goes on in Santa Maria, I stopped at the sheriff's this morning to ask what the state laboratory had reported so far. There isn't much as yet, but they find that the bullet in the pool was from Carmencita's gun, which establishes her death, they think, as suicide."

"I don't believe it," I said stubbornly.

Suddenly I remembered something. Tom Brandon had had a

narrow crescent-shaped scar on the back of his head, buried under his dark hair. I remembered how he happened to mention it. A Polish painter was staying in Santa Maria. He wore his hair in a long bob and we laughed about it till we learned that the bob covered a scar on the back of his head. Then Brandon had said that he had a scar from an automobile accident.

"I remember the sheriff said there was a scar on what was left of Arkwright's scalp," I said. "Tom Brandon had a scar, too."

"The sheriff might be interested," said Patrick.

He left soon after that and I didn't see him again till he called for me that evening to take me to Mona's for dinner.

His car was splashed with mud, though we had had no rain in Santa Maria Valley.

Soon after Patrick left the shop the church bell started tolling and I closed the shop to go to Carmencita's funeral. Julia also came. We were the only Anglos there.

# CHAPTER 34

Mona's dinner that evening made me resolve not to feed Patrick Abbott again until Mrs. Dominguez could give him a swell Mexican dinner, the gourmet kind where you do up chicken or turkey and artichoke hearts and such with shredded almonds or spicy Mexican sauces.

We started off with chilled crab in an appetizing Spanish sauce, served with tiny crisp hot cornflakes. Then a filet mignon, with a butter-and-parsley sauce if you wanted it, and new green peas and buttered shoestring carrots and scalloped potatoes. Next a delicious avocado salad with the lemon and garlic hovering like a bouquet, and finally ice cream, colored a pale caramel and tasting dreamily of rum.

Mona ate little. She looked worried. She wore a hyacinth crepe with a bolero of fuchsia velveteen, a pearl necklace, diamond bracelets, and several rings. I had on one of those black taffeta ensembles which are supposed to double for anything from a rodeo to a formal dinner and look it. Patrick wore his dinner jacket, Michael his navy serge suit, and Luis lived up to Mona's elegance in a white full-sleeved satin shirt, red sash, and sleek black braided trousers, and of course all his silver and turquoise necklaces, bracelets and rings.

I looked carefully at his rings. None was the ring Patrick Abbott had dropped in my living room.

The spacious dining room with its massive furniture could have accommodated thirty as easily as five. Slim tall candles lighted the big oval table softly. Heavy curtains were drawn over the windows, as well as across the French doors opening onto the east terrace. The two graceful dark-skinned Mexican girls, Rita and Lupe, in gay Spanish costumes, served.

"I had to argue Michael into coming," Mona said, after we were seated. "Sonya's in the hospital."

"Hospital?" I asked, almost as surprised as if I hadn't guessed it.

Michael smiled. "Touch of flu. We thought she needed watching."

"We?" I said, not thinking how it must sound.

Michael said, "Mona was the one who insisted on the hospital. She can get so much better care."

"I had to beg Michael to come to dinner on bended knees," Mona said whimsically. "I did it on your account, Mr. Abbott. I hear you've struck up a friendship over your painting," she went right on. "But I don't like Michael's taking pupils and I've said so. He needs all his time for himself."

She made no secret this evening of her infatuation with Michael. She couldn't keep her eyes off him, or her hands either. But I decided soon that it was all on Mona's side. Michael did his best to avoid being petted.

"I'll have just to eat and run, you know," he said.

Mona touched his arm. "Henpecked!" she accused.

"But Sonya's condition may be serious," he said. "I'm not too happy being away like this, Mona."

"I didn't mean it the way I sounded, Michael darling."

"We're afraid of pneumonia," Michael said to me.

The Mexican girls served the chilled crab and poured some white wine and Mona talked about her day at the hospital.

Patrick Abbott listened to her patter as if it were of gravest importance.

She had put Patrick on her right and Michael on her left. I sat between Patrick and Luis.

We talked about winter, about skiing in the mountains, wonderful days when the snow lay white and deep all the way to the blue mountains.

"You'll miss it, Michael," I said.

Michael said, "You don't know how much."

"It's ridiculous for him even to think of leaving," Mona said.

"You're really going?" Patrick Abbott said.

"Definitely," said Michael. "Sonya's illness will hold us up a bit. We can't get away with Mona next week. But it's all settled."

"I shall postpone going myself," Mona said.

"You mustn't," said Michael, a little embarrassed.

Mona reached over and patted his hand. "You promised not to speak of it again, Michael."

"Yesterday was a marvelous summer-style day," I said. "We went out to Julia's."

"Superb view out that way," Patrick said.

Mona raised her brows. "You get around, Mr. Abbott."

"He went out with me," I said, not meaning to mention our having visited Arkwright's, but Patrick promptly added, "We drove out with Mr. Trask." He seemed not to notice Mona's frown. "He took us out to that Arkwright house, Mrs. Brandon, by way of the trail past Mrs. Price's."

I thought Mona's face went suddenly white.

"Why should Trask go there now?" Mona asked.

"He was interested in what might be clues to the solution of that murder, Mrs. Brandon."

"I thought that was settled."

"I believe the sheriff is continuing to investigate."

"Sounds like locking the stable door after the horse is stolen," Mona said, with her lips curling. "Exactly like Trask. A thoroughly incompetent official."

"Oh, Mona, I don't agree!" Michael said, saving me the trouble.

Mona said, "If we ever had a real murder here we'd have to call in the FBI or somebody."

"What do you mean by a real murder, Mrs. Brandon?" Patrick asked.

"Somebody who mattered," said Mona, tersely. There was a brief silence.

"The sheriff had seen some spots on the floor he was rather curious about. Some ink spots," Patrick said then. "Mr. Trask took me there to have a look at the spots."

"Sounds very jolly," Mona said sarcastically.

"Yes," Patrick Abbott said, cheerfully. "We examined them thoroughly this time. Or rather *it*, since there is now only one large black spot. It was ink, all right. Tomorrow we'll go back again and get more of the wood under the spot for analysis."

"Indeed!" Mona said. She stabbed at her food. I wondered if Patrick didn't realize that she was annoyed. I also wondered what he was up to. He'd gotten specimens of that wood yesterday.

"How is your arm, Mr. Abbott?" Mona asked then. Her eyes sparkled maliciously.

"My arm?"

"You scratched it, you said, on a nail."

"Oh, that," Patrick said, smiling. "I have a confession to make you, Mrs. Brandon. It wasn't a nail. I was shot."

"Shot?" Mona repeated.

"Somebody shot at me through Jean's window."

"Such things don't happen," Mona said looking at me.

"Some kid playing with a gun," I said.

"That seems logical," Mona said, too quickly. "I never could see why you wanted to live over there with the Mexicans anyhow, Jean. Yes, I think that explains it."

"When was all this?" Michael asked.

"Night before last," I said.

"It happened not five minutes before you arrived at Jean's, Mrs. Brandon," Patrick said. "That was why I was in such a hurry when we met at the foot of the hill."

I saw an artery throbbing in Mona's tense throat. "Were you trying to find the doctor?"

"No. Only trying to catch whoever fired that shot."

"You and Sonya were at my house," Mona said then, to Michael. "I took a letter to the post office, ran into Luis near the plaza, and did some errands, then I went to see Jean a minute. I thought something queer had been going on there. I must say you were pretty cool, Jean."

"Cool? I was scared to death," I said.

"Why didn't you tell me what had happened?"

"I guess I was too scared."

"Anyhow, after a while," Mona said to Michael, "Mr. Abbott came back to Jean's with his arm bleeding and told me he caught it on a nail."

"Well, it was only some crazy kid," I said. "I feel sure of that. And luckily Pat wasn't hurt very much."

Luis had finished the course. He laid down his fork. He seemed in his own world, far above our talk.

Patrick Abbott said, "The more I think of it the more certain I feel that the shot meant business."

You could feel the tension, except in Luis, who seemed to pay no notice.

"But that's absurd!" Mona snapped. "Why should anyone want to do that, Mr. Abbott?"

"Well," Patrick said, with a little bow of his head and a gay smile, "I happen to be a detective."

"A what?" Mona shrieked.

Michael laughed aloud at her, and I said impatiently, "I thought that was a secret, Pat."

"When a secret gets out," Patrick said serenely, "you might just as well admit it. And mine's out."

Mona asked sternly, "But what are you doing in Santa Maria?"

"I'm trying to take a vacation, Mrs. Brandon. And trying to learn a little about painting, which I should like as an avocation at least. Unfortunately when I came up here I agreed to look into a case as a favor to a friend. That is why I was investigating the ink spot. My friend is in the Secret Service. The job up here possibly has to do with counterfeiters, hence my interest in green ink."

"Green ink?" Michael said, in a puzzled tone.

"Counterfeiters use green ink for printing money."

"Oh, of course," Michael said. "Stupid of me."

"But why should such dreadful people come to an out-of-the-way place like Santa Maria?" Mona asked.

"That's probably why, Mrs. Brandon. Because it *is* out of the way. It hasn't much police surveillance. It's a paradise for such outlaws. All they need is someone outside to circulate the counterfeit money."

"Do you mean to say," Mona said, leaning forward in her chair, "that you think Arkwright was a counterfeiter?"

"Oh, an ink spot doesn't prove anything, Mrs. Brandon. It's just a clue, and I'm afraid even as such it's been found too late. If he was one of a gang you may be sure the others have left by now. But we'll have another look-around tomorrow. I mean, at that house. I don't have to tell you that I'm speaking confidentially."

"Of course not," Mona said, too swiftly.

I thought of all the ears around us, of Luis, of Mona and Michael and myself, and wondered what on earth was wrong with Patrick Abbott.

"Tell us more about counterfeiters," Mona insisted. "I'm fascinated, Mr. Abbott."

"Of course," he said, "if it won't bore you?"

Patrick Abbott talked, after Mona urged him a second time, telling some tale about counterfeiters in New York City who wound up finally in the Pennsylvania mountains west of Harrisburg. They were caught and sentenced, and all because one of them went to a local dealer and ordered an unusual amount of green ink. Several people were killed during the hunt, which took months. Two engraved plates confiscated, which were for a ten-dollar bill and a twenty, were so perfect that the fraud had already cost the government half a million dollars before the criminals were apprehended. Patrick said that a master engraver of extraordinary ability had made those plates. And they never caught the engraver.

I wondered why Mona listened to this recital with such absorption, but her comment at the end explained it.

"My former husband," she said, "or I suppose I should say my husband, was very clever at all kinds of engraving. Would you care to see some of his work?"

"Very much," Patrick said.

I glanced at Luis. I felt worried. He was watching Patrick Abbott but shifted his inscrutable almond eyes when he caught me looking at himself.

"It is all so very interesting," Mona chimed in, when Patrick finished his story. "What exciting people you meet, Mr. Abbott! Well! Do you know, you are the first detective I've ever met."

Patrick, needless to say, looked thrilled.

Michael chuckled. The atmosphere was easier. The food—we were then on the steak course—was so marvelous. And the wine! A Spanish wine suggestive (so Patrick said) of a rare vintage, *l'Hermitage.*

"Nice situation that Arkwright house has," Patrick said. You could sense tension again. "I wonder if it might be for sale."

"I shouldn't think anyone would care to buy it!" Mona snapped.

"I'd like it myself," Patrick said.

"Better not let it get out that you want it," I offered. "Mr. McClure will make you pay for it through the teeth."

"I don't think there'll be any competition," Patrick Abbott answered. "The Mexicans won't go near the place now, and nobody else will want it."

"Why do you?" Mona asked, suspiciously.

"This view is magnificent," Patrick said.

"Rather simple, that house, isn't it?" Mona tried to conceal her apprehension. "What is it like inside?"

She looked at me. So did Patrick. I hesitated, wondering if I should mention the ugly things with which poor Carmencita had tried to prettify her sad abode, the strips of cheap linoleum, the store lace curtains.

"It's a well-built adobe," I said. "Pat could fix it up."

"I couldn't be bothered with any old doby," Mona said. "Particularly one away out there."

"The place wouldn't be so out of the way," Patrick said, "if the trail past Mrs. Price's was fixed up. We managed to get over it in Mr. Trask's old Buick. But he preferred to ford the river and come back the long way."

"Quicksand there," Luis said suddenly.

It was the first time the Indian had spoken.

"How do you know, Luis?" Mona asked sharply.

Luis replied with the utmost dignity. "Indians all know that, Mona."

"Oh, fiddlesticks!" Mona said.

"Mr. Trask said the same thing, Mrs. Brandon," Patrick Abbott said. "But another car had gone through there lately and he said he knew the car and thought if it could make it his could. We made it."

"I think nobody better drive car through there," said Luis.

"Shut up, Luis," Mona said.

She looked terrified. I knew then that it was her car that had gone through the creek. Her station wagon, that day she met Daisy. We'd had no local rain since to wash away tracks.

I said, "All the Indians know where the quicksands are, don't they, Luis?" The Indian nodded. I said then, "That is one reason why Mr. Trask knew the Indians hadn't killed Arkwright, you know. He said the other afternoon—remember, Pat? —that the Indians would have dumped the body in the quicksands in the river near where it lay. Nothing holds up an investigation like the absence of the body, he said, and the clever Indians would have got rid of that body. He said—"

"Oh, for God's sake!" Mona suddenly shrilled. "Can't you talk about something else? Can't you see that I'm frantic from hearing about all that? Can't you—"

Michael leaned over and took Mona's hand. She quieted down immediately and I felt that he saved her thus from more hysteria, and from telling something, perhaps, that she would, regret.

The talk then veered to pleasant things.

Michael looked at his watch after he had his salad. If Mona would excuse him, he said, he'd get along to the hospital. No, he wouldn't wait for dessert, but would like coffee. One of the girls brought it at once.

Patrick asked Mona if she knew London. They talked Europe and New York then till we left the table.

In the hall Patrick spent a few minutes looking at Brandon's steel engravings. It was impossible to tell from his face how they struck him. Luis disappeared soon after dinner. At nine o'clock I suggested that Mona must be tired and we'd better go.

It was an unpleasant night. The smoke from the chimneys of the village mingled with fog and made driving difficult. Julia's car was parked at my gate and she was sitting by the fireplace in the living room.

"I came in to ask if you had any news from Daisy," she said.

# CHAPTER 35

PATRICK WOULD stay only a few minutes. He had a cigarette and mentioned that he'd been to Santa Fe. I asked if that was where he got the mud on his car. He said it was. He'd run into a rainstorm fifty miles south, he said, just after he got through the canyon. We told Julia we'd been to Mona's for dinner.

"You'd better stay all night, Julia. The fog's terrible."

"All right," she said.

"Think you can make it all right?" I asked Patrick, as he left to drive to the ranch, meaning the fog.

"In time. Good night. Be seeing you."

Julia and I had a cigarette by the fireplace and I told her that Sonya was in the hospital. It was still early but Julia began to yawn and then told me good night and went to bed.

She had just turned out her lights and closed her door when I heard a car turn up my hill. I was still sitting at the fireplace. The car parked at my gate. High heels clicked along the flags. Mona Brandon's footsteps.

She had changed to a tweed suit.

"I had to come," she announced, on entering. "Your detective friend, Jean—I must talk with him."

"He went home ages ago."

"But whose car is that?" she demanded suspiciously.

"Julia's."

Mona breathed importantly. "I'm wild to talk with that detective. Where do you think he is?"

"Have you tried Warner's Ranch?" Mona shook her head.

We were standing just inside the front door.

"I don't want to phone. It would be all over town in no time. And the night's impossible to drive any distance in, even for Luis, who could see in a fog if anyone could." She glanced about. "Where's Julia?"

"In the guest room."

Mona dropped her voice to a whisper. "She positively must not overhear what I'm about to say, Jean. I've got to get something off my chest. It's about Daisy Payne. She killed that man Arkwright."

"Mona!"

"Shush! I've been sure of it all the time. I can't keep it back any longer. That's why I want to see your detective."

I said, "You must be out of your mind, Mona. Daisy couldn't do a thing like that."

"Are you accusing me of lying?" Mona snapped.

"But what you've just said is terribly serious, Mona. By the way, where *is* Daisy?"

"She's gone. She went away just to spite me, really. She doesn't dream that I suspect the truth."

"You're positive, of course," I said, sarcastically.

"Certainly. But Daisy really left town because we had a row about her gun, not because she thought I suspected her of murder. She thought I'd feel bad if she went away."

"Her gun?"

"Do I have to be catechized?" Mona rasped. "All right, then,

I'll tell you about the gun. Daisy came over the morning after the party and said she'd lost her evening bag with the gun in it in my house the night before. I told her I couldn't be bothered. It was that horrible morning when they found that awful Mexican woman in the swimming pool. Everything was ghastly. Of all the times for Daisy to pick to make a row about that silly gun! Also she started yapping about her knife. She said that both disappeared at my house, the gun at the party, the knife some time before. It was perfectly silly and I said so."

Mona linked her hands together. Her long blood-red nails flattened against the white backs of her hands.

"After you left tonight I got to thinking about her. Trask evidently suspects that I was out that way. You said he knew whose car made those tracks. So it's bound to come out unless I act first and tell what I know. Daisy's crazy, I suppose. Stark staring mad. If she knows I've told about seeing her out there I'll be in danger. People are always killing other people because they think they know something they want kept quiet."

"That's only in story books, Mona. Daisy wouldn't hurt a fly!"

"I know what I'm talking about, Jean." She dropped her voice. "I saw her out at the place myself. Right after the murder."

I wondered how Mona would feel if she knew that I already knew about their meeting on the trail.

"I'll tell you all about it, Jean. Carmencita was a disgrace to this valley so I decided to run her out. Obviously that place was a kind of love nest, so I thought that by having the road fixed up so everyone would use it to go to the Picnic Rocks they'd move. Frankly I meant to do something of the sort wherever they went, buy up the property or something, but get them out. So just by chance that same afternoon when Daisy killed the man I asked Michael to drive me out there to look the ground over.

"I would have taken Luis, but he was missing the way he always is lately, so I asked Michael. But you know how Sonya is. I simply couldn't have her trailing along, so I told her I wanted Michael to drive me into Santa Maria and didn't want her to find out we went elsewhere because it would have meant an awful row. Well, anyhow, just as we got into that arroyo in front of the Arkwright house, we saw Daisy. She was coming from behind the house. She had a calf slung over her shoulder and she put it in her station wagon. I could see that she was terribly flustered at being discovered. I asked her why she had come here and she told me some fishy story about coming for the calf." Mona paused. "A few days later, we found out about Arkwright. Then I knew everything."

"Everything?" I asked. I felt hypnotized.

"My dear! It's as simple as *a b c*. It's a case like *Lady Chatterley's Lover*, you know. In that story a titled woman was crazy about a plain simple man and went right after him and got him. But in this case the man must have put up a fight or something and Daisy in a fit of hysteria knifed him."

I felt like laughing, the whole thing was so ridiculous.

Mona said angrily.

"Why couldn't it happen? It's Nature, taking her revenge on the overcivilized."

"I think you are making some pretty tall statements, Mona."

"Do you think anyone would doubt my word?" she blazed.

"Well," I said, taking another tack, "why haven't you told this to the sheriff?"

"That hick? Why should I?"

I was so overwhelmed by this demonstration of her *amour propre* that I couldn't answer.

"I think," she said, giving me a superior glance, "that what I should or shouldn't tell is for me, not you, to decide. Anyhow, it may never come out. I'd much rather it didn't. If it should, it would mean a fight for me with Sonya when she learned I'd gone out there with Michael."

"Well," I said, "just why have you come here with this story, Mona? What is it you want?"

"I've told you. I want to hire your detective."

"He's not looking for a job, Mona."

Mona flashed a smile.

"I'll make my offer so attractive he can't resist." Suddenly she looked worried again. "I'm scared. I sensed from what Mr. Abbott said tonight that they were going to carry the investigation of that Arkwright murder further, so I decided it would look better if I got my own detective and sent him to the sheriff to represent me."

"I think you mean a lawyer, don't you?" I said.

"I mean exactly what I say, Jean. And Patrick Abbott's the one I want. I like him. He could go everywhere with me and protect me."

She turned toward the door.

"We've got to go to the hospital, fog or no fog, before going back home tonight. I hope Sonya appreciates it."

I went into the guest room and sat down on Julia's bed. I told her what Mona had said.

"Do you think that Arkwright was Brandon, Jean?" Julia asked.

"No. I don't."

"Does Mona?"

"Search me. She refers to him as that man, and so on. She pretended when she came here the other night that Brandon was dead."

"Who thinks he's really Brandon?"

"Gilbert, for one."

"Oh, Gilbert!" scoffed Julia.

I said, "Mona's almost as good a liar as Gilbert, at that. But the purpose of their lies differs."

"How's that?"

"Gilbert makes an art of lying. He gets his thrill out of making a good lie that somehow hangs together and is therefore an end in itself. But Mona lies to cover up something. I wonder what?"

# CHAPTER 36

NEXT DAY was one of those very busy days in the shop which are the rule in the summer season but seldom happen later than September. The weather, while not bright, was not oppressive. Mrs. Dominguez was back on the job, which meant I could leave Julia and the cat to her. I had breakfast at the Castillo. Rose was back, too, looking sad but even more queenly. When I opened the shop it had been cleaned and the fire laid.

Julia came in after a while and I left her in charge while I went to the bank. I deposited Mona's check and Luis's money, which I had remembered to bring this morning. I heard nothing from it so apparently it was good money.

That day many tourists came to Santa Maria. All day long they would drive into town, circle the plaza, then drive out past Mona's, look at the place from outside its walls, then drive back to the plaza, park and have lunch and afterward dally around town.

Julia came back about noon.

"I've got a letter from Daisy, Jean. She's in New York."

"Really?" I remembered that Gilbert had said so, too.

"She's trying to get to England. She seems to be in good spirits, said she was sorry about leaving like that. You know,

Jean, when there's murder in a place everybody gets upset. People kind of lose their bearings at such a time. Distrust things vaguely. Feel scared. That's honestly why I stayed with you last night. I was scared."

"What of, Julia?"

"Just scared. Can't you get away now for lunch?"

"Think so," I said.

We'd just got seated in the Castillo when Joe Padilla came from the bar to ask what we'd have. He said the drinks were on him because he had a new baby which they were naming Julia Jean in our honor.

Then Rose gave us a piece of news.

"You see that house burn down last night, Miss Price?" she asked Julia.

"What house?"

"Where Carmencita lived. Arkwright house."

"For heaven's sake!" said Julia. "Who told you?"

"The neighbor Gomez. He's in town today." Rose left us.

Julia said, "I'm glad it burned. I couldn't see the place without thinking of Carmencita. Funny thing about Carmencita, Jean. No matter what she did you wished her well."

"I wonder how it happened to burn?" I said. I thought of Mona and Luis last night, and her saying they were going on to the hospital. Had they burned it? Why?

When Patrick Abbott came into the shop late in the afternoon I asked him if he knew about the fire. He did.

"The house wasn't any good anyhow," was all he said. "It's the situation that's fine."

He didn't seem much interested. He'd come to ask me to go to the movies tonight. He also asked Julia, who was still in the shop. I said I couldn't leave the shop Saturday nights, so he dated Julia. The movies are fun on Saturday night. The cowboys from the ranges beyond the mountains always come to see the horse operas.

There was a lot going on around the plaza all day. For one thing there was a rally. Elections were to be held next week. A rally is interesting in Santa Maria because all the country people come into town. You realize then how many more Mexicans there are around here than Anglos. At the rally Mr. Trask, among others, made a speech. I didn't hear it but everybody said it was a fine speech, and he didn't need an interpreter either the way some of the candidates did, since he spoke both Spanish and English. I don't know why I'm setting all this down except to show that it was just a normal Saturday.

All day long people were in and out of The Turquoise Shop. In the evening these were usually friends, dropping in to be social. There's a lot of drinking around the plaza on Saturdays. A lot of people get drunk and there are always a few fights. The jail is always crowded after any Saturday night.

Patrick showed up at six o'clock and took me to supper at the Castillo. Rose hung around our table off and on. She asked if Miss Payne got her bag back.

"I found it under a table there at Miss Brandon's and left it on the bar when I went home," she said.

"Did it have her gun in it?" I asked. Rose blushed.

"I think."

"Didn't you look?" I asked, to tease her.

"No, Miss Holly. But one of the boys who was helping us did, and I saw it in the bag."

"That's all right, Rose. Everybody knows she carries it."

"Miss Holly," Rose asked then, "can I have the Santo Carmencita left at your shop? My aunt say she left it with you, Miss Holly."

I didn't know if I should admit having it, till Patrick Abbott said, "Perhaps she means the one you showed me the other day, the one wrapped in newspaper."

"I pay you for it, Miss Holly. Whatever you say."

"You can have it as a gift, Rose, if the sheriff says I can give it to you."

"Is there some special reason for your wanting that Santo, Rose?" Patrick asked. "I mean, other than its having been your sister's?"

Rose said yes, that it could perform miracles.

I asked her then where Carmencita had got it. She said Mr. Brandon himself had taken it to her after she went to prison, that he had asked if there was anything she wanted and she had asked him for the Santo.

# CHAPTER 37

SHORTLY AFTER ten o'clock I found myself alone in the shop. The air was stale. The hearth was littered with ashes and cigarette remains, and the whole place had a tired pushed-about look. I felt the same way. I had told Patrick and Julia that if I weren't in the shop after the show was over they could find me at home. So I counted the money in the till, put it in the safe, covered the counters, banked the fire and put up the screen, and locked up.

It occurred to me as I was walking along my side of the plaza on my way home that Julia probably wouldn't go home tonight because she'd be there alone. In Santa Maria so many people lived alone and thought nothing of it, but the recent doings had made us kind of jittery. I convinced myself that I didn't feel afraid for myself, only for Julia out in the country.

I headed into the road which leads along the foot of the mesa past my house. After the street lamps on the square the darkness was intense. I got out my flashlight and followed the bright little circle of its light. The road was rutted and a misstep might mean a twisted ankle or a bad fall, but it was easy going with a light. The air was hazy again, though not so thick as last night. I couldn't have seen anything anyhow so long as I used the light, for the guiding circle blacked out everything else.

All at once I had a feeling of being followed.

Someone, at least, was walking behind me on the road, someone without a light who made no effort to catch up or to pass me. I lagged for a few steps as an experiment. The person also lagged. So I walked very fast. He did the same thing.

A lot of Mexicans live in another valley on the other side of the mesa. Some of them used a path which joined up with the top of my lane. All Saturday night, sometimes, they would go sauntering over the hill, feeling very merry, or fighting, and they made a practice of smashing their bottles on the stile where the path and lane joined. If the man was a drunk with an empty bottle or two he might mistake me for the stile.

I walked still faster.

Suddenly my flashlight went out. Just failed, like that. Short circuit, I thought. I paused to jiggle it, forgetting for the moment my pursuer. I became aware of intense silence. The man had also stopped!

Then I was really scared. I hurried on without bothering with the light. His stopping like that proved he was following me purposely, and he wasn't walking clumsily, like a drunk, but was biding his time, waiting for me to turn into my lane, no doubt, before closing in on me.

I walked as fast as I could then, not picking my way as I should have done in the dark, and since I couldn't spot holes in the road I hadn't gone far till I twisted an ankle. I went on, limping and hurrying. My chances of getting away were very slim, what with the walled-in rutted corral on my right and the fenced-in pasture on the left, and no house on this road before mine. My best chance was to arrive at my house enough in advance to get the key from under the flowerpot and open the door, go inside, bolt the door and turn on the lights. That might scare the man away.

I hurried faster, peering at the ground I couldn't see and listening for the footsteps behind me. I seemed to have gained slightly on him as I turned into the lane and began to climb the short hill. The footing was better now. I began to run.

That was a mistake. Halfway up the steep slope I stepped on a loose stone and fell down.

The man following me—I was sure, of course, that it was a man—stopped dead still. I couldn't hear a sound, save those I made as I scrambled back onto my feet and rushed on up the hill.

I'd lost the useless flashlight.

The man following me had no flashlight. Possibly needed none. The Mexicans usually didn't, nor the Indians. People always said that Indians could see like cats in the dark.

An Indian had been hovering about my house.

Now that I was really desperate I began to act with a curious precision. I got to my gate, opened it, closed it, fastened the latch, and sped along the flagstones. I stooped down and got my key. I found the lock without fumbling.

As I turned the key my gate was opened by someone who was familiar with it.

Then he laughed. It was Gilbert Mason.

# CHAPTER 38

"Here's your flashlight," Gilbert said. He giggled.

"Cute trick!" I muttered, stepping inside and snapping on the lights.

My hands were shaking. He followed me in and laid my flashlight on the chair near the door. He had his briefcase. I was thinking, as I put a trembling match to the fire, that I'd been stupid not to think of Gilbert, who was capable of just such a stunt and who had trained himself to see in the dark.

He followed me over to the fireplace, still giggling.

"I'm glad you think it's funny," I said.

"I'd no intention of scaring you. Till I saw you were already scared. Then I decided you needed a lesson. What's the matter? Think you're slated to be murdered?"

"I didn't think ahead that far," I rasped. "Sit down, Gilbert."

I closed the slats of the blinds, then went to my room, dropped my bag and coat, went into the bath and washed the dirt I'd got on my hands when I'd tumbled, then saw that my stockings were done for, and changed them. When I came back to the living room Gilbert was sitting in the wing chair with the briefcase on his knees and gazing at the fire. I forgot how mad I was because his face looked so ghastly.

"Like some coffee, Gilbert?"

"No, thanks."

I went into the kitchen and put the kettle on the stove in case he changed his mind about coffee, and came back to the fireplace. I still felt jittery, but what Gilbert said now made sense. I'd been a fool to get in a panic like that.

"I meant to catch you in the shop, Jean," he said, in a decent tone, "but I waited for your regular Saturday-night herd to stampede, and then got there just too late. I saw you as you left the plaza for home, so I followed. Listen, Daisy's coming back."

I didn't say anything.

"I may turn my evidence straight over to the sheriff, after all," Gilbert said, significantly. "It was my plan, of course, to bide my time and watch her get into a state where she shivered every time a door closed softly or a leaf fell behind her back. But maybe I won't."

"Why do you hate her so, Gilbert?" I asked, wearily.

"Hate?" he sneered. "You know I'm above hate and love and all that sort of bunk. I don't hate Daisy. But I'll get a certain satisfaction out of seeing them both get their just dues."

"Them?"

"Mona and Daisy."

I glanced at my watch and saw that it would be half an hour perhaps before Julia and Patrick Abbott would show up. "Daisy doesn't know that I know," Gilbert said then, in a confidential tone. "I mean, that I know she killed him. She doesn't know I've got the knife, either. She thinks Mona's the only one who knows. And O'Hara. And he won't tell, of course. Anyhow, he doesn't know everything. Mona knows everything, that is except that I also know, but she's not telling. She wanted Brandon out of the way too much. That was sheer luck for Mona, to be rid of him so easily. After that Carmencita had to be got rid of. So Mona scared Daisy into doing that. Then Sonya, but before that it got to be too much for poor old Daisy, who bolted after polishing off Carmencita."

For the first time I was positive that Gilbert was insane.

I remembered that the thing to do with nuts was to act cooperative.

"Would you care to talk to me about it, Gilbert?" I said, in a nurselike voice.

"Of course," he said. He gave me a sly look of pleasure. Then he said, "You mentioned coffee—"

"Half a minute!" I said, flying to the kitchen, but making the preparations last ten minutes.

Twenty minutes to go now. Maybe less, maybe more.

"Mind you, I'm no clairvoyant," Gilbert said, when I was on the sofa again, watching the time, and he was pouring himself a second cup of black coffee from the tray. "That's bunk. I use my brain. Put two and two together and make them add up to the right answer. See? But it doesn't take an expert in human behavior to know that old-maid-Daisy was frustrated to the point of insanity and likely to blow up any time. You remember how she was about Brandon? Mona laughed at her. And that made it all the more serious to Daisy. She thought Mona wonderful, too, you see. She waited. Armed herself to the teeth and bided her time."

He paused. I smiled cooperatively, so he went right on, speaking quietly and confidently.

"When Mona wants anything she goes after it. If it's a man, like O'Hara, she's ruthless. Mona has money and lets it do her dirty work. Daisy works differently. Daisy is really good, as the saying is, but she's stingy, and anyhow she hasn't anything like the money Mona's got, and she's also ugly as hell and handicapped in going after what she wants by being a real lady and therefore inhibited. So she waits. She never gave up the idea of Brandon, never, but she waited till Carmencita threw him over for good, and then went after him. The calf was just an excuse. She could have got that calf anywhere, if she had really wanted it. But it gave a plausible reason for her trip out to that house. If the calf hadn't turned up she'd have thought up something else. She meant the whole thing to be secret.

"Julia was in Hollywood, luckily, and Carmencita was in Santa Maria. At last, after all these years, the moment was right. The funny thing is that all these coincidences give her away, when you think of it. They're too neat. She knew Julia was absent, knew Carmencita was in town, knew that anyone seeing her turn into the lane would think she was having a look at Julia's place in Julia's absence for Julia. Besides, at that time of day, a station wagon is fairly invisible at a distance on the desert. I mean, after she got beyond Julia's she was unlikely to be noticed from the highway two miles and more away. But unfortunately she met Mona on her way back.

"She hadn't gone there to kill him, Jean. I daresay she made him a proposition. He was a pauper now. She had enough for two and a house, and so on. She imagined he would again be a good artist and fulfill his promise. She felt sure that no one else knew that Arkwright was Brandon, except Carmencita, and she could be bought. No one was ever to know the real truth. Arkwright would vanish and Brandon would presently return openly to Santa Maria."

Gilbert set his cup and saucer on the coffee table.

"I know the inside of Daisy's mind as though it were my own, Jean. I know each step of her plan, how she put it together piece by piece, each little piece dovetailing into the one before and after it. It was very perfect. But when Brandon turned her down—she hadn't allowed for that—she flew into one of her insane rages and cut his throat. Then she met Mona."

I wondered how Daisy could have killed the man without getting any blood on her. That ruined Gilbert's concoction, didn't it? But I kept mum, an eye on my watch.

He talked on. "There had been that accidental meeting with Mona. Mona didn't want to be seen out there so made Daisy promise not to talk. Mona saw blood on Daisy's clothes. Daisy said the calf had had a nosebleed. Later the man was found dead and Mona accused Daisy of the crime. But Mona wasn't talking. She'd been out that way herself, hadn't she? Any kind of scandal and everybody would find out Arkwright was Brandon, and she'd be in for it, too. But she didn't say so to Daisy. She just scared Daisy crazy and kept her so."

"How did you get the knife, Gilbert?" I asked.

"I went out there. Found it at the scene of the crime."

"Keeping it makes you an accessory after the fact."

"You're telling me?" he said, irritably.

"Of course I know you'll do what is wise, Gilbert," I purred.

Gilbert flowered under this treatment. I wondered why I had never thought of it before.

I looked at my watch. Ten more minutes and they might be here.

"Now we get to Carmencita," Gilbert said. "Mona made Daisy shoot Carmencita. With Carmencita's gun. That is why Daisy's bag and gun were left in the bar, you know. As a blind. It was lying in there on the floor when you were at the bar with Abbott, Jean. During the entertainment. Didn't you see it?"

"I saw her bag."

"I had half a notion to snitch it myself," Gilbert said. His eyes glistened. "Well, to make a long story short I went to Mona's the next morning, after the party, knowing it would be overrun with sheriffs and such, and it was. I went to the house. I didn't go near the pool. I loathe that sort of mess. No, I went into the house, by that door from the east terrace which opens at the foot of the small stairs. I walked through the hall. I heard Mona screaming at someone. This may be interesting, I thought, so I turned left at the intersection of the halls, and then ducked into the dining room. Mona was in the white room, just opposite. I put my ear to the crack in the partially open dining room door.

"Meanwhile Mona was ranting continuously. Then Daisy spoke up. That was the first I knew that the other party was our Daisy. They were both in a frenzy. They were quarreling specifically about Daisy's bag and gun. Mona declared Daisy had not left her bag in the house after the party. Daisy said she had and demanded it. Mona cussed like a fishwife and ordered Daisy to get out pronto or she'd turn her over to the sheriff. Daisy screamed that if she did she'd tell why she'd done what she'd done. Mona laughed and said no one would believe Daisy, and that everybody thought she was crazy anyhow." Gilbert giggled. "It was priceless. I took notes."

"But what happened?" I asked.

"Oh, they started tearing hair soon after that and then I saw Daisy rush out of the room with blood streaming down her face, Mona after her, wiping those bloody red nails of hers on a white velvet robe. Real blood on them this time. Daisy's." Gilbert tittered.

I looked at my watch. Five more minutes.

"Between ourselves," Gilbert said, dropping his voice as though he was afraid of being overheard, "I followed Daisy from the house that night and saw her shoot Carmencita and push her into the swimming pool."

He was leaning toward me. His eyes glistened and there was moisture on his forehead.

Suddenly he seemed to fold back into the chair. His head lurched forward, and he slid onto the hearth rug in a dead faint.

I bent over and lifted one of his arms. It was limp. The hand felt cold. I felt frantic. I dashed to the kitchen for a basin of water and a towel. I had a wet towel on his forehead and was sponging his poor lost face, wondering what else to do, when Patrick and Julia arrived.

"Oh, the poor thing!" Julia cried, on seeing Gilbert.

Patrick Abbott knelt beside him, lifted an eyelid, felt his pulse, then said for me to get some ice to put in the basin of water. It took several minutes to bring him to.

Some time during this period I said to Patrick that something must be done to find Tom Brandon, in order to stop talk. "The sheriff's doing all he can," Patrick said. As soon as Gilbert revived he protested against being pawed over, as he put it, but he did condescend later to wait a while in order to ride with Patrick Abbott as far as Daisy's lane. Before they left Patrick came into the kitchen when I went to fix some drinks.

"If I were you, Jean, I'd be careful about having Mason here when you're alone."

"He followed me home. Scared me to death," I said.

Patrick looked serious.

"He's his own worst enemy," I said. "He told me quite a tale tonight. Remind me to tell it to you some time."

"Where does he come from?" Patrick asked.

"New York. Mona met him there one winter and decided he was a genius and invited him to live here at her expense. It kind of bothers me lately that he talks against Mona. He never did that before."

Patrick said, "By the way, we've located the counterfeiter's hideaway. I didn't get a chance to tell you at dinner. It's in the woods on the mountains a few miles above the Arkwright place. I phoned the state police in Santa Fe this morning. They sent a photographer and this afternoon we went to the place and took some pictures and got some loot. The fingerprints match those found on the mirror and razor I took that day from the house."

"So Arkwright was your man?"

"One of them, anyhow. We ought to hear from the FBI tomorrow or next day. If the prints are successfully identified we should know plenty more than we do now. One thing bothered me, though. There were a couple of engraved plates in the place and considerable counterfeit money, which tallied with what you took in, incidentally. But the plates were so crude. Too crude, in fact."

I thought of that remark later. At the moment I remembered that I hadn't told him about Mona's coming to see me last night, and hurried to speak of it. "Have you seen Mona today, Pat?"

"No."

"She came here after you last night."

"What does she want with me?"

"She wants to hire a detective."

Patrick said gravely, "Sounds like nice work."

Julia came out then and said that Gilbert wanted coffee, not a highball. I still had the kettle boiling and made him a fresh cup. He was silent after that. We sat around and talked and sipped our drinks. I asked if anyone had had any word about Sonya. No one had so we decided she was getting along all right. Gilbert didn't comment.

# CHAPTER 39

I was awakened Sunday morning by something walking on my recumbent frame. My cat.

Then Mrs. Dominguez looked in at the garden window. It was Sunday, but she had come to make up some of her lost time. I had bolted the door, for a change, and had to get up and let her in. By the time I had my bath, she had breakfast ready. Then Julia appeared, dressed and ready to go home.

"Do you think Carmencita really killed herself, Mrs. Dominguez?" Julia asked, as we sat in the kitchen, sipping our orange juice.

"*Sí, sí.* Why not?" Mrs. Dominguez answered, surprised.

"Why?'

"I think she unhappy."

"She was going to be married," Julia said.

The brown-skinned woman rolled her eyes. "She was so wicked, Miss Price. She could not forget, I think."

I asked her if she knew when Carmencita had gone back to the house for the Santo. She said last Sunday night, which was when Julia had seen the figure in the lane. "She show me when she come back, Miss Holly. I scold. Maybe someone see her, I say. What they think? She laugh."

"Mr. Brandon gave it to her, didn't he?" I asked.

"*Si*. In person. He take it himself."

"Why?"

"Carmencita ask for it. She saw it in the place when he made her picture and he ask could he do anything for her and she say she like that Santo."

Not at all compromising, you might say. Carmencita was a maid in the house and had plenty of chances to see the saint. So its only importance lay in the fact that she had gone back to the house for it that night. Did her going out there for it have any connection with her death? No—I reminded myself—she was a suicide. If her family thought her a suicide she must be one. They should know her well enough for that.

Patrick Abbott had asked us to the Warners' Ranch for Sunday dinner, but Julia was invited to friends in Santa Fe. She left right after breakfast.

I wanted to do a little work in the shop, so I dressed for the day in my best tweeds and oxfords and walked to the plaza about eleven o'clock, leaving word with Mrs. Dominguez that Mr. Abbott could find me at the shop if he came to the house first. It was a beautiful day again, clear and almost as warm as summer. I felt good. It is not my normal state to feel depressed and confused and irritable, and I walked along the road blithely, hearing the meadowlark again, smelling the meadows, my scare last night quite forgotten.

I arrived at the plaza, noted its pleasant Sunday morning look of dalliance, and entered the shop. Mrs. Dominguez had been here, too. Last night's disorder and litter had been disposed of. I left the door open, not wanting to start the fire and thinking that the warmer air from outside would take the chill off the room. Then I brought my account books from the safe and perched on the stool behind the turquoise case, laying the books on top of the dust sheet, and started checking up yesterday's sales.

I didn't expect callers this morning. But ten minutes after I'd arrived at the shop there was a crash of brakes out in front as Dr. Johnson made a sudden decision to park. He came in.

"Morning, Miss Holly." I said good morning. "Mind if I talk to you a minute?" I said of course not. The doctor looked worried. His clothes were mussed and careless, and a lock of lank hair hung over his sallow forehead in front of his pushed-back felt hat.

"Sit down," I said.

"I'm in a jam, Miss Holly," he said, after sinking into one of the Mexican chairs by the fireless fireplace. I waited for him to go on.

"I think perhaps you can help out. It concerns Mrs. O'Hara."

"Sonya?" I twirled my pencil.

"You know her well, of course?"

"I wouldn't say I do, Dr. Johnson."

"Has she any close relatives?"

"I don't know. Why?"

"You know she's in the hospital?"

"Yes. Mona mentioned it Friday night." I started feeling uneasy. "I hope she's not worse?"

"She's going to die."

"What?"

The doctor brushed his hand wearily across his long sallow jaw.

"Oh, what a shame, Dr. Johnson. Do they know it?"

"They?"

"I mean Michael and Mona."

"Oh, yes. They know it. O'Hara is very upset."

He hesitated, biting into his lower lip.

"It's Mrs. Brandon who is making the trouble, Miss Holly. I'm fond of Mrs. Brandon. She's a wonderful woman and she has done a lot for this town, but she is hellbent on doing something now that she will regret someday. Not to mention what it may mean for the rest of us."

He was silent again, as though floating off into some dark sphere of his own.

"I'm so terribly sorry," I said. "The poor thing! I knew Sonya had a touch of flu—"

"Flu?" he flared up angrily. "She had nothing of the kind!"

"Oh?"

"She was taken to the hospital early Thursday morning, soon after midnight, with a bullet in her spine. She shot herself. The bullet pierced her left lung, barely missing the heart, and lodged in the backbone. She bled so much internally before I could get there and operate that I doubt if she ever had a chance. I told them then that recovery would be a miracle. She's a healthy woman and she's put up a game fight, but when pneumonia developed I immediately told them both exactly what it meant, along with that wound."

"When was that?"

"Yesterday afternoon."

"How long has she got?"

"It's a matter of hours."

There was a silence.

"But how did it happen?" I asked then.

"She shot herself. I told you that," Dr. Johnson said, touchily. "The gun was in her hand when they found her."

"They?"

"O'Hara and Mrs. Brandon discovered her simultaneously. A very fortunate coincidence, too. I mean, it removes all suspicion of its being anything but suicide."

I said, "Where did it happen?"

"She was at home, in Michael's studio. It seems that they had spent the evening with Mrs. Brandon at her house." That would be correct, I thought, remembering that Mona had come to my house that evening—it was the night the shot came through the window and the ring was lost—and that she had mentioned having left the O'Haras at her house. They were in and out of each other's houses all the time, of course. "Well, after they got home it seems that Michael went back to the big house to take Mrs. Brandon some book which they had and she wanted. When he got back Mona had remembered that she might go to Santa Fe next day and she wanted to take along the key to the little gate in the wall near the O'Hara house in order to have a duplicate made. There was only one key. Michael had this, so Mrs. Brandon walked as far as the gate so he could give her the key as soon as he let himself out. And damn lucky thing she was with him, too, for as O'Hara opened the gate they both heard groans coming from the cottage, which is not far from the gate, as you know. They ran to the house and found Sonya lying face down on the floor. The gun was still in her hand!"

"Good Lord! Had they heard the shot?"

"Of course not. Why should they, with all that shrubbery and the wall and all between them and that house? A small automatic doesn't make much noise."

"A small automatic?"

"It was Miss Payne's little gun, Miss Holly. The one with the turquoise grips."

"Oh," I said. Then I said, again, "Oh!"

The doctor sighed. "Well, they loaded her into O'Hara's car and rushed her to the hospital. Mrs. Brandon drove. I was up the valley on a baby case. I didn't get back to town till almost three o'clock. Miss Edwards had done all she could. But they wouldn't let her get another doctor, and by the time I got there—well . . ."

"There isn't anyone else in Santa Maria who's capable of taking care of a case like that," I said. I meant his being a good surgeon as well as a general practitioner.

He threw me a numb glance.

"It was a bad wound," he said mechanically, grinding it out as if he had turned it over and over and over in his mind. "She had lost so much blood. Then pneumonia. She never had a chance. She hasn't been in her right mind since it happened, even."

I sat thinking about it.

"Well, Sonya has the Russian temperament, you know. I suppose she was jealous and shot herself on an impulse. Don't let her death worry you like this, Dr. Johnson."

"Her death?" the doctor barked. "That's not it. Mrs. Brandon insists that I withhold the true facts from the death certificate."

"What?"

"She wants me to state that the death was caused by pneumonia."

"Well, wouldn't it be?" I asked.

"Of course not. The pneumonia's secondary. The gunshot is the primary cause. But Mona seems to think the truth will reflect on herself, for some reason."

I could hardly restrain a smile. "Well, it would. It'll make a scandal. You can't blame her for wanting it kept dark."

The doctor mustered up a mite of dignity.

"I'm speaking from my standpoint. It is a matter of pro-

fessional ethics. She is asking me to falsify on a death certificate. That is a serious professional offense." He reiterated, testi-
ly, "The pneumonia followed the gunshot wound. That makes it
only contributory. If I issue a statement saying that she died of
simple pneumonia, I commit a crime. If Mrs. O'Hara had been
shot with intent to murder, for instance, instead of being a suicide, I would be what is called an accessory after the fact. So
would O'Hara, Mrs. Brandon, and two nurses who know the
truth. One is Miss Edwards. The other is the special nurse they
had me send to Santa Fe for."

"For heavens' sake!" I exclaimed. "But you won't do what
Mona wants, of course?"

The doctor took out a cigarette. He didn't light it. He turned
it round and round in his slender surgeon's fingers until it fell
apart, when he eyed it with vague surprise and cast it at the
fireplace.

"I've tried to explain all this to Mona, Jean. I've argued
till I was black in the face. She's determined to have her way,
regardless."

"She's a fool about scandal, Dr. Johnson. It's her vanity."

"Scandal? Listen, girl, she's going to land us all in the pen.
I've told her so. But that makes no difference. She won't listen.
But whether she likes it or not, there is only one thing for her to
do. Face the truth now and get it over with."

"What does Michael say?"

"O'Hara agrees with me."

"I suppose you know that people say Mona is in love with
him?"

The doctor shrugged. "Gossip."

All at once I remembered something.

"Where was Luis while all that was going on, Dr. Johnson?"

"You mean at the time of the shooting? Asleep, I suppose. What difference does that make? Well, I've got no business telling you all this, Jean. But I thought maybe you could help me make Mrs. Brandon listen to reason."

I sniffed.

"She never has, Dr. Johnson."

"I know that. She's a wonderful woman, but she's reckless."

I said, "You are certain that it was suicide?"

"No doubt of it. Sonya obviously stole Miss Payne's gun for that purpose. I saw it myself that night. That is, the bag which held it. Under a table in the bar."

My temper rose, the way it always did at the way Mona pushed people around.

"I'd go ahead and do what I thought right, Dr. Johnson. What right has she to dictate to you like that?"

For a moment the doctor did not speak. Then he said huskily, "It's my wife."

"Your wife?"

He nodded desolately. "I . . . well, Miss Holly, I owe Mona Brandon seven thousand dollars. She's got a mortgage on everything I own, my house, my office, my equipment, my car, even on my wife's car. But my wife knows nothing about all that."

I saw it all. The silly extravagant Mrs. Johnson, with her clothes which tried to rival Mona's, her string of little real pearls, her cabriolet, her parties. The doctor adored her.

"Mrs. Brandon threatens to foreclose at once and she has the legal right, unless I do as she says. That means ruin. I'm not young enough to get started all over again. And it would kill my wife."

"Women don't kill that easily!" I snapped.

"I know what I'm talking about," the doctor snapped back. "Lily would die."

I said, "What's Mona's proposition if you do as she says?"

"She'll cancel every cent I owe."

"Not bad," I said sarcastically. "Afterwards you'd have to walk her chalk line, of course. And you'd always be scared pink every time you'd think about how many people know the truth."

"Sure," the doctor agreed.

"It's fantastic, Dr. Johnson. The way she owns all Santa Maria. She's got us hogtied."

He nodded. "We think we live in a free country. But nobody in Santa Maria dares lift a finger unless she says yes. I've often wondered why she wanted to stay here after Brandon left her. I think it's because she's dictatorial by nature and doesn't care to live where anyone else might be considered as important as herself." He looked at me. "But it's different with you, Jean. You're independent of her, and you're not afraid of her. That's really why I stopped in. I thought maybe you could talk to her, make her listen to reason."

I smiled, thinking of my five-hundred-dollar order lying in my safe. I independent?

I said, "She would know you had talked. If I went to her, that would make things worse."

He appeared not to have thought of that.

"Maybe you're right," he said, slowly.

He got up and went without further discussion, got in his car and drove away.

# CHAPTER 40

AFTER THE doctor left I couldn't get my mind back on my accounts, so I put the books back in the safe, locked up, and went to the Castillo. I sat down at a table by the front windows, where I could see Patrick Abbott when he stopped at The Turquoise Shop.

Sheriff Trask, walking across the plaza, saw me in the restaurant and came in.

"Good morning," he said. He wouldn't sit down. "I've got Tom Brandon on my mind again, Miss Holly. You haven't had any more hunches as to where he might be, I reckon?"

I shook my head.

"Ever since that Arkwright hombre was found, Miss Holly, people have been coming on the sly and asking if I don't think he was Brandon. I reckon you know that, though. Mr. Abbott said right off that the thing to do was to locate Brandon and let the town know where he was. Well, that would stop the talk, I reckon, only we haven't located him."

"If he's in Europe," I said, "it may be a long time before you do. Have you talked with Mrs. Brandon?"

"Sure. Phoned her right after we found the corpse and three or four times since. She apparently thinks Brandon's whereabouts none of my business. I can't figure her out. Once she told me he was dead. I asked when and where and she was uppity and then said she really knew none of the details. I phoned her again last night and told her I had to know immediately where he was, dead or alive, so after objecting some more she told me to wire her lawyers in New York, that they might have some definite information. I asked for their address. She said she'd look it up and call me back. After while she did call back and said that she couldn't find the lawyers' address. I asked if she hadn't any correspondence or anything and she said it was all in her vault at the bank and that if I could wait till Monday she would get the address for me. Since today was Sunday I decided to let it ride, instead of insisting on her getting Mr. McClure and getting into the bank last night. I figure she knows their address all right." Mr. Trask added, "She's the kind of woman that given enough rope hangs herself anyhow, Miss Holly. So she shall have rope. Until Monday."

Suddenly I had an idea.

"It just occurred to me that Brandon had an agent in New York, Mr. Trask. I couldn't call myself a real agent, you know. I've only had a few of his pictures. I should have a note of that name and address, though, somewhere in my files. I'm not very systematic about that sort of thing. If you'll come along to the shop I'll try to find it." I was all cleaned up, however, and the files would be dusty. "I'd rather do it this afternoon, if you don't mind."

"Sure, Miss Holly. No hurry, since it's Sunday. If you could look it up in time for me to get off a wire tonight."

"Of course," I said.

Mr. Trask said, rather apologetically, "I don't want to be too hard on Mrs. Brandon. She's pretty upset about Mrs. O'Hara."

"So you know that?" I said.

"I've had to be out at the hospital a lot, on account of that bus accident, ma'am. I reckon I shouldn't have said what I did about Mrs. Brandon. But she sure can be mighty aggravating."

I said, "Mr. Trask, I heard you say to Mr. Abbott that there was a scar on Arkwright's scalp. What sort of scar?"

"Kind of thin, and curved a little. A small white scar."

"Tom Brandon had a scar like that," I said. He took it very calmly.

"Lots of people do, Miss Holly. Well, I'll be getting along. If you happen to see Mr. Abbott will you tell him three-thirty here on the plaza will suit me fine? Thanks again, ma'am."

Patrick Abbott drove up a few minutes later. I told him what the sheriff had said. He said they were going up to the counterfeiter's place again.

"Want to come along?" he asked.

"Of course," I said.

We drove out to Warner's, passing Mona's place on the way, seeing Daisy's closed-up house and further away Gilbert's humble dwelling. I talked all the time. I told Patrick everything the doctor had said. I said wasn't it funny that a doctor would get so upset. He said that doctors in personal crises got more excited than anyone else. I said what did he think we ought to do. He said nothing. I asked why. He said the doctor would do the right thing, not to worry. Then he said, when I kept worrying, "Trask knows all about it, anyhow, Jean. The Santa Fe nurse came to him about it. She got wise, and she's not hypnotized by Mrs. Brandon the way you Santa Maria people are, you see. I'm just telling you so you'll enjoy your dinner. Mrs. Warner has made her special pecan pie in your honor."

"Thanks," I said. Then I said, "You do talk things over with the sheriff, then?"

"Off and on."

"Even on your vacation?"

"I have learned a lot from your sheriff. I couldn't pass up a chance to improve my own knowledge, you know. There aren't many like him."

Warner's Ranch was a very swell place, five miles north of Santa Maria. There was a big sprawling ranch house with eight or ten guest cottages. During the season they had a lot of dudes, at fancy prices. As we put away the hearty chicken dinner at the long dining-room table in a room with pine-paneled walls and a big open fire, the talk ran to winter sports. They had a good life out here, I thought. Mrs. Warner was a tall strapping whole-hearted woman. Warner had come out here first from New York to get rid of tuberculosis. I think he'd been a stockbroker.

Soon after three o'clock we came into town, met the sheriff, and drove in his car south and east and then headed up along an old trail which led up to a deserted logging camp in the moun-tains. A short distance up the trail we found a bridge out. We left the car and walked. Here the overgrown road followed a mountain stream.

It was the stream which passed the Arkwright house.

Trask said, "I reckon that's what he did with the fishing boots. Walked in the river part way to cover up his trail."

"Anyhow they gave him a good excuse for coming up here."

"We're pretty high," I said. My ears rang from the altitude. The white-barked aspens which abound only above eight thou-sand feet were all about us. "Too bad this place is so hard to get to now. It's lovely."

We arrived at the abandoned camp. It would be about three

miles from the Arkwright house and perhaps a thousand feet higher. Patrick Abbott led the way to a cabin which looked somewhat better than the others, took out his keys and inserted one in the new padlock on the door. "We put this on yesterday," he said to Mr. Trask. "Had to break the one that was on the door in order to get in." We entered what looked like a place fixed up for roughing it. There was a table, two chairs, a small wood stove, and canned food and utensils on some shelves. In a corner near the stove was a large pile of split wood.

"We found the outfit under that wood," Patrick Abbott said. "Press, plates for two bills—a five and a ten—watermarked paper, plenty of green ink. It was all in a waterproof box, and locked up. Not a very good hiding place, of course, but after all the chances of anyone's coming along and breaking in were fairly remote. Hikers would think it a weekend cabin. If one should break in and make a fire he'd have to burn an awful lot of wood to get down to the tin box."

Mr. Trask pushed back his hat.

"Well, if you hadn't had an eye for green ink, Mr. Abbott, I don't reckon anyone would have found it very soon. I doubt if anybody comes by here once in a year, if that."

"How did you find it?" I asked.

"An Indian did the real work," Patrick said.

"It was Mr. Abbott who thought of hiring the Indian, Miss Holly. So he ought to get the credit."

"I guess you're both being modest," I said.

"Not me, ma'am," laughed the sheriff. "But I've been tied to that hospital lately hand and foot, so I haven't been doing much scouting round."

"So Arkwright was a counterfeiter," I said.

"Looks like it," Patrick Abbott said.

"Is that why he was murdered?"

"Possibly," Patrick said.

"Who did it?" I asked.

"That's what I'd like to know, ma'am," Mr. Trask said, with a rueful grin.

"Don't you know?" I quizzed Patrick Abbott.

"Of course I know," he said, surprisingly, "but it doesn't shape up the way it should as yet. I can't figure out why those engraving plates were so crude, Trask. If the paper hadn't been practically perfect that money could have been spotted a yard away as phony. I don't get it."

"Anyhow, now you'll have to work on it," I said, thinking it might lead to solving the entire mystery.

"Not at all. It's Uncle Sam's job now."

The sheriff looked disappointed.

"You're not going to hand it over to the Secret Service now, are you, Mr. Abbott? Just when we're getting things nice?"

"They'll probably come and take the job," Patrick said.

"I suppose it was his gang," I said. "They always belong to a gang, don't they?"

"It's the usual thing, Miss Holly," said Mr. Trask.

Back in town we went to the shop. I went through loads of papers but I never found the agent's address.

I washed up then and Patrick and I dropped in at the Castillo for cocktails. There were lots of people in the restaurant so we sat at one of the tables in the bar. A crowd of cowboys stood at the rail, cracking jokes with Joe Padilla.

"Do you think Arkwright was Brandon?" I asked Patrick Abbott.

"We'll soon know definitely."

"How?"

"If he was a criminal with a former conviction, his fingerprints and life history will be on file with the FBI in Washington. If he's a past counterfeiter, the Secret Service will have him listed too."

We had martinis.

I said, "The longer this goes on the harder I find it to figure out where Mona fits the picture."

"Let me know when you solve it," Patrick Abbott said.

"Go right ahead. Laugh."

"I'm not laughing."

"Have you seen her about that job?"

"As a matter of fact I haven't."

"Why would she want to hire a detective if she wasn't guilty of something or other? Why should she think her life is in danger? Why is she in a state of mind all the time? She's always arrogant and bossy, but I've never seen her carry it so far." I said then, "You know whom I feel sorrier for all the time? Michael O'Hara. What with this and that."

Patrick nodded soberly. "I could never be the artist O'Hara is," he said then.

"Few people are, if that's any consolation. The worst of it is that Michael's a goner any way you look at it. If Sonya dies he will blame himself and be all knocked out for goodness knows how long. And if she lives he'll have to spend his life taking care of her. There's no real justice, is there?"

A few minutes later Michael came into the bar. He stopped at our table a moment before going into the restaurant.

"Sonya is better," he said. He looked happy. "She took a turn for the better about three this afternoon. It did go into pneumonia, just as we feared."

"Miss Holly," Rose reported a few minutes later, "you think Mr. Mason is sick? For long time now he eat nothing but coffee. Black coffee, and if I say anything he say 'Rose mind your business' but today he not come at all."

I looked at Patrick Abbott.

"We'd better have a look at him," he said, rising at once.

# CHAPTER 41

HALF A mile from the plaza, and halfway to Mona's, as I have said before, a lane angles to the left. A street, you might call it, but it is really a dead-end lane, which stops at Daisy Payne's gate. To the right by a stile, over an adobe wall, a path crosses a field to Gilbert Mason's cottage.

Daisy's brick house, which she had tried to make look like something from Edwardian England, had a high brick wall in front and lots of shrubbery and a garden at the back, and vines. It was dark tonight and somehow forbidding. We picked our way along the path with Patrick's flashlight. The poet's house was a pale blob in the starlight. The windows were dark. The crash curtains were drawn against the panes, as Patrick Abbott's flashlight revealed, for there was no glow from inside. No smoke rose from the chimney.

Patrick knocked at the front door. The noise echoed back flatly. He knocked again, using the handle on the flashlight. No reply. He tried the latch. The door was bolted on the inside.

"Good heavens!" I muttered, certain something terrible had happened to Gilbert.

Patrick walked round the house. I followed.

There was another latch on the back door similar to that on

the front. It yielded immediately. We entered the kitchen. The place was colder than outdoors. Following Patrick's light, we walked through the kitchen into the only other room, which served Gilbert as a living room, bedroom, and study. Relief came over me like a wave when there was no one in the house.

The bed was tidily made, but had dents in it, as if someone had been lying on top of the crash cover.

Patrick Abbott stalked across and touched it with his hand.

"He hasn't been gone very long," he said.

"How do you know?"

"Elementary," he said, with a grin. "The bed's still warm."

I shivered and said anyway I didn't like the look of things.

"Don't get morbid. Chances are he's gone down town for supper. Maybe he got hungry enough to decide to eat."

"We should have met him on our way here."

"Not necessarily."

He circled the room with the light. I saw that sugar bowl on the table then, but I didn't think about it till later on.

I was shivering. The nights are always chilly here and most people have a hearth fire summer and winter. Automatically I went over to the empty fireplace and spread out my hands to imaginary flames. The hearth was scrubbed clean as a plate. It had been so warm outside I wore no gloves. I took them out of my coat pocket now, and put them on.

"This is the cleanest place I ever saw in my life," Pat said then, as if he were echoing my own thoughts.

"It's always spotless," I said. "Well, shall we go?"

"Let's wait a while. Perhaps he'll return."

"Okay. Maybe we can find a lamp in the kitchen."

We went back into the kitchen and found a lamp, two candles, and virtually nothing else on the cupboard shelves. The lamp had no oil in it. Patrick got out matches and lighted the candles and we carried them in and set them on the mantel. The candles were in low tin holders, the saucer kind with a curved ring for a handle. Against the white adobe walls, they made a good light.

Patrick put his flashlight in his coat pocket and got out his cigarettes. Gilbert would loathe the smell of tobacco in his house, but I didn't say so. I started holding my gloved hands close to a candle flame to absorb its midget warmth.

Patrick said, "He sure doesn't keep much around."

"Gilbert prides himself on being tough. Ascetic."

"Maybe I can find some wood outside and make a fire."

"In that clean fireplace? He'd murder us!"

"All the same I'm going to do it. If he's sick, as Rose thinks, we'd better get this place warmed up."

Patrick went out and searched the woodshed and the yard, and returned. "I'll not be making a fire after all. There's nothing, not even a twig, to use for a fire. Mason must anticipate a mild winter." He looked around. "You say he writes? What with?"

I didn't answer. I was feeling more and more worried.

"We might as well sit down, Jean."

"I think we ought to go," I said. "We can leave a note explaining. After all, Gilbert shouldn't object to our barging in. He walks into other people's houses."

Patrick said, "We won't stay long. This place has me interested. I knew Mason was a very queer bird, but I didn't know how queer till I came in here. Sit down, Jean."

I gave in and sat down on one of the two hard chairs.

Patrick took the other, facing me across the empty fireplace. I thought I shouldn't have wanted to sit on the bed where Gilbert had lain. For some reason I felt about it as I do the beds of really sick people! Maybe Patrick felt the same. But he didn't say so. He was taking a visual inventory of the room, where he sat. There were—besides the bed and the two chairs—a cupboard, a chest, and table, on which there was nothing but a sugar bowl of a dead-white semi-porcelain matching a few other pieces in the kitchen cupboard. The lid was on the bowl. All the furniture had been given a natural buff-colored finish, waxed, and polished. The walls were eggshell white, and of course spotlessly clean. The curtains and bedcover were of unbleached crash, made double. I called Patrick's attention specially to the walls. Gilbert had mastered the Indian art of giving the interior of a room a beautiful finish which is softer than calcimine, by applying a coat of liquid white adobe to the walls with a piece of sheepskin and patting it smooth and glossy with the palm of the hand. It takes a long time to do it properly. Most of the Anglos couldn't be bothered. Gilbert was very proud of this special accomplishment. The floor had the same look of vivid cleanliness. There were no pictures or ornaments of any kind in the room. The aspen poles supporting the ceiling had been cleaned inch by inch and then varnished.

There was no bath. Gilbert took his frequent baths at the wash-stand in the kitchen.

"Mrs. Brandon gives him an allowance, you said? Why?"

I said, "Because she thinks he has talent, I guess. Needs leisure to develop it."

"I wonder how old he is?"

"I don't know exactly. Twenty-five or six, maybe."

"You think he has talent?"

"Yes, I think he has," I said. I had said it so often.

"How long has he been out here?"

I had to think.

"Six years."

Patrick Abbott said, "Mrs. Brandon may have a lot of money but she doesn't strike me as particularly patient."

I laughed. "Gilbert has a genius for making himself a nuisance. I daresay he has a special way with him when it comes to Mona. Listen, I'm catching cold. Let's go, and leave the note to explain using the candles, and your cigarette ashes, and so on."

"Okay," Patrick said. "But I'll throw the ashes outdoors."

I wrote the note on a pad I had in my bag and decided to leave it on the table under the edge of the sugar bowl. As I picked the bowl up to use it as a weight for the slip of paper, I used too much strength, thinking it would be full of sugar and heavier than it was. The lid tumbled off and went spinning around on the table.

"Look!" I cried out.

The bowl was full of paper money!

Patrick whistled, and then whipped out his magnifying glass, then fetched a candle to the table and examined the notes one by one, while I stood by, my throat feeling tight with anxiety lest Gilbert should return suddenly to the house. They were all twenty dollar bills. They amounted to three hundred and forty dollars.

"Put them back!" I urged. "Let's get going. If he should come in, and find you looking at his money—"

Patrick Abbott calmly took his time. Finally he returned the money to the bowl and put on the lid. I laid the note on the studio bed. I held one candle while Patrick put out the other and carried the cigarette ashes outside.

We walked back to the car in silence.

"Mrs. Brandon must give Mason a pretty good allowance," Patrick said, after we reached the car.

"One dollar a day," I said.

He whistled. "Can a man live here on a dollar a day?"

"Apparently Gilbert does. And saves on it," I said.

"Apparently," he said.

He didn't believe it any more than I did. Gilbert always had his meals at the Castillo. Breakfast was thirty cents up, lunch started at fifty cents, dinner at sixty-five. He could snack, but even so it would take a long time to save all that out of a dollar a day. My thoughts kept stealing to that murdered man, his stripped wallet, the stained knife in Gilbert's briefcase, and about Gilbert's phenomenal knowledge of this and that which he attributed to his crystal mind. I remembered seeing him come in from outside that night at Mona's about the time of Carmencita's so-called suicide, asking for brandy though he usually did not drink, of his saying last night that he saw Carmencita killed, of his maniacal hatred of Daisy, supplemented lately by something of the same kind toward Mona herself.

"Was that good money?" I asked Patrick, after we were driving back to the plaza.

"Looked all right under a powerful glass."

"Perhaps we should have taken it," I said.

"We hadn't what is called a warrant," he said.

"How do you suppose he got it?"

"Maybe he saved it."

"Pat," I said, and my voice sounded small, "do you think he did it?"

"What?"

"Murdered Arkwright and took that money?"

Patrick slanted a glance at me. "I had rather gathered that you thought Mona had Luis Martinez do it?"

"That's really more like it, Pat. Gilbert honestly couldn't do such things."

"I don't wonder you're all mixed up. I feel sorry for any investigator, no matter what the crime, in a place like this. What with people wanting to cover up for their friends or worrying about what will happen to their business if they antagonize Mona Brandon and with everybody knowing what everybody else will do before they do it, well—"

"There's Gilbert!" I interrupted.

"Sure enough," Patrick Abbott said. He angled in to the curb. "About time we had supper," he said. Michael was still in the restaurant.

# CHAPTER 42

It did me good to see how happy Michael looked. He really loved his funny fat Sonya, then. Well, I'd never be guilty again of wondering why people married other people, and so on.

We sat with Michael at a table toward the front.

"We've just been to Gilbert's house," I said to Michael. "We were afraid he was sick. His door was unlocked and we walked in expecting goodness knows what. But there he sits, and okay, apparently, even though he doesn't look it."

"Mona says he's been very difficult lately," Michael said.

We had coffee and sandwiches. Michael had finished. He refused a drink. He started talking again about Sonya. He said that last night they'd given her up. He talked about the oxygen tent, which meant more thanks to Mona, he said. She had donated two of the tents to the hospital recently.

I listened glowingly, thinking now that about the grandest thing that could happen would be for Sonya to get well.

"It's worse for the one who isn't ill, in a way," said Patrick Abbott. "I mean, on the nerves. You look as though you could do with a night's sleep, O'Hara."

"I think Michael looks marvelous. Considering," I said.

Patrick agreed.

I slipped another glance at Gilbert. He was pensive and superior.

"How's the painting?" Michael asked Patrick Abbott.

"Terrible."

"Everybody has to start."

"Thanks for the encouragement, O'Hara."

"I won't be able to go on with the lessons," Michael said. "I'll have to take care of Sonya. We can't afford a nurse, you know. Mona's paying the hospital bill herself. She insisted on it, and all I can do is call it a loan till I get back to New York to start earning again."

"It's a darn shame, your having to go to New York," I said. "But people have to live. Listen, Michael, when did Sonya first get ill?"

"Wednesday night. It came on suddenly. I guess it was pneumonia all the time. She's got type 3. It's the worst. Swoops down and finishes off its victims fast." Michael smiled a pallid smile. "Mona is wonderful in a crisis. She went along to the hospital just as she was that night. What with one thing or another we shall be indebted to her always for Sonya's life."

Then Michael asked, "What have you been doing all day?"

"We drove up to that old logging camp above the Arkwright place," I said.

"Oh. Is there a road up there?"

"You couldn't exactly call it a road," I said. "We walked after getting to the woods."

"Must be a nice view."

"Lovely."

"I'll miss Santa Maria and its views," Michael said. "And the people. All the nice people, Jean."

Michael then spoke of how they had happened to come to

Santa Maria, about saving money for years to take time off from commercial work, meaning to go to Paris, but meeting Mona in New York and being offered the cottage, and saying how glad he was that they had come here instead of going to Europe.

"But a man owes his wife a decent living," he finished.

He went out soon, saying he was going back to the hospital. I said to Patrick, "Do you think they'll keep the attempted suicide from getting out?"

"Why not?"

"It was a very sudden illness?"

"Pneumonia often is."

Rose came and said indignantly that Gilbert wasn't eating again. There weren't many people now in the restaurant. The waitresses stood around talking to each other. Mr. Kaufmann was at the bar, having an earnest conversation with Joe Padilla. We had finished our coffee and were about to leave when Mr. Trask came in. "Saw you through the window," he said. We asked him to sit down. He signaled Joe for a beer and Rose went to fetch it. "Just come from the hospital, by the way," the sheriff said. "Lot of cheerful-looking people out there this evening, with Mrs. O'Hara making such a change for the better."

"It's true, then?"

"Yes, ma'am."

Then Gilbert pranced over and joined us. He sat down, resting his threadbare elbows on the table.

"There he is, Miss Holly," Rose said, eyeing Gilbert angrily as she brought the beer. "You make him eat, Miss Holly. For a week now—"

"Shut up, Rose!" Gilbert said.

"For one week!" Rose yapped. "Nothing but coffee!"

Gilbert stuck out his chin. "Nine days," he corrected her. His glance lorded it over us. "Nine days. It wouldn't hurt the rest of you to try it. Clears the brain. I've gotten so I know everything."

The sheriff was rolling a cigarette. His keen glance came up to Gilbert. "I don't know if that would be an advantage or not, Mason."

"It wouldn't hurt you, Trask," Gilbert said, disagreeably.

"How's that?"

"We might get some action on the local murders."

The sheriff put a cigarette between his lips and felt in his pockets for a match.

"Think so, Mason?" he said with another slantwise glance.

Gilbert promptly got up and walked out. The sheriff watched him go with an ironic look in his eyes. I told him then about Gilbert's fainting at my house last night.

"Mason just wants you to pay attention, ma'am," the sheriff said quietly.

"It was a real faint," Patrick Abbott said.

"If he's starving himself like that he might die," I said.

"Chances are he'll land in the hospital first, ma'am. Good thing. They make them eat in the hospital." He then said, "By the way, Mrs. Brandon just called and gave me the address of her New York lawyers. Said it just happened to come to her. Still think I ought to go ahead and wire them for possible information about Brandon, Mr. Abbott?"

"Might as well," Patrick Abbott said.

After I was home in bed I remembered that we hadn't told Gilbert about going to his house. It bothered me, considering Gilbert. I thought about the money in the sugar bowl. I thought about Rose, trying to get him to eat, worrying over him the way all women did, and of the sheriff's indifference, which was much like Patrick Abbott's boredom with Gilbert. Men disliked him instinctively. Women mothered him.

I could tell by the night sounds that the weather was thickening again. Suddenly I sensed someone at the window on the lane, which I had thoughtlessly opened again.

This time my flashlight, repaired, was lying on the table.

I reached for it and snapped it on in time to see Luis's Scottish blanket before he moved on.

What did he want? The money? No, that couldn't be. Because the first time I saw him at the window was before he paid me the money for his things. Then what?

# CHAPTER 43

As I look back through what I have set down I feel as if I'd been behaving, ever since that morning when Gilbert said that Arkwright was Brandon, like a first-class snoop. The worst was not being able to put a finger on any of it. Something was happening, some evil influence seemed always at work, but what exactly? You'd think that in a little place like Santa Maria everybody would know everything about everybody else. On the contrary. The Anglos, for instance, were seldom natives, and came from everywhere, often, as in Gilbert's case, having no ties anyone knew of with the past. They said they were so and so, came from such and such, and if they settled down and behaved themselves according to our casual standards, they were all right. No one would dream, for instance, of suspecting Mr. McClure of highway robbery—we had had two unsolved ones—just because he was crazy about money, and because we had not known him since infancy. Same with the rest of us—Julia, Daisy, the O'Haras, the Johnsons, myself, all of us.

But I didn't feel the same way about Mona. She was the only one. Her selfishness was so immense. I couldn't get away from the feeling that she was in some way malevolent, that she was working toward something she was determined to have and that

Luis Martinez was her tool. Silly and melodramatic as it may seem, each day added some little item to increase my belief that Mona was behind everything. I would reproach myself for it, too. Why should you hate her so? I would say to myself. What has she done to you? Nothing worth the mention. A few slights and insults, and no more. Forget it, I would order myself. It is none of your concern. Let other people settle their own difficulties with Mona. Let it alone. And then I would think of the man who might be Brandon as a heap of bones in the desert and wonder how he could settle anything. Or Carmencita's relations, gullible little people who felt gratitude because Mona had given the poor dead girl a nice funeral. What could they do against Mona Brandon? I would think of her greed for power over anyone and everyone. Something must be done, I would think, angrily, and then I would think nothing could be done, that every town had its Mona, dictating to its little people like the Dominguezes and the rest of us, that there was nothing to be done about it, that the only way was to forget it, not think of it at all. No, better to stand aside, be the complete bystander that Gilbert accused me of being that grim Monday morning a week ago. Better to forget it, except as a show. Look on. Not get involved. That was the only way.

Then I would think of Luis or Gilbert or Daisy or the O'Haras, all under her thumb in one way or another, and I would start all over again. Down with all tyrants. And so on. Round and round. Over and over.

The next morning was Monday again, and a double for the one a week ago. Purple mountains. Black sky. The cottonwoods a tawny lacework. A little, sullen wind. Snow hanging over us, as before. I opened the shop at nine o'clock, put on my smock, and kept my mind made up to report Luis Martinez's meanderings to Patrick Abbott, and even to the sheriff unless Patrick had a better idea. I'd had enough. If I could understand it . . . but I couldn't.

Then Luis came into the shop. He opened the door, stepped in and said, from the door, "Mona say will you bring them things to the house this afternoon? Half-past-four, Jean."

"You mean that silver she bought, Luis?"

"Yes."

"Luis?" I called as he started out. He paused. "What were you doing at my window last night, Luis?" He looked blank.

Then he grinned!

"I come by. I stop to look at weather. I think it snow today. 'Bout suppertime maybe."

"Can you tie that?" I thought, after he'd gone.

Julia arrived next. I was sitting at the case. She came in and sat down by the fire.

"I just ran into Mona at Penney's," she said. "She was quite nice again, acting like other people for a change."

"Really?"

"I asked about Sonya. She said she was doing fine, said they thought she was out of danger. Mona's leaving tomorrow for New York."

"Oh. So that's why she wanted me to bring the things this afternoon."

"What things?"

"I told you, Julia. The silver pieces she bought to use as Christmas presents."

"I'm glad she's leaving," Julia said. "Things are so peaceful in Santa Maria when Mona's away. I hope she stays all winter and has a wonderful time."

"Know when Daisy's coming back?" I asked.

"Not definitely."

Patrick Abbott didn't show up till along in the afternoon. Gilbert Mason didn't appear all day, but I went home for lunch and didn't know if he'd been at the restaurant or not. Mr. Trask dropped in and said Mona's lawyers had wired him to try Quito, Ecuador, for Tom Brandon. He'd cabled the chief of police in Quito but if they run their affairs like the Mexicans he doubted if he'd get an answer for a week.

At four o'clock I banked the fire, put up the screen, put on my coat and took the basket of silver again from the safe. I hadn't had a customer all day, and I thought, as I closed the safe, hearing someone enter the shop, that it was just my luck to have one come in now.

It was Patrick Abbott. "Closing up so early?" he asked, as I came out.

"I've got to take this silver to Mona's."

"May I drive you there?"

"Thanks very much."

"How about a drink first?"

"I could do with some coffee," I said.

We had it at a drugstore, then drove east from the plaza. Black clouds were boiling up behind the eastern mountains. "Luis said it would snow today," I said, "but there isn't much time left. By the way, Pat, Luis keeps hanging around my house. I wonder why?"

"I don't think it's anything, Jean."

"Why not?"

"Well," Patrick said, after a moment, "I think I can explain it, partly. He has a girl who works as a maid at a ranch on the other side of the mesa. An Indian girl."

"Pretty late for making calls, Pat."

"Time means nothing to an Indian. That girl is the reason for his buying those things in your shop, by the way."

"You mean, he's getting married?"

"Something like that. It's a secret."

"But what does Mona say?"

"I'm afraid she doesn't know it."

"But if he's legally adopted—"

"He isn't. Even if he were, he's of age."

"How does he get in and out at night?"

Patrick smiled. "He had himself some keys made."

"How did you learn all this?"

"From the sheriff, child. I told you he knew plenty. Here we are."

"Did you see Mona about your job?"

"Come to think of it, I didn't."

"Julia tells me Mona's going away tomorrow."

"Mr. Trask mentioned it too."

"He seems to know everything," I said.

"He needs to."

Pedro hesitated about letting Patrick drive in, since Mrs. Brandon had told him I would be alone, but he gave in and in a moment we were moving along the winding drive. "I'll wait," Patrick said, when I got out at the door. "It may snow at any minute so I'll wait to take you home."

I rang. Lupe admitted me, took the basket while I removed my coat, and then preceded me to the white sitting room opposite the dining room. Mona was lying on a chaise longue at one side of the small white fireplace. The room was almost pure white, with a tawny fire on the hearth, tawny roses in white bowls, and Mona in a tawny velvet tea-gown.

*Mucho* glamour, I thought. Was this for me? Decidedly not,

for as soon as I was seated in the white chair opposite Mona, the basket of silver on an ottoman beside me, she said impatiently,

"Why haven't you a phone?"

"A phone?" I said. "Heavens, I don't need one."

"It would have saved you making this useless trip this afternoon."

"Useless?"

"I'm not up to looking at that stuff, Jean. I've got a headache."

She could have sent me word, I thought.

But I said, "That's all right. I'll leave the basket and you can look at the pieces whenever you like. There's a list, with prices and notes about old pieces and all. You can exchange anything you wish to later. If you'll sign my copy of the list."

Mona's roving eyes fastened on me.

"Why?"

"Matter of form. You needn't, unless you like. But inasmuch as you're going away—"

Her eyes narrowed.

"How did you learn that?"

I said, "I didn't know it was a secret."

She laughed harshly and dropped it.

She was drinking. Straight gin. There was a decanter on the table at the head of the chaise longue.

Then I noted something else. The lost ring! It lay on the table next the decanter.

Or, at least, a ring like the one Patrick had dropped that night in front of my fireplace. I saw the azure shield-shaped stone, but I was too far away to get the details of the silver mounting. If I could see the symbols inside the ring meaning *Forever Unto Death*, that would clinch it.

I must get the ring, of course.

I saw then how I could get it without perhaps exciting her notice. There was an open box of cigarettes on the table near the ring. Mona couldn't see the things on the tabletop without twisting to look over her shoulder. I would take a long step, get a cigarette and the ring. Then with any kind of luck she wouldn't miss it till after I'd gone. I wondered why she had taken it from my house that night. Well, it all hung together. The ring had been found on the desert near the site of that murder. Mr. Trask had thought it might be a clue and Patrick Abbott had brought it to show me on the chance that I might know to whom it belonged. I hadn't, but it looked like the sort of thing Luis collected. The ring had become really important when it vanished from my house. And there it lay, or one too like it for words.

Mona asked, "Don't you want a drink?"

"No, thank you."

"There are cigarettes in that box beside you."

"Thanks."

She meant a box on a table next my chair. There went my immediate excuse for getting a cigarette from the other table and grabbing the ring. I'd have to rise and admire the alabaster box, or something, and then take the ring. It might be clumsy but I must get that ring.

Mona's next remark put me off, however.

"I'm not up to looking at jewelry this afternoon, Jean, but I've got plenty to say to you on other subjects. You owe me an explanation. Why didn't you send that detective to me as I asked?" She eyed me belligerently. "Of course you told him what I said."

"Yes. I did."

"When?"

"Saturday night, to be exact."

"Why did you wait so long?"

"That was the first time after you talked to me that I thought of it. But you could have sent for him yourself, you know."

She frowned.

"What did he say?"

"He said it sounded like nice work. But he is on a vacation, Mona. He doesn't want a job."

"Vacation? Why is he spending it with the sheriff?"

"I think it's the other way round. The sheriff has been going to Patrick Abbott. After all, they don't confide in me."

Mona reached over her shoulder for the decanter and refilled her little gin glass.

"You aren't usually so dumb, Jean."

"Why not quiz Patrick Abbott, Mona? I really know very little about anything."

She did not answer immediately. She sipped the crystal liquid and eyed me with condescension, as if she knew a great deal that would interest me, should she care to speak.

Suddenly it occurred to me that the ring was a plant, that she had put it there purposely, meaning for me to take it. I felt confused then. Should I take it? Or leave it?

I asked a question, deliberately to evade further talk about Patrick Abbott, while making up my mind what to do now about that ring.

"How is Sonya this afternoon?" was my question.

Mona's laugh was small and bitter. "Better, of course."

"Do they think she'll recover?"

"Why? What reason is there for her to live?"

I looked down my nose. What she had said was so terrible that it made the taking of the ring seem unimportant.

"Oh, don't put on an act, Jean! You know as well as I do that she's nothing but a ball and chain. What chance has Michael got so long as he has Sonya on his hands?"

I felt guilty when I remembered that I had said almost the same thing, but anyhow not because I wanted him myself.

"Sonya ought to die," Mona continued sullenly. "In fact, Michael will never be rid of her satisfactorily any other way."

She watched me over her glass, her eyes glistening.

"I'll admit that I put up a great show of trying to save Sonya. I helped Michael get her to the hospital and saw that she had proper nursing and all the rest. But I didn't want her to live. Never. I only did what I did so that if she died no one would blame me. Or accuse me."

My eyes met hers and looked away.

"I was so sure she would die. I counted on it. Johnson was absolutely sure. But Sonya's got the constitution of an ox. Peasant, I should say. So she's going to get well." She gave a little sniff. "It was all so perfect. She wouldn't know a thing. She wouldn't suffer. Johnson said that pneumonia was a merciful death. She would never know what happened, he said. It seemed as good as settled. Then, mind you, they put her under an oxygen tent and now she's improving every minute. And I myself provided that tent!"

"But poor Michael!" I burst out.

Mona's glance fairly knifed me.

"Why so?"

"Michael cared about her."

"Rot. Michael loves me. That's why she shot herself."

"Shot herself?" I couldn't've sounded more shocked if I hadn't already known it.

Mona laughed.

"We covered it all over very prettily, didn't we! Nobody even guessed it. We counted on her dying, of course. And we thought for her sake as well as our own that it would be better if the scandal never got out. But now she's going to live and it will come out anyhow. Sonya will talk. She will brag about how she held onto Michael by trying to kill herself. There is nothing some women won't resort to."

I had entirely forgotten the ring.

Mona's face twitched.

"It's going to make us so much trouble. Her living, I mean. There will have to be a divorce and all the rest. Everything will be dragged out and aired to the rabble. People will start nosing around, wanting to know all about Tom Brandon and all the rest. We'll have to hear all about Carmencita again. Again and again. It would have been so easy if she had only died." She made a small sound in her throat. "And why not? What is there for her to live for?"

There was a light tap on the door. Lupe entered. Mona glared.

"Shall I serve the tea now, ma'am?" the girl asked softly.

"Get out!" Mona shouted at her. The girl shrank back into the hall. "Shut the door!" It was already almost shut. "And don't stand at the keyhole, mind."

The door closed.

The knob turned and was still. There was a tiny silence. The fire crackled. I stood up. This was no place for me, assuredly. "Sit down!" Mona commanded me.

I sat down. But I had no intention of listening to her much longer. She must have had too much gin.

"Michael is going to divorce Sonya and marry me. You might as well get it straight, Jean, and then you can tell all the snakes that it came directly from me. I shall make Michael a great artist. I can buy Sonya off. I don't care what it costs. The important thing to me is Michael."

Not to mention yourself, I thought.

"Michael must be saved. It doesn't matter what happens to people like Sonya. Little people don't count. I'm fed up with them all. People like Sonya and Gilbert and Daisy seem to have been put up on this earth just to plague me. Daisy comes here making scenes. Sonya shoots herself to give me trouble. Gilbert starves himself to spite me."

"What's that about Gilbert?" I said.

Mona frowned irritably. "I said he was starving himself to spite me. Just because I told him to go on relief, which is where he belongs, he gets mad and starves himself. Comes up here every day and brags about how many pounds he's lost and how clear his brain is. Just to persecute me, mind you! After all I've done for him, too."

"So that's it," I said. "But Gilbert couldn't go on relief."

"Why not?"

"He just couldn't."

Mona sneered, "You sympathize with him, I suppose?"

I said, "I'm sorry for Gilbert. He's such a misfit, Mona. Unless some sort of miracle occurs he'll be unhappy all his life. I do sympathize with him. His temperament makes him so helpless."

Mona sat up straight. She swung her tawny slippers onto the white rug. As she turned to set the glass beside the decanter I noticed the tendons twitching in the backs of her hands.

It was all somehow deliberate. I couldn't help feeling that she was working herself deliberately into a frenzy.

I had put out my cigarette. I stood up to go.

"What do you mean by criticizing me like that?" Mona demanded.

"I'm sorry."

She asked again, her eyes hard and narrow, "Why didn't you send that detective to me?"

I looked down at her.

"All I could do was tell him you wanted to see him. I told you that. If he didn't come I dare say he wasn't interested."

"You're lying!"

"I suppose," I said, "that it doesn't occur to you, Mona, that there might be one person in the world who doesn't jump when you say frog."

Mona leaped to her feet and took a step toward me. Her eyes were like swords. Her hands worked like claws.

"You never told him! You're lying!"

I said, as quietly as I could, "He's outside now. I'll insist on his coming in so you can talk to him yourself."

"Outside? Here? What for?"

"He's waiting for me."

Mona Brandon shrank away a little, seeming suddenly smaller, and at bay. "You two-faced bitch!" she muttered, in a low venomous tone. "So that's your game, is it? You take my money and come here with your junk and keep me in this room while he snoops around my place. So that's it!"

I was too disgusted to speak. It was my moment, the time for me to speak out and say my say, to tell her what I thought of her arrogance and selfishness and suspicion. But I was so appalled at her accusation I was speechless.

She pointed a dramatic finger at the door.

"Get out!" she yelled.

"With pleasure," I said.

"Take your junk with you." She pointed at the silver. "I never wanted it in the first place. I only bought it because I felt sorry for you."

Felt sorry for me? I felt my blood rise, but all I could do for some reason was pick up the basket and say, "I'll send back your money."

"Shut up and get out!" she screamed.

I turned toward the door. She sank back on the chaise longue and started emitting one scream after another, as though I were murdering her. I stopped and stared. Now what? Then the door burst open. I expected to see Lupe. It was Michael O'Hara. He gave me an angry glance and hurried to Mona, who collapsed with small whimpers onto his shoulder. I paused long enough to observe this and then went on into the hall and out of the house. I had forgotten all about the ring.

The thing that bothered me most was that Michael obviously blamed me for Mona's hysterics.

# CHAPTER 44

PATRICK ABBOTT'S car was not on the circle. I walked a little way and saw it parked next some laurels along the drive. He was not in it, however, so I got in and sounded the horn, and after a couple of minutes he came from the direction of the swimming pool.

"Hi, there," he said. "Didn't expect you back so soon."

"Mona's changed her mind about wanting the silver," I said.

"She'll probably ask for it again tomorrow," he said, getting in and starting the motor. We drove toward the gate.

"Mona called me a bitch. She accused me of bringing you here to snoop while I kept her occupied inside the house."

Patrick looked serious.

"I'm sorry. I'll tell her myself that you had no part in my snooping."

"You weren't, were you?"

"I had a look about the place while you were inside."

We left the grounds and turned toward the village.

"The fact is, she jumped on me right away because you hadn't come to see her about the job. But I saw that ring on a table near her chair and I decided to stay long enough to grab it. Then she jumped on me again because you hadn't come to see her and I

227

said you were outside and could come in and explain it yourself. She promptly threw a fit. Then Michael arrived, looked
daggers at me, and comforted her. And in the mess I forgot
to get the ring."

"It makes no difference, really, at this stage."

I didn't quiz him about that "this stage." I was still too upset
over the quarrel.

"As a matter of fact Mona was drinking gin, which probably
helped put her into the state she was in, Pat. She is all in a dith-
er, mind you, because Sonya O'Hara is going to get well."

I told him all that had happened.

We drove slowly toward the village. The snow storm was
holding off but indubitably coming this time. You could feel it,
for certain.

I said that Mona had undoubtedly planned a rendezvous
with Michael. I told Patrick about all the glamour.

"Poor Michael!" I said. "Why doesn't he just get up and walk
out on it all, anyhow?"

"She probably doesn't show her worse side to Michael."

"I should hope not!"

Patrick parked in front of The Turquoise Shop. I went inside and put the silver back into the safe, wrote a check for five
hundred dollars, put it in an envelope, addressed it to Mona,
and took it to the post office. It was getting dark. The lights
had come on around the plaza. The wind soughed in the naked
cottonwoods.

Meanwhile Patrick had vanished, but he turned up as I got
back from the post office.

"How about a drink, Jean?"

"I could use one," I said.

We sat at the long table in the Castillo Bar. Joe Padilla

brought our martinis. There were two cowboys drinking beer at the rail and talking their witty soft-voiced talk. Joe went back to the bar and stood listening to them.

Patrick Abbott said very casually, "A man six feet tall or over could leave Mrs. Brandon's house by way of the east terrace, walk to the swimming pool, commit a murder, and be back in the house inside of five minutes, or even less. If he knew the arrangements for the evening he could go while the Indians were dancing and have a fifty-fifty chance of not being seen on the grounds."

"So it was murder?" I said.

"Of course it was murder."

Everything seemed intense.

"That's what Gilbert said," I said. "But you and the sheriff gave the impression that you considered it suicide."

"Did we?"

"You know you did. He said that the investigation was continuing, but he didn't seem excited about it."

"The sheriff's got plenty of what it takes," Patrick said.

"Nothing seems to happen."

"Plenty's happening," Patrick Abbott said. "Like another quick one?"

"No, thanks."

We sat on a while longer. I liked the old-time bar in the Castillo. It was solid mahogany and immense, with a mirror behind it reaching to the ceiling, and with little brackets on which stood fancy bottles of wonderful colored drinks nobody ever drank. Joe was always at the bar. He wouldn't let one of the girls come behind the bar ever, because he said it brought bad luck. Men didn't like buying drinks from women, he always said. Joe wouldn't serve a Mexican at the Castillo Bar either, though he was one himself. Now the cowmen in their high-heeled boots and wide hats stood talking and wisecracking in their soft southern voices and Joe stood beaming. A fly buzzed against the mirror. Joe swatted it, but kept his ear on the cowboys.

"So Mona did do it," I said, in a low voice.

"What?" Patrick Abbott asked.

"You know what. Or had it done. It's all the same thing. You're always talking about motive. She is the only person who has sufficient motive, as well as enough nerve and enough money, to put it over. She's crazy about Michael. I never realized how crazy till today. She said the things you might feel in your blackest states but never say, unless you're like Mona."

"She's crazy about him, all right," Patrick Abbott said.

"Then you agree with me?"

"Did I give you that impression?"

Mrs. Dominguez's little boy, Tony, eased in through the front door, looking for someone. He saw me. He ran to our table, put down a letter, and then beat it.

"Well?" I said. I sat looking at the pure white envelope and the spidery, black handwriting.

"What is it?" Patrick asked.

"That's Gilbert's writing," I said.

"Aren't you going to read it?"

I pushed it aside. "Not now. Mona is enough for one afternoon, thanks. I think I should like that drink after all, Pat."

Patrick signaled Joe, gave the order, and then said, "Perhaps you'd better read the letter, Jean."

Good thing he insisted, too.

# CHAPTER 45

"My dear Jean," the letter began stiffly. It was written in ink on white typewriter paper with a very fine penpoint. Each slanting spidery letter was meticulously formed and placed. There were six tightly packed pages, which must have taken him hours to write in such a precise script. "This is my confession. Imagine writing it to, of all people, you, my pet!"

There followed a paragraph of slams at my unsympathetic character.

Then he laid off me and went to town on Mona, for two pages, calling her vulgar, greedy, vain, bad-tempered, and so on. He was bitter about her, he said, because at first he had thought her an angel, then had learned she was a cheat. He felt no gratitude to her whatever. What she gave him over a year was less than half the price she paid any day for some useless trinket.

Next he discussed himself, spoke of his father in New York who had been old before he was forty from supporting as a laborer too many brats, of his mother who stank of hard work, of his schooling in high school, working his way through a midwestern state university, getting a job then in a mail-order house.

"I didn't know why I was so different from other people,"

he said. "I was a poet, of course, cursed with special nerves and imagination. I saw and felt and understood and suffered with a special heat. But I did not know why then. It's ironic to speak of this to you, Jean. You're no more intelligent than the others. You actually pity me, for instance. That's nonsense. I've been happy in Santa Maria, utterly happy, with my life so entirely as it should be, my little house so repletely my shell, so perfect, so just enough. And people like you and Julia pity me. Fools!"

A frenzy of hard spidery words then poured vitriol on Daisy and her phlegmatic arrogance.

"It was Daisy I wanted to get even with when I thought up that murder. The first one. Brandon." My eyes narrowed onto the page. "*That was why I stole the knife.*"

"Maybe you'd better read this," I said, pushing the first pages at Patrick Abbott. I saw him pick them up as I read on.

"It was so easy. I mean the deed itself. Believe me, there's nothing hard about taking the life of a man. I'll admit as we stood talking there in that out-of-the-way spot, with the dusk falling, that I was rather perplexed about how to do it. Should I stab him in the back, or what? Then he started away and I did it. Swiftly. I leaped and grabbed his hair and slit his throat. But the blood! It was a fountain, I had it all over me, nasty, sticky, funny-smelling stuff, so I ran away in a panic, because of the blood, and was a quarter of a mile from the spot before I realized that I was still carrying the knife. I had meant to leave it beside the body, then walk out that way in a day or two and discover the corpse myself, with the knife beside it. Daisy's going out there for the calf was sheer coincidence, pure luck. I got home and bathed and burned the bloody clothes, but I delayed doing anything more for a day or two. I wrapped up the bloody knife and put it in my briefcase. Then I got to thinking about

Mona. Mona had told me to go on relief, and I decided Mona too had to suffer. And that decision spelled Carmencita's doom. She had to die too, under circumstances which would reflect on Mona. That was why I asked you at the party not to tell anyone about my having the knife, for I had arranged for Carmencita to come to the pool and told her I'd give her money, so I could shoot her with her own gun and it would look like suicide, and turn the whole town against Mona."

"For gosh sakes!" I said, pushing the page over to Patrick Abbott. "This doesn't make sense, at all."

At this point Gilbert said at great length that he had discovered that he got more pleasure from the actual doing of murder than from his schemes for vengeance against the people he didn't like. Living suddenly seemed stale. Hadn't he done everything, after doing murder? There was nothing left now—save dying himself—which interested him in the least, so he decided to starve himself to death. He had been going without food for several days already to spite Mona for cutting off his allowance, so he decided to carry it to the limit. He told Mona he was starving himself to death to get even with her. Since he had now lost all interest in the murders, and their consequences, he was really glad that nothing definite had come out at the inquests which incriminated anyone else.

He was ready. He had burned all his papers and had cleaned the hearth of their smoke. There was money enough in the sugar bowl on his table to pay for his cremation. But starvation was too slow. He'd gotten bored with dying by inches so he was taking a quicker way out.

"Don't feel flattered because I address this to you, darling," he wound up. "There was merely nobody else.

"Adios! Gilbert"

I pushed the last page at Patrick Abbott, heaved a bored sigh, and picked up my drink and finished it. I was amazed when he pocketed the letter and reached for his hat.

"Come on, Jean. Let's get going."

"Where?" I asked, trotting after him. He handed a bill to Joe across the bar and didn't wait for change. We were in his car and moving before he spoke.

"We'll stop first at the sheriff's office," he said, turning off the plaza.

"Why?"

"He'd better come with us to Mason's, just in case. Also he can call the doctor."

"You don't think Gilbert's really done anything?"

Patrick made no answer. There was a light in Mr. Trask's office. He jammed on the brakes and dashed in. He came right out, alone, and we drove east at a wild pace.

"Is he coming?" I asked.

"He has to go to the hospital. Sudden call. Dr. Johnson's out there, too. Mrs. O'Hara is worse again. By the way, when I told Trask about your seeing the ring—while you went to the post office—he told me he'd heard from his cable to Quito for news of Brandon. He was quite surprised to get such quick action."

I couldn't put my mind on that. I said, as we whizzed into Daisy's lane, "I'm not worried about Gilbert, really. People who threaten to kill themselves never do."

"That's where you're wrong," Patrick said quietly.

"If it's true," I said, suddenly feeling desperate, "I blame myself."

"For what?"

"For everything. I've known all along that Gilbert was off his head a little. Nobody knew it as well as I did. He has always sat around the shop and raved on and I never paid any attention to it. It didn't do me any harm and he got it off his chest, so I just let him rave. I'd sit there working and he'd talk, and it went in one ear and out the other. But this week I was worried about the awful things that had happened and it got on my nerves and I wouldn't honestly listen. He was trying all the time to tell me that he'd done it. And I wouldn't half listen."

"Done what?" Patrick said, slowing down to stop.

"Killed those people."

"Holy smoke!" Patrick barked.

"He's ill," I said, as we got out of the car. "He's a mental case. Don't let them do anything to him, Pat. He's crazy."

"Me, too," Patrick Abbott said, focusing his flashlight on the stile. He climbed over and turned the light back for me to follow. We started across the field. He walked ahead. I trotted to keep up with his long swift stride.

"It's no joke," I said.

"Joke?" he said. "It's about as funny as a corpse. I never saw such a lunatic fringe. I'll be one myself if I hang around here much longer. The place is crawling with nuts. I doubt if it's worth trying to be an artist if it means that you have to live in places like this."

"I love Santa Maria!" I snapped back.

We were getting close to the house. I could see a slim gash of light where the drawn curtains didn't quite meet. It was very dark. The snow clouds shut over the earth like a lid. The wind blew slightly.

We got to the gate. Patrick flashed his light over the little white hovel. "My little house, so repletely my shell, so perfect, so just enough," I remembered from the letter.

"Ever see a dead man?" Pat asked me suddenly. I shivered. I

never had, except in a coffin, which is not the same thing. "Well, watch yourself, just in case," he said.

He tried the front door latch. It lifted easily. We stepped into the white spotless room.

Gilbert lay on his back on the couch. On his two chairs, one at his head and one at his feet, burned his two candles. If they had been new to start with they had been burning for some time.

Patrick put his light on Gilbert's face, which was darkly red. He bent over him and lifted an eyelid. "Looks like atropine," he said.

"Is he dead?" I asked.

"Can't you see he's breathing?" he said irritably. "Here. Hold this light!"

He took out a clean handkerchief, stepped to the table and dumped the money from the bowl into it, tied it in a knot and put it in his pocket.

"Do you think he stole that from Arkwright?" I asked, in a small voice.

"Mason saved this money dollar by dollar. He withdrew it on Saturday from the bank. I'm merely taking it now so it won't be stolen."

Patrick pinched out the candles.

"I'll have to carry him to the car, Jean. Please hold the flash so it will light the path. Be disastrous to fall."

He picked Gilbert up as though he were a child.

"He doesn't weigh much," he said, as we left the house.

"Where are you taking him?"

"To the hospital, idiot!" Patrick yapped, with annoyance.

# CHAPTER 46

I AM not likely to forget that rapid transit to the hospital. I drove, Patrick Abbott beside me with Gilbert in his arms. "Don't talk, drive!" he ordered me, whenever I ventured to ask a question. We dashed into the town and skirted the plaza and headed south, slowing up only when I turned into the hospital lane. We weren't five minutes en route after we got into the car. Mona's car was standing in front of the hospital, and Luis loafed under the light at the main entrance. The Indian saw us arrive without any change in the set expression of his dark handsome face. A nurse appeared from somewhere and led the way to the emergency room and then tore off upstairs after Dr. Johnson. I hung around in the hall. In a minute or two Mr. Trask came hurrying downstairs. He looked pretty grim. Then the doctor came, running down the steps like a kid, his face very serious, and at once after he disappeared into the emergency room, out came the sheriff and went swinging back upstairs. I stood there in the hall, bewildered and fidgety, smelling the acrid odors of the hospital, noticing the clean dark linoleum, so highly waxed it reflected the wall lights, wondering if I couldn't somehow do something somewhere. I felt very useless.

Presently Patrick Abbott appeared and asked why I didn't wait in the public waiting room next the office.

"How's Gilbert?" I asked.

"They can't tell yet."

"Think he'll get over it?" I said, hating to use the word *die*.

"Impossible to say. Depends on how much poison he took and how long ago he took it."

He abandoned me and I walked into the waiting room and sat down. It was a large square room with windows on two sides. There was a chandelier in the middle of the ceiling which cast a naked light over the empty chairs that faced the table in the middle of the room. Two were rocking chairs. The table was piled with old magazines, their pretty-girl covers dog-eared and creased from handling, which made them look pretty desolate. The room was furnished with a melange of battered furniture donated by various well-wishers in Santa Maria, mostly old pieces of oak or willow-work which had already served enough time.

I began hearing a queer whispering sound. For a moment it seemed almost malicious, until I recognized it for what it was. Snow! Snow was falling at last, in small hard flakes which a rising wind brushed against the windowpanes.

At last I heard footsteps. They converged toward this room. Sharp high heels, the dulcet padding of a nurse's rubber soles, the solid tread of men's feet.

Mona Brandon entered first. She wore a green tweed suit and a little felt hat. She was crying, just a little, dabbing at her eyes with her handkerchief. She gave me a sharp look and sat down.

Miss Edwards came next. She was middle-aged and calmly professional. Then Patrick Abbott entered, then Mi-

chael, and last of all Mr. Trask. Three tall handsome creatures, I must say.

When I saw Michael's tight face I guessed that Sonya was
dead.

It was true. A sudden relapse had carried her swiftly away.

"Sit down, all," said Mr. Trask. Miss Edwards and Michael
sat down. But Mona faced the sheriff indignantly.

"How dare you?" she demanded. "At such a time!"

"Sit down, Mrs. Brandon!" the sheriff said, his voice as easy
as ever, his look of authority very definite. Mona flounced into
a chair.

Patrick Abbott and the sheriff seated themselves.

Mona's angry eyes now landed on me.

"Why are you here?" she demanded. "I insist on privacy for
whatever it is you're going to ask us, sheriff. Send her away! And
that nosy sleuth of hers, too. Send them out! They do nothing
but snoop around after me."

"This is my party," said Mr. Trask, quietly. "I'll decide who
stays or goes, ma'am."

Mona looked dramatic.

"But don't you realize that Mrs. O'Hara has just died? Can't
you understand how we feel?"

"Yes, ma'am. Please accept my sympathy. I don't like this any
better than you all do. But Miss Holly has had a letter which
brings up a lot of questions which need investigation." Mona
shot a frantic look at Michael O'Hara. Mr. Trask said, "It's from
Gilbert Mason." A scornful smile instantly drove the fear from
Mona's set face. "He's tried to kill himself."

"Tried!" Mona said, sarcastically.

"He's in a bad way, ma'am. The doctor's with him now."

Mona said, "How like him to pick a time like this!"

Mr. Trask said, "He wrote a letter to Miss Holly in which he makes a full confession of the murders of the man who called himself Arkwright and the woman Carmencita Dominguez."

Mona's eyes brightened.

"Oh!" she cried, looking excitedly from one to the other of us. "I knew it! I had a hunch about Gilbert all along but I didn't dare say so. He's insane, of course. I've known it for ages. But one doesn't say those things, does one! I felt so sorry for him. Well, that explains everything, doesn't it?"

I glanced at Patrick Abbott, who was watching Mona with a queer look in his eyes, as though she were some strange specimen under that magnifying glass of his.

Mr. Trask said, "It happens that Mason wasn't eating much lately, and—"

Mona interrupted him. "He was starving himself just to spite me. I told you so, Jean." She flung me a glance. "Well, after all it's a good thing he took this way out before something *really* terrible happened. I wouldn't be surprised if he was a homicidal maniac, running at large, planning to murder us all one by one in our beds."

"Well," the sheriff cut in, "I doubt if we'll ever know what he was planning to do next. Depends on how much atropine he swallowed. But he makes a number of statements in his letter that I'd like you to help me clear up, Mrs. Brandon, ma'am. He says for one thing that this man Arkwright was your former husband, Tom Brandon."

Fear glazed Mona's eyes.

"That's a lie!" she cried.

"What makes you think so, ma'am?"

Mona swallowed. "Because Tom Brandon is living in South America."

"Yes, ma'am," the sheriff said easily. "Mighty glad to know it, too. He's there all right. I cabled today to make sure and got an affirmative answer this evening. You could have saved me a little trouble by giving us his address a week ago, ma'am."

Mona avoided an explanation. She said, "After all I've done for him, Gilbert slanders me in a farewell letter. It's incredible."

The sheriff did not press her then for an answer to his question about Brandon.

He said, "Mason is the kind who would resent anybody who held any authority of any kind over him, Mrs. Brandon. I understand your position."

"Well, thank goodness somebody understands it," Mona said. "If you only knew what I've had to put up with—"

"Yes, ma'am. Excuse me for interrupting, but you ain't the only one who was mighty glad to hear that Brandon was alive and well in Quito, Ecuador. I was myself. People kept saying that that dead man was Brandon. I couldn't make it click. There was a lot of circumstantial evidence which was sort of confusing. The dead man had a small crescent-shaped scar on the back of his head. So did Brandon. They both had dark hair, good teeth, and were about the same size. The dead man kept away from people. So did Brandon, though not to the same extent. Then there was the gossip." Mona started to protest. The sheriff held up his hand. "Luckily we had a sample of the corpse's hair and we got some fingerprints at the house and also at a cabin he used up in the woods. We had word from the Identification Bureau in Washington that the prints identify the man as one Simkovitch, alias Arkwright, a professional crook, with a past record as a counterfeiter."

Mona stood up. "I should like to go home, Mr. Trask. This is very interesting, but—"

"In a minute, ma'am. Sit down."

"But why should all this concern me?"

"I'll thank you to sit down, Mrs. Brandon," said the sheriff, softly as ever. But Mona sat down.

"Were you and Brandon divorced, ma'am?"

"That's none of your business!" Mona yelped.

"I'll thank you to answer the question, Mrs. Brandon."

"Well, yes, we were."

"Did anyone in Santa Maria know about this divorce?"

"How dare you?" Mona screamed, jumping up.

"Sit down and answer the question!"

Mona sat down.

"Only one person."

"Who was that, ma'am?"

"Michael O'Hara," Mona said, in a very low tone. "Why does that concern you?"

"It may and it may not, ma'am."

I glanced at Patrick Abbott. He was quietly attentive.

Michael sat with his chin sunk on his chest. His red head had a wilted desolate look. This must be terrible for him, at such a time.

"In the, letter, ma'am," the sheriff continued, "Mason says he killed the man, who he seemed convinced was Brandon, intending at first that suspicion should fall on Miss Daisy Payne."

"What a crazy idea!" Mona cried.

I looked at Patrick Abbott. He was watching Mona.

"What exactly do you make of that from Mason, Mrs. Brandon?"

"He was insane," Mona said promptly. "Daisy wouldn't hurt a fly, really." I gasped, thinking of what she had said to me about Daisy. "I should have done something about Gilbert, Mr. Trask, but I couldn't bear to report him to whoever it is you report them to for locking them up."

The sheriff let it pass.

"Mason was pretty hard up, wasn't he, Mrs. Brandon?"

Mona tried to look benevolent.

"Well, I gave him only a small allowance, Mr. Trask. It was all he seemed to want. Naturally I did a lot for him in little ways, too. On the side."

The sheriff said, "We found three hundred and forty dollars in his house."

Mona stiffened with anger.

"What?"

"How would you account for his having that money, Mrs. Brandon?"

"Well, I don't know where he got it," Mona yapped, "but for him to pretend he had none, and to starve himself just to torture . me—"

"Haven't you any opinion about that money, ma'am?"

"Opinion?" Mona looked blank. Then she brightened. "You mean he stole it from the man he killed, Sheriff?"

"No, ma'am," the sheriff said softly. "That money belonged to Gilbert Mason and nobody else. He saved it bit by bit from the allowance you gave him and put it in the bank."

"Why, the dirty double-crossing—"

The sheriff lifted a hand. "Mason drew his money out on Saturday. We've checked it with the bank. Evidently he had suicide in mind at the time, for he says in the letter how he wants the money used." The sheriff leaned toward Mona slightly and asked in a crisp voice, "Mrs. Brandon, why did you withhold the facts of your former husband's whereabouts?"

"How dare you!" Mona barked.

"Answer the question, please, ma'am."

"What right—"

"You're just wasting everybody's time, ma'am."

Mona suddenly seemed to collapse inside.

She said, "When they came here about a year ago, and Carmencita began strutting around Santa Maria as if she owned it—just to annoy me, of course—I thought then maybe the man really might be Tom Brandon. But about six months ago I wrote my lawyers in New York and they traced him to Ecuador."

"Why didn't you tell me that?"

"Oh, I didn't want it all dragged up. Seemed to me it was my own business."

The sheriff let it ride.

"Do you really believe that Mason killed Arkwright and Carmencita, Mrs. Brandon?"

"He says so, doesn't he?"

"But if he hadn't said so, would you have any suspicion of anyone else?"

Mona frowned. Then she said, "Well, yes, I did have. I thought once or twice that Daisy Payne did it."

"Why?"

"She went out to that place, you know. About the time he was killed. I saw her myself. And since I'm positive she's a nymphomaniac—"

"A what, ma'am?"

"Really, Mr. Trask! Haven't you had any education at all?"

"I reckon not enough anyhow, Mrs. Brandon. Miss Payne just seems like a cranky old maid to me. She went out there plainly and simply to buy that calf and haul it into town herself because she's too tight to hire somebody to do it for her. It don't take much education to figure that one out, Mrs. Brandon, ma'am."

Mona suddenly buried her face in her white red-tipped hands. "Why must you torture me?" she wailed. "What is all this? I insist on having a lawyer."

Mr. Trask ignored her. "So far as I have been able to find out," he said, "Carmencita Dominguez never did know much about the man she lived with. He wouldn't be likely to confide in her to any extent, because he was a jailbird who had broken his parole, and he was already up to his neck in another counterfeiting plot, and he would be afraid she would talk to her kinfolks. She wasn't much of a woman to ask questions, anyways. I doubt if she ever knew that Arkwright had her get that house because he wanted to be close to a man in Santa Maria, a master engraver of such talent, and so unprincipled, that his very existence is a threat to our government. This man, already guilty of counterfeiting, has lately added three murders—"

Mona jumped up. "I refuse to sit and listen—"

The sheriff ignored her.

"Sorry, O'Hara," he said.

# CHAPTER 47

MICHAEL JUMPED up and ran out into the hall. Patrick went after him, then the sheriff.

I heard a shot and some yells. I felt sick.

I stood up, and sat down again when it occurred to me that Michael had probably shot Patrick Abbott.

Miss Edwards rushed out into the hall then, and Mona Brandon sent a frenzied look around the room, after which she slipped out by way of the other door leading to the office.

I heard a tangle of sounds. Footsteps, voices, a motor whirring in front of the hospital. I could smell gunpowder and the sweetish smell of blood.

Dr. Johnson joined the group in the hall and began giving orders.

Patrick looked in. He was all right, anyhow.

"Where's Mrs. Brandon?"

"She beat it. I heard her car go. Why?"

"O'Hara was asking for her," he said.

He went away.

I got up then and went to the door. There was a great pool of blood on the blackish linoleum. The handyman, whom they'd call an orderly in a bigger hospital, was coming with cloths and a bucket. I turned back and went into the office and then went out and stood in the main hall, near the entrance. It was twenty-two minutes to eight. It was just sixty-five minutes since we left the Castillo to go to Gilbert's. I could hear the man in the outer hall cleaning up the blood. I could smell some sort of antiseptic. The man finished and went away and after his footsteps died away the place became very quiet. I could again hear the whispering of the snow on windows. I felt numb.

Then Miss Edwards appeared. "How is he?" I said.

"Still alive. He's making a statement."

"You mean Gilbert?"

"No. O'Hara."

"How's Gilbert?"

"He's going to be all right."

"What will happen to him, Miss Edwards?"

She moved her shoulders. "Goodness knows. Those people are always a problem. Neither sane nor insane."

"I mean Michael."

The nurse blinked.

"Oh. He can't live. It's fortunate they can get a statement. Removes suspicion from other people, you know. He's bleeding to death, internally, you know. He shot himself in—"

I felt relieved. "I thought perhaps one of them did it."

"No, he shot himself. In the chest. Poor fellow. Mrs. Brandon ought not to have run away like that. Well, I must find somebody to clean up that blood."

She must be upset herself, I thought. The blood was already cleaned up.

After Michael died, I went into town with Dr. Johnson. Patrick Abbott and Mr. Trask stayed behind in some sort of huddle in which I was certainly not wanted. The snow was rather fun, like driving through an ocean of feathers.

"Mrs. O'Hara took a turn for the better after I talked to you Sunday," Dr. Johnson said. "I felt like a fool for having gabbed I thought she might actually get well." Then he said, "I think I should tell you that I telephoned the sheriff myself tonight when I was certain she was dying." He drove me home and left me at the gate. Mrs. Dominguez was hovering about and wondering if she should stay or go home. I had a hot bath and then she brought my supper to me in bed. Toby strutted about. My house seemed bright and cozy and opulent. Gilbert had thought his perfect. Mona loved hers. There were certainly a lot of different kinds of people in Santa Maria.

# CHAPTER 48

I HEARD a car slogging up my snow-covered hill. Mrs. Dominguez went to the door. I thought it would be Patrick Abbott, but it was Julia Price, the Santa Maria grapevine. Some nurse had phoned somebody from the hospital and the news was all over, even phoned to Julia in the country, who had managed to drive through the snow to hear the story direct. I told her all I knew. We felt sorry for everybody, even Mona.

The snow was still falling at midnight. Julia said then that somebody would have to come next morning and dig her car out of the lane.

As I walked to the shop next morning, in the deep tracks of Mexicans who had gone on earlier, Santa Maria had that hallowed look which it has in perfection only after the first snowfall.

I wore my high laced boots and my sheep-lined coat and a stocking cap. Winter was here.

I stopped at a garage near the plaza to send aid for Julia's snowbound car and then opened the shop, lit the fire, and changed the boots for some oxfords I'd brought with me. I folded the dust sheets and put the shop in order. Then I pulled a basket of huaraches near the fire and began pairing them to put them away in the storeroom until spring.

Patrick Abbott rode up on one of the Warners' paints. He trailed the reins over the pony's head and came in.

"Hiya," he said.

"Hello," I said.

"Glad to see you got home all right," he said. His face was ruddy from the spicy air. His eyes sparkled. He wore a sweater under his suede jacket, and high boots.

The snow began tumbling off his boots and melting into little pools on the hearth.

"No thanks to you, though," I said.

"I asked the doctor to take you," he said.

"Oh." Then I said, "Better take off that jacket. It's colder out than it looks."

Patrick took off the jacket and hung it with his wide hat on the peg over the Indian head belts. He sat down and got out his cigarettes.

"How's Gilbert?" I asked, having heard on the plaza that he was still alive.

"He'll be all right."

"Isn't it queer that he imagined he'd murdered those people?"

"Happens all the time. Cigarette?"

There was no hurry about the huaraches. I took off my gloves and tossed them into the basket with the shoes and had the cigarette.

"I wonder how he knew before anybody else that Daisy had gone to New York?"

Patrick smiled.

"He saw her on her way to the bus. She asked him to tell people she'd gone. He did. Only, he dramatized it."

I shook my head over Gilbert.

"What will happen to him, Pat?"

"Oh, he'll just go on being himself. Unless he makes a success sometime of his poetry. Then he'll be a nice guy. Maybe."

I asked, "What about Mona?"

"Mrs. Brandon has gone for an indefinite stay in the East."

"Luis drive her?"

"As far as Santa Fe. She's taking a train."

"And he's coming back?"

"I told you Luis was getting married. Going to move back to the pueblo. By the way, he says he stopped on your hill like that because he can tell from there what the weather'll be like next day. He was always on his way home from calling on his girl, who works on a ranch over the hill. Luis had no idea he was scaring you."

I said, "I feel silly."

"Everybody's been on edge, Jean."

"Thanks."

I said then, "Poor Michael."

"Poor? A man who cheats and murders?"

"But he was such a fine artist!"

"That makes it worse."

I sighed. "I can't believe it. Or understand it, either. I wish you would begin at the beginning and tell it all."

Patrick Abbott crossed his long legs and told the story.

"O'Hara killed Arkwright because he threatened to expose him for his part in a former counterfeiting crime. A few years ago O'Hara engraved two plates for a gang of counterfeiters. He was paid in good cash. He came here to work on his pictures, meaning never to get mixed up with any such outfit again. It was his first and only offense. But one of the gang, this so-called

Arkwright, got out on parole, tracked him down, and eventually O'Hara killed him. He killed Carmencita because she suspected him and he was afraid she would talk. Sonya was on the list because he didn't think he could shake her any other way, and he planned to marry Mona Brandon."

"So he was in love with her after all?"

"Not at all. O'Hara loved only one thing—his work. The reason for all his crimes was an overwhelming desire for freedom and leisure in order to paint. He made the plates for the counterfeiters to get money to come here and be free from having to do commercial art. He had used up that money and faced having to go back to New York when suddenly Mona Brandon fell in love with him. To be married to her would mean freedom forever from financial worry. So he proceeded in a calculating and fairly ingenious fashion to get rid of all the obstacles in his way to that end."

"So he wasn't planning to go back to New York really?"

"No, indeed."

"Didn't you honestly come here to work on this case, Pat?"

"Of course not! I came here for a vacation. I walked into your shop to buy a picture because I liked it, and for no other reason. Then the sheriff showed up and mentioned a green ink spot that had mysteriously turned black. Even if I hadn't already agreed to take a casual look into counterfeiting operations suspected up this way I would have been a sucker for a case where a green ink spot turned black overnight in the house of a man just murdered. Then I saw Carmencita. My interest in Arkwright practically doubled instantly. She was so beautiful, you see."

"Oh."

"Next, Carmencita met a violent end. When the girlfriend of a man who's murdered dies mysteriously soon after, chances are it is because she knows something, or is suspected of it. What did she know? Perhaps why and when the ink spot turned black.

"I kept thinking about her. And that ink spot. I asked myself questions. For instance: Who would arrange the rendezvous at the swimming pool? Certainly someone whose presence in that area, if noticed, would not excite undue suspicion. That reduced the likely suspects, tentatively, to Mrs. Brandon, the Indian, the O'Haras, one of the staff, possibly Gilbert Mason.

"Who would want Carmencita dead?

"Mrs. Brandon? Perhaps. But not enough to kill her, surely, since she no longer wanted Tom Brandon back, whether he was Arkwright or not. There was also a faint possibility that he might be Brandon and that the two of them were blackmailing her. But neither Carmencita nor Brandon was the blackmailing type.

"Gilbert? If he had killed Arkwright, perhaps. But Gilbert's bad deeds were reputedly in his mind only. We never seriously suspected Gilbert Mason.

"One of the staff? Mr. Trask knew them all. None would have sufficient motive. They were all good, quiet, decent Mexican people, except the very respectable Scottish housekeeper.

"The Indian? Not for any reason of his own, and Mrs. Brandon, as we have said, would not be likely to desire Carmencita's death enough to hire Luis to bump her off.

"The O'Haras? Well, it wasn't hard to imagine Sonya doing murder, but the most likely motive in her case would be jealousy, and she was jealous of Mona Brandon, not Carmencita. Michael? Well, if the green spot meant that Arkwright were a counterfeiter there might be some hookup between him and Michael O'Hara if O'Hara were an expert engraver—but O'Hara, though very versatile, and though interested in all kinds of things, took no apparent interest in the art of engraving.

"But I asked myself, why not? One reason that O'Hara was so popular was because he was at pains to seem interested in anything and everything anyone spoke to him about. But his attention bounced right off the subject of engraving.

"He was the answer to some of the questions, however. For instance, he might be seen in that part of the grounds without attracting undue notice. And while the Indians were dancing he sat with his wife and Mrs. Brandon near the exit to the stairs leading down to the library. He could have slipped out for a few minutes during all that period of noise and stir and be missed by no one but the two women. His excuse, if they asked, time out for a smoke, a drink, or to go to the washroom. We didn't question him or them about this because we didn't want him to know he was being watched. But he confirmed our suppositions in his deathbed statement.

"Another thing that made me think O'Hara was our man was his expert knowledge of people. He alone of the probable suspects was clever enough to anticipate that public opinion would have it that Carmencita killed herself as she did to spite Mona Brandon, and that Sonya shot herself out of jealousy. He counted on this public opinion to distract the attention from himself. I'd've hated being in his shoes while his wife lay there in the hospital, apt to revive at any moment and speak up—he'd been afraid to shoot her a second time lest it look like murder—but I guess he would have lied out of it. He was popular. She wasn't.

"Well, anyhow, having decided that O'Hara was the one, we assumed that he had gone to the Arkwright house after the inquest, thinking that the coast was now entirely clear, in order to obliterate any clues which might implicate himself in some way. Carmencita, unfortunately, went out there at the same time to get her miracle-working Santo and walked in on him as he was pouring common black ink from a bottle he found in the kitchen on that green ink spot. He wore gloves.

"Since he could hardly give any plausible reason for what he was doing, he decided to buy her off. He talked to her, learned she wanted money for her trousseau, and arranged the rendezvous at the pool. A queer one, except that the girl knew the grounds intimately and trusted O'Hara, as all women did. How, then, would he arrange for her to get into the place at night? By the little gate, of course, since she would probably not be noticed. Therefore he would provide Carmencita with a key. He had the only key to the gate. But it's easy to get a duplicate made, and there would be locksmiths in Santa Fe. O'Hara had gone to Santa Fe on Monday before the party, presumably on an errand for Mrs. Brandon.

"So, on Friday, when I took those things from the Arkwright house to Santa Fe for examination and the photographing of the fingerprints, I made the rounds of the locksmiths, and sure enough at one I found that a Yale key had been duplicated on Monday for a tall redheaded man. In his confession O'Hara said that he had mailed the key to Carmencita from Santa Fe. She gave it back to him at the pool, since she wouldn't need it to get out. He threw it away that same night.

"Naturally, the key tied him up decidedly with the death of Carmencita, if the locksmith could identify him as the man who had the key made. But before arresting O'Hara we wanted to know more about Arkwright, and how O'Hara fitted into that picture. The hideaway hadn't yet been located. We still had nothing but those ink spots on that score. But while in Santa Fe that afternoon I went through some Secret Service records on file at police headquarters and I came on that story about the green ink, which I told at dinner that night at Mrs. Brandon's. I chose it because the engraver hadn't been rounded up with the rest of the gang, and also because of the green ink, since whoever went to the Arkwright house that night apparently had green ink on his mind. I also remarked that Trask and I would be going out again next day to look for more clues in that house. That was a calculated indiscretion. I had no intention of going back there or buying it, either, but wanted to stampede O'Hara, if guilty, into doing something to incriminate himself further. He did. He left the dinner table, drove out there the long way, and set fire to the house. Its wooden interior was of pine and burned like kindling. Then he went back to the hospital. That was a foggy night, you may remember, and O'Hara said in his confession that he didn't bother with even ordinary precautions because of the weather. We had two men watching the house."

"Why didn't you arrest him then?"

"We hoped his wife would still make a statement. And Luis hadn't yet found the hideaway."

"Luis?"

Patrick grinned.

"Trask okayed Luis for the scouting job. I knew the Indian badly needed a hundred and three dollars and thirty-five cents."

"The amount he owed me!"

"Exactly. He would take no less. And no more, either."

"I feel awful," I said.

"You should. I could have relieved your mind but decided you should suffer a little for being so suspicious of a man whom your sheriff trusts implicitly."

"I feel worse. But go on, Pat."

"That's about all. The fingerprints in the hideaway matched those we got in the Arkwright house. The FBI successfully identified them as those of a man with a criminal record, named Sim-kovitch. The hair, teeth, and the small scar on the scalp also tal-lied. Simkovitch, alias Arkwright, had been sentenced to federal prison for a part in a counterfeiting crime in which the engraver was never caught. That engraver was O'Hara, needless to say.

"When Sonya died—suddenly after all—we closed in on O'Hara. We were going to do it that night anyhow. He shot himself, but fortunately was able to make a statement which supplied the missing details."

"For instance?"

"Well, he told us he met this so-called Arkwright at an art-ist's affair some years ago. Didn't know at first that he was a criminal. O'Hara was crazy to get away from it all and paint. Arkwright knew it and finally talked him into making the two plates which were confiscated three years ago when the gang was rounded up. As I previously said O'Hara was paid for the plates in good cash and called it quits. But Arkwright intended to make counterfeiting his career so he didn't squeal on O'Hara, just bided his time, got out, came here, and turned on the heat. They met actually only four times, since to be seen together was hazardous. Always at that spot where the murder was done.

"O'Hara realized from the first that he would have to kill Arkwright. He kept stalling him along, saying he was working on the new plates, finally saying he would deliver them. Instead he took a butcher knife with him and a spare suit of jeans exact-ly like the ones he wore that night. He killed the man, buried the knife and the bloody jeans in the riverbed, washed himself, put on the other jeans, and went home. Trask says the shifting quicksands in the river may have carried away the knife and the clothes and would have disposed of the corpse had O'Hara only realized it."

"Oh. And what about the ring?"

"Some Boy Scouts found the ring and gave it to Trask, who suggested I show it to you. We really thought some sightseer had probably dropped it, since so many went out to look at the place where the body was found. I showed it to O'Hara when we had the painting lesson. I was struck by his lack of interest— it was like his indifference to engraving. So I said I was going to your house for dinner and would show you the ring. I mentioned that you were a whiz at that sort of thing and would no doubt identify the ring. That evening the O'Haras were with Mrs. Brandon when she announced that she was going to your house. Now, the ring belonged to O'Hara. Mrs. Brandon had given it to him recently, but he was afraid to wear it because of his wife, and, alas, it had been in the pocket of the spare suit of jeans he had taken with him when he killed Arkwright. He imagined that Mona would see the ring at your house, hear where it was found, and suspect him of murder. That would spoil everything.

"Right then he had Daisy Payne's gun in his pocket, all ready to polish off his wife later that evening. So he left his wife at the Brandons, rushed home, got in his car, drove north of the plaza and up your hill by the lane to the Mexican cottages, ran across the corral, and arrived outside your window as I was show- ing the ring. Mind you, Mona was on her way, and he thought about that, lost his head, fired the shot. He intended to shoot you and me both, grab the ring, and beat it. But he missed. So he bolted. He went home, put away his car, and was back at Mrs. Brandon's when she got home. She assumed he'd been there all evening. Actually, fate played right into his hands with the ring. Mona discovered it at your house and quietly pocketed it to return it to him, since it was their secret. She thought he'd dropped it there the night before, when he and Sonya came to your house after the party. She gave it back to him yesterday afternoon, when you saw it on the table, and he destroyed it before going to the hospital last night."

"But why did she carry on like that?"

"Too much gin. Plus the knowledge that her man might be slipping away from her, with his wife on the mend. She just picked on you in general, you know."

"And why did she come to my house the night the shot was fired through my window?"

"Out of curiosity, plain and simple. To sound you out about what people were saying about Carmencita's death in the pool. Like many arrogant, selfish people, Mona Brandon is hypersensitive to the opinion of those she pretends to despise. She knew that you had many friends and would have heard the gossip, and she was trying to get you to talk. She would think it beneath what she calls pride to come right out in the open and tell you why she wanted to know what was being said."

"But she carried on so!"

"Of course. Tried all her tricks. Put on all her acts."

"Yes," I said. Yes, that would explain it all right. "Listen, what made you say that you couldn't understand why the engraved plates found in the counterfeiter's cabin were too crude?"

"Because we thought that O'Hara might have been collaborating with Arkwright already, and the plates weren't up to his standard. He explained that—said that Arkwright had picked them up before coming here and one of the reasons for his putting pressure on O'Hara was that the money they printed was so bad that he felt in constant danger of being tracked down."

I said, "Well, I think you're wonderful."

"Of course," Patrick agreed. He grinned. "But I'd be a lot more wonderful if I had a nose like your cat's."

"Toby's?"

He nodded.

"Toby bit O'Hara that night after he shot Carmencita. He bit me after I ran out and fired off my gun. He nosed out that shell. Toby ought to be a detective."

I laughed.

"He's allergic to the smell of gunpowder. A Mexican once took him for a skunk and he still has some buckshot under that handsome pelt."

"Well, if I had known that . . . oh, well, it's finished."

I sighed.

"I can't believe it. Michael was so nice."

"Nice? Clever, you mean. Gifted. Ruthless. Sly. He took such pains to make people like him, simply because he understood you all so well. Better than you did yourselves sometimes. He flattered Mona Brandon, was candid with you, cool and businesslike with me. He should have done something constructive with such a talent. He certainly was a better artist than criminal, though. He walked right into our traps."

"So you did work on the case?"

"Oh, no. Just helped the sheriff out a bit."

"You're modest."

"Me? You ought to see me strutting around on a case of my own!"

I said, "I was dead sure Mona was mixed up in it."

"Yes. If you hadn't been so hellbent on having Mona guilty you might have seen things more clearly, Jean."

"You don't like her, I hope?" I asked, feeling kind of anxious.

"Well, she's awfully attractive," Patrick said.

I sighed. Then I put on the gloves again and went back to sorting the huaraches. Patrick Abbott was silent. After a while

I looked up to see why. He was looking at me. He had a queer look in his eyes. But very nice.

He said, "Still she's hardly my ideal woman."

"But really!" I said. With sarcasm.

"I never have cared much for women who screech and yelp if they don't get everything they want when they want it. Other peoples' husbands, for instance. But I do like women who are easy to look at."

"So I've noticed!" I snapped.

"Still, I'm not partial to blondes. I like them slim, with white skin, black hair, amber eyes, long lashes, competent hands, minds of their own even though cockeyed, sympathetic even when it's not quite bright to be so, with a shop in which you love to sit around and prattle, lots of friends—"

"You seem to have someone in mind!"

"I have. Definitely," Patrick Abbott said.

I could feel my color coming up like a sunrise. I looked at him again. He was watching me. With an eyebrow up I must admit that he was putting me in a state of great mental confusion, but it was very agreeable.

## THE END

# DISCUSSION QUESTIONS

- Were you able to predict any part of the solution to the case?

- Aside from the solution, did anything about the book surprise you? If so, what?

- Did any aspects of the plot date the story? If so, which ones?

- Would the story be different if it were set in the present day? If so, how?

- Were there any historical details that the author included that surprised you?

- What role did the setting play in the narrative?

- Did you learn anything about the region or the era in which the story was set while reading the book?

If you enjoyed *The Turquoise Shop*,
try one of these titles, available now from...

# OTTO PENZLER PRESENTS
## ═ AMERICAN MYSTERY CLASSICS ═

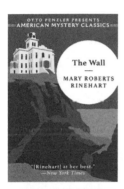

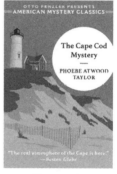

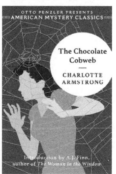

H.F. Heard, *A Taste for Honey*

Dolores Hitchens, *The Cat Saw Murder*
*Introduced by* Joyce Carol Oates

Dorothy B. Hughes, *Dread Journey*
*Introduced by* Sarah Weinman
Dorothy B. Hughes, *Ride the Pink Horse*
*Introduced by* Sara Paretsky
Dorothy B. Hughes, *The So Blue Marble*

W. Bolingbroke Johnson, *The Widening Stain*
*Introduced by* Nicholas A. Basbanes

Baynard Kendrick, *The Odor of Violets*

Jonathan Latimer, *Headed for a Hearse*
*Introduced by* Max Allan Collins

Frances and Richard Lockridge, *Death on the Aisle*

John P. Marquand, *Your Turn, Mr. Moto*
*Introduced by* Lawrence Block

Stuart Palmer, *The Puzzle of the Happy Hooligan*

Otto Penzler, ed., *Golden Age Detective Stories*
Otto Penzler, ed., *Golden Age Locked Room Mysteries*

Ellery Queen, *The American Gun Mystery*
Ellery Queen, *The Chinese Orange Mystery*
Ellery Queen, *The Dutch Shoe Mystery*
Ellery Queen, *The Egyptian Cross Mystery*
Ellery Queen, *The Siamese Twin Mystery*

H.F. Heard, *A Taste for Honey*

Dolores Hitchens, *The Cat Saw Murder*
*Introduced by* Joyce Carol Oates

Dorothy B. Hughes, *Dread Journey*
*Introduced by* Sarah Weinman
Dorothy B. Hughes, *Ride the Pink Horse*
*Introduced by* Sara Paretsky
Dorothy B. Hughes, *The So Blue Marble*

W. Bolingbroke Johnson, *The Widening Stain*
*Introduced by* Nicholas A. Basbanes

Baynard Kendrick, *The Odor of Violets*

Jonathan Latimer, *Headed for a Hearse*
*Introduced by* Max Allan Collins

Frances and Richard Lockridge, *Death on the Aisle*

John P. Marquand, *Your Turn, Mr. Moto*
*Introduced by* Lawrence Block

Stuart Palmer, *The Puzzle of the Happy Hooligan*

Otto Penzler, ed., *Golden Age Detective Stories*
Otto Penzler, ed., *Golden Age Locked Room Mysteries*

Ellery Queen, *The American Gun Mystery*
Ellery Queen, *The Chinese Orange Mystery*
Ellery Queen, *The Dutch Shoe Mystery*
Ellery Queen, *The Egyptian Cross Mystery*
Ellery Queen, *The Siamese Twin Mystery*

Patrick Quentin, *A Puzzle for Fools*

Clayton Rawson, *Death from a Top Hat*

Craig Rice, *Eight Faces at Three*
*Introduced by* Lisa Lutz
Craig Rice, *Home Sweet Homicide*

Mary Roberts Rinehart, *The Haunted Lady*
Mary Roberts Rinehart, *Miss Pinkerton*
*Introduced by* Carolyn Hart
Mary Roberts Rinehart, *The Red Lamp*
Mary Roberts Rinehart, *The Wall*

Joel Townsley Rogers, *The Red Right Hand*
*Introduced by* Joe R. Lansdale

Roger Scarlett, *Cat's Paw*
*Introduced by* Curtis Evans

Vincent Starrett, *The Great Hotel Murder*
*Introduced by* Lyndsay Faye
Vincent Starrett, *Murder on "B" Deck*
*Introduced by* Ray Betzner

S. S. Van Dine, *The Benson Murder Case*
*Introduced by* Ragnar Jonasson

Cornell Woolrich, *The Bride Wore Black*
*Introduced by* Eddie Muller
Cornell Woolrich, *Waltz into Darkness*
*Introduced by* Wallace Stroby